Sometimes you need your closest friends in the face of trouble – but other times, only an enemy will do. Veronica finds an unlikely support in ex-best friend Bailey when she finds out she's pregnant – and there's no way she's having the baby. Together they embark on the road trip of a lifetime. Brilliant writing and cracking dialogue in the face of crazy circumstances, weird dangers and stupid accidents make this an outstanding debut by a great new writing duo. I loved *Juno* and *Booksmart*, and *Unpregnant* is similarly silly, serious and sensitive – what a movie it will make!

BARRY CUNNINGHAM
Publisher
Chicken House

UNPREGNANT

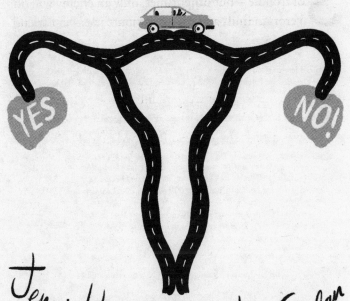

Jenni Hendriks & Ted Caplan

Chicken House

2 Palmer Street, Frome, Somerset BA11 1DS
www.chickenhousebooks.com

Text © Jennifer Hendriks and Theodore Caplan 2019

First published in the United States by HarperTeen,
an imprint of HarperCollins Publishers,
195 Broadway, New York, NY 10007.

First published in Great Britain in 2020
Chicken House
2 Palmer Street
Frome, Somerset BA11 1DS
United Kingdom
www.chickenhousebooks.com

Cover and interior design by Helen Crawford-White
Typeset by Dorchester Typesetting Group Ltd
Printed and bound in Great Britain by CPI Group (UK) Ltd, Croydon, CR0 4YY

The paper used in this Chicken House book is made
from wood grown in sustainable forests.

1 3 5 7 9 10 8 6 4 2

British Library Cataloguing in Publication data available.

PB ISBN 978-1-912626-16-8
eISBN 978-1-912626-81-6

For our children

MILE 0

Sitting on the icy-cold toilet seat in the third stall of the girls' bathroom, I desperately squeezed my thighs together and concentrated on not peeing.

'Ronnie, you done in there? We gotta book it if we're gonna make it to first period,' Emily asked. No, I wasn't almost done. And a late slip was the least of my concerns.

'Uh, go ahead. I've got . . . girl issues.' Just not the monthly kind.

I prayed Emily would leave quickly. That second glass of orange and guava juice this morning had definitely been a mistake. Curse its pulpy goodness. Finally, she opened the door. The bathroom echoed with pounding footsteps as everyone hurried to class, then . . . silence. I remained frozen, straining to hear the slightest sound of a student, or worse, a teacher, approaching. But there was only the occasional drip from a tap. Everyone was in homeroom. I let out a sigh of relief. And almost peed.

It was time to find out if my nightmare was over or only just beginning. I slowly unzipped the front pouch of my backpack and winced as the sound reverberated off the tiled walls. Even though I was alone, I couldn't shake the feeling that someone would know what I was about to do. I reached deep into my backpack, felt around the pens and broken pencils scattered at the bottom, and found what I'd hidden there. I sat back down and studied the object in my hand. It felt heavier than I remembered.

I'd read the instructions last night. Then again when I woke up. And once more after breakfast. I was nothing if not a good student. But now that the moment had come, my throat constricted with panic. What if I missed the stick? What if I did it wrong? I only had one of these and I couldn't mess it up. I took a deep breath. I had a freakin' 4.56 GPA, a membership in the National Honor Society, and was going to Brown University in the fall. I could damn well pee on a stick.

I ripped open the thick foil and pulled out the pregnancy test. The little plastic window stared back at me, blank, waiting to tell my fate. Trying not to think of what I was about to do, I stuck the thing between my legs and peed.

For a moment I was lost in the bliss of a rapidly empty-ing bladder, then a stab of panic struck. I'd forgotten a step. The instructions had said to pee a little first and *then* stick the test down there. Would not doing that invalidate the results? I looked down to see if the test was working. The fibrous wick was soaked, and the little plastic window was turning a light grey. Was it supposed to do that? Or did that mean I'd broken it? Should I stop peeing?

Then, in the window, a thin pink line began to appear. My stomach dropped, until I remembered the little pamphlet had called it a control line. Two lines needed to appear to indicate pregnancy. I hoped the line meant the test was working right. Especially since I was out of pee. Careful to keep the test as flat as possible – as per the instructions – I pulled it from between my legs. Three minutes. I could read the results in three minutes. They were going to be the longest three minutes of my life.

I looked anywhere but at the little window. I wasn't the type to fix my make-up obsessively or smoke illicit substances, so the girls' bathroom wasn't exactly a place I'd spent a lot of time in over the last four years. Forty-five seconds of staring at the stall walls told me I hadn't missed much. The only thing to distract me was one mildly amusing caricature of our principal and several dire warnings about the diseased genitals of the football team – no surprise there. I dared a peek at the test. Still one line.

Hope exploded in my chest. Maybe I was just late. Maybe this was me panicking over nothing. Like when I thought I'd bombed the second essay on my Advanced Placement English test. Even though I hadn't fully elucidated the thematic similarities between Dickens's *Great Expectations* and Thackeray's *Vanity Fair*, I'd still scored a five.

I had been under a lot of stress with college admissions and prom and finals. Not to mention being in the running for valedictorian. I was probably just late. I blinked. Was that the faintest whisper of a second line appearing? Leaning towards the stall door, I tried to angle a little more light on to the window. If I could just—

The door to the bathroom slammed open.

I jumped. In slow motion, I saw the test bounce from my hands, brushing past the tips of my fingers. Lunging forward, I made a desperate grab for it, but found only air. Tipping end over end, it fell to the floor, landed on the tile with an impossible-not-to-hear crack, skittered under the stall door and spun to a stop right in the dead centre of the bathroom floor.

OK, this was not the time to panic. I needed to keep it together. Maybe they wouldn't see it. Maybe they were blind. And deaf. Maybe there would be a massive earthquake and the school would collapse and we'd all die. Missouri had to have a fault line somewhere.

Clomp. Clomp. Clomp. From under the stall door, I saw a pair of scuffed black combat boots walk over to where the test lay, perfectly highlighted by a beam of sunlight. A hand reached down, chipped green nail polish on bitten-down fingernails.

'Whoa.'

Who was it? Who now held my pee-covered future in their hand? I peered through the crack in the stall door. Oversized black T-shirt. Ripped skinny jeans a size too small. Faded turquoise hair with black roots that looked like it hadn't seen a brush in days.

No. The high school gods couldn't be that cruel. Bailey Butler. Jefferson High's very own black hole of anger and darkness. If you said hello in the halls, she'd flip you off. Not to mention what she'd do if you tried to sit with her at lunch. She had a whole table to herself in the cafeteria because she literally barked at people when they tried to sit down. Rumour had it that when the quarterback of the football team had said something to piss her off, she'd bought a pocketknife and engraved his name on it. She was sullen. She was cynical. She was deeply unpleasant to be around. She also used to be my best friend.

Bailey lifted the test to her nose and sniffed. 'Still fresh.' She scanned the bathroom, her gaze stopping when she saw my white Adidas Superstars. 'Oh, this is going to be fun.'

Would she still know my voice? It'd been almost four years since we last spoke. Just to be safe, I pitched it low and gravelly. 'Uh, if you could just slide that back under here, that'd be great.' I stuck my hand out beneath the door and hoped she was feeling merciful.

Bailey snorted. 'Nice try. But I'm pretty sure Batman can't get pregnant.' Through the gap in the door, I saw her begin to pace back and forth, hands behind her back, the corners of her mouth curling upwards. Great. I knew that smile. It was the one I imagined Catholic priests wore when they carried out the Spanish Inquisition.

'Chloe McCourt?' Bailey ventured. I sat on the toilet in stony silence. No way was I playing this game. I'd just wait her out. Bailey narrowed her eyes. 'No. Calvin broke up with her. No way she landed another dude already after she burnt his football uniform in the quad; I don't care how big her titties are. Hmmm. This is a tricky one. Ella Tran? She's dumb enough to confuse her mints with her birth control.'

'Give it back.' I tried to make my lowered voice sound forceful, but it just came out desperate.

Bailey squinted, examining my shoes. 'Well, there's always long-time subscriber to the Penis of the Month Club, Olivia Blume . . .'

'No!' I burst out, offended.

'Oooh. Judgy. A clue. Who thinks they're better than everyone else?' Bailey tapped her chin. 'Faith Bidwell?' Bailey wasn't going to give up. I had to end it before someone else came in.

'Darn it. Don't tell anyone. Can you hand it back now?' I waited with my hand extended. I wasn't sure she bought my B-plus performance, but Bailey walked towards the stall. Maybe she was getting bored of the game. I felt a flutter of hope. But then instead of bending down to hand me the test, she leapt up and grabbed the top of the stall door.

'Holy donkey balls!'

I yelped. Bailey was hanging over the top and grinning down at me.

'Bailey! Get down!' I frantically waved her away.

'Am I dreaming? Life cannot be this perfect,' she crowed.

My cheeks went red as I fumbled with my clothes, trying to yank my underwear and jeans on without exposing myself to Bailey's laughing eyes.

'Do you mind?' I glared up at her.

Amazingly, Bailey slid down without protest. My clothes back on, I banged open the stall door. She was waiting for me.

'Veronica Clarke, as I live and breathe,' she drawled. 'Hold on. I want to remember this moment for ever.' She reached into her back pocket, pulled out her phone and aimed it at me.

'Don't you dare—'

She snapped the picture, then smiled as she studied the result. 'Just how I'll always remember you.' Bailey flipped the phone around to show me the picture. I was half lunging at the camera, my mouth open in a snarl.

'Don't post that!' I yelped before I could stop myself. Total humiliation via social media was the last thing I needed right now.

Bailey smiled lovingly at the picture before pocketing her phone. 'Relax. This is too special to share.'

'Are we done now? You got what you wanted. You embarrassed me. You mocked me. You made my day worse than it already was. Now can you please give the test back?'

Bailey looked at my outstretched hand and cocked an eyebrow. 'I see you're still wearing your purity ring. Just keeping up appearances? Or is this some sort of virgin birth thing?' I snatched my hand back, my cheeks aflame. Trust Bailey not to miss any tiny detail that could be used to torture me. 'Wow. You really are the full cliché.'

'I am not a cliché!' I sputtered.

'A prom queen, valedictorian, Christian pregnancy is pretty damn cliché.'

'First, I'm up for valedictorian but Hannah Ballard has a lot more extra-curriculars than me. Even though I took more APs than her and I think that my charity work should be a factor—'

'Oh God, you are such a nerd—'

'And I was in prom *court*, not prom queen. So totally not a cliché,' I finished.

'You're right. I stand corrected. My deepest apologies.

You are full-cliché adjacent.'

'I know it's nearly impossible for you, but could you stop being a bitch for one minute?'

Bailey looked at me, mildly confused. 'No. Why would I do that?'

Something inside me snapped. After a week and a half of worry, stealing a pregnancy test from my older sister, not peeing all morning, now I had to deal with Bailey being Bailey? That expression about seeing red — it's not true. You actually see white. It was like a flash went off. The next thing I knew I was diving towards the hand holding the test. Bailey snatched it out of the way just in time, dancing back a few steps as I stumbled forward.

'Damn, girl. Chill. You're not getting this back until you promise me something.'

'Never gonna happen,' I snarled as I recovered my footing and launched myself at her a second time. She fell back against the sink, laughing at my futile attempts to wrest the test from her grip. Finally, I managed to grab her arm. I was using all my strength to try to get her to drop the test when I felt something cold and sharp against my neck.

'I said chill.'

I froze, then cautiously turned my eyes to look at our reflections in the bathroom mirror. Bailey was holding a black plastic box against my neck. It took a moment to register what the thing was, since up until now I'd only seen them on cop shows. It was a Taser. She had a flippin' Taser.

'Oh my God. How did you get that into school? You could be expelled! And, like, less than a month before graduation!'

Bailey snorted. 'Of course that would be your first thought when someone pulls a Taser on you.' I released her wrist. Bailey lowered the thing and stepped away from me. 'Now, where were we? Oh yeah, the promise. I'll give you the test back if you can promise one very important thing: that your procreation partner wasn't Kevin Decuziac.'

I held back a groan. She knew Kevin was my boyfriend. The whole school did. He was the star of the soccer team. He played in our church band. Everyone liked him, even my parents. Sure, his grades were only OK, but his goofy sense of humour more than made up for it. And, most importantly, he was totally devoted to me. Only Bailey could have a problem with Kevin.

Seeing my expression, she crinkled her nose in mock horror. 'EEEEEEEEEWWWWWW!'

'I don't know why you're surprised,' I grumbled, defensive.

'I don't know, I guess I keep hoping you'll use that AP brain of yours and break up. Or that he'll die of Ebola or something. Ugh! Ugh! Ugh!' She made a choking sound, as if she were a cat with a hairball. 'I can't believe you let that clingy jock-hole inside you!' She bent over, pretending to gag some more, and I noticed in her enthusiasm to act out her disgust, she'd placed the Taser on the edge of the sink.

I walked over and snatched it while she was busy pretending to vomit all over the floor. It took her several more dry heaves before she noticed the little black box pointed at her. When she did, her eyes widened a fraction and she smiled.

'Well, colour me impressed.'

'Hand it over.' I tried to make my voice sound threatening, like my dad's when he was mad at my brother for playing with one of his autographed baseballs.

'Do it.'

'What?' I lowered the Taser an inch, confused.

Bailey stepped closer, totally unconcerned by the not-lethal-but-still-probably-very-painful weapon pointed at her. 'I've never used it. I want to know what it feels like.'

Suddenly all the anger drained out of me. Bailey was still the same. Still the sort of person who would do something stupid, like let who-knows-how-many volts of electricity course through her just so she could say that she tried it. And it still irritated the crap out of me.

Bailey looked thoughtful. 'I wonder if I'll foam at the mouth.'

'I'm not going to tase you.'

Bailey sighed, disappointed. 'Figured.'

We stood staring at each other, not sure what should

happen next.

'Come on, Bailey. We're friends.' It was the wrong thing to say. A cynical sneer twisted Bailey's lips.

'We are?'

'I mean . . . well . . .'

'Is it seventh grade again?' Bailey widened her eyes in feigned surprise. She looked down at her chest. 'Hmmm. I've got a sweet pair of double Ds, so probably not.' She glared at me. 'Which means . . . not friends.'

She was never going to give me the test. So I did the only thing I could think of. I took the Taser, dropped it in the sink and put my hand on the tap. A drop of water splashed on to the black plastic.

'Give me the test or the Taser gets a bath.' Real alarm flashed across Bailey's face. I turned the tap a fraction of an inch. Another drop of water plunked on to the Taser. 'Pretty sure this thing's not waterproof.'

Bailey took an involuntary step towards me. 'Don't. My mom'll kill me. It's her favourite after the pink Glock. She's super into self-protection nowadays.'

I smiled and held out my hand, waiting. With a sigh, Bailey slapped the test into my palm. My knees almost buckled under the wave of relief. Without a second glance at Bailey, I fled to the nearest stall and locked the door.

'Oh, come on now,' she called after me, 'I thought we were besties. Don't you want to share the moment?'

No. I didn't want to share the moment. I didn't want to be having this moment at all. And now that it was here, I couldn't face looking at that stupid test.

Bailey started singing an old Hannah Montana song. *'You're a true friend, you're here till the end . . .'*

Trying to block her out, I took a deep breath and looked down. Two little pink lines, side by side.

Positive. It was positive.

My body went cold. My vision blurred. Bailey's song became a muffled drone. I saw two fat tears splash on to the plastic stick in my hand.

The singing stopped. I heard a thump and looked up to see Bailey hanging over the stall door again. I couldn't even feel embarrassed at the tears and snot running down my face. It didn't matter. All that mattered were those lines.

'Damn.' There was no elation in her exclamation. She even managed to look a little sorry for me. For some reason that made me cry harder.

When I exited the stall a few minutes later, my face blotchy but the tears gone, I was surprised to see her still waiting for me, perched on the edge of the sink, combat boots swinging.

'Sorry, that sucks.'

I wanted to glare at her, but couldn't even meet her eyes. 'Can you not tell anyone? Please?' I barely managed to whisper the words. Even to me they sounded pitiful and unconvincing. Who would hold back on this piece of gossip? I knew my reputation. Straight As. Varsity volleyball. Captain of the debate team. Clear skin, nice hair, cute nose. Most Liked *and* Most Likely to Succeed. Which meant that as much as everyone pretended to love me, most of them couldn't wait for me to mess up. I could just picture Hannah Ballard's smug face when she learnt she would be valedictorian. I was pretty sure pregnancy was an automatic disqualification. Which was so unfair. It's not like this would affect my grades and—

'God. Whatever you're thinking right now, just stop. You look like you're about to poop. I'm not gonna tell anyone.' Bailey's voice jerked me out of my panic spiral.

'Why not?' The question slipped out before I could stop myself.

Bailey shrugged. 'Because everyone in this school is an asshole.'

Buzz. My phone vibrated in my backpack. Again. And again, my stomach twisted in on itself. I couldn't relax. It was like there was a giant neon sign on my forehead flashing PREGNANT. Every time I saw my reflection as I walked through the halls, I imagined what it would look like in a few months, my stomach jutting out over my toes, the outline of my belly button poking through my T-shirt. I wasn't sure if the nausea I was feeling was an early symptom or nerves. But that wasn't the worst part. The worst part was the reason my phone was buzzing in my backpack every three and a half minutes. The worst part was Kevin.

I wasn't ready to tell him. I'd managed to avoid him all day. Luckily we didn't have any classes together. And during lunch I'd hidden in the library, a place I was pretty sure he'd never stepped foot in. But that hadn't stopped the texting. I pulled out my phone.

Kevin: 😘 ⏰ 🏢 🚗 ?

Kevin: 🤍 🤍 🤍 🤍

Kevin: ?

Kevin: ?

Kevin: 😬

Kevin: 🥺

Kevin: 💔

I sighed, stuffing my phone into my backpack. I couldn't avoid him for ever. But what was I supposed to say? *Hey, sweetie, despite using a condom every single time and sometimes more than one, I still managed to wind up pregnant.* It was every teenage guy's nightmare. Luckily, school was over for the day. In five minutes my ride home would be here and this would be a problem for Tomorrow Me. I scanned the parking lot, looking for Mrs Hennison's dented Toyota Sienna, ready to make an Olympic-speed sprint when I saw it.

Suddenly my vision went black as two hands covered my eyes. I yelped.

'Guess who, babe?'

Clearly, my luck was continuing to suck. 'Hey, Kevin.' He took his hands off my eyes and spun me around. Grey-blue eyes, hair that naturally swooped and curled in a glorious mess, and a smile that made me melt. It was the sort of smile that said every time he saw me, he couldn't believe his luck. He studied my expression, concerned.

'Whoa. Did I scare you?'

'No. Well, I mean, a little.'

He reached towards me and began rubbing my arms. 'Is everything OK?' He searched my eyes. I looked away, sure they would reveal my secret. 'You didn't answer my texts.'

'Sorry. I . . . uh . . . got busy.' Before Kevin could probe further, a friend of his patted him on the back as he walked past.

'See you at Conner's?'

'Hell yeah,' Kevin assured him with an elbow bump, and turned back to me. 'Did I tell you Conner got into University of Florida? Quinn's going to Arizona State. Hudson's joining the Marines. Everybody's freakin' leaving.'

'I know. Senior year. It's crazy.'

He glanced down. A flash of annoyance crossed his face. 'You trying to rub it in?' he asked. I blinked, momentarily confused. Then I remembered I was wearing my new Brown University hoodie.

'No. My parents got it for me. You know. They're

super excited.'

He toyed with the zipper for a moment, then grinned. 'You could always fail your finals. Then you could go to Missouri State with me.' It was my turn to get annoyed. We'd been over this before. I squirmed out of his arms.

'Can we not . . .'

He made a pouty face. 'Aw, come on. I was only teasing.' He pulled me back towards him. 'What's wrong?'

'Nothing.' I couldn't tell him. Here in the parking lot, in the middle of all our classmates, with Mr Contreras directing traffic nearby, was not the right time or place to break this sort of news. Though I had no idea what the right time or place would be.

'Seriously, I was just teasing. You know I'm totally going to drive to Rhode Island to see you every weekend.'

'I know.'

'I love my hot Ivy League lady,' he said with a playful grin. His charm was hard to resist. My heart twisted. I was going to ruin everything.

'I love you, too.' My voice sounded flat, even to my ears.

'You sure?' He looked down at me, searching.

'Yes.' I put as much conviction as I could behind the words, hoping later he would remember.

Kevin grinned, pleased. 'That's all that matters.'

I hoped so. But I doubted it. He kissed me again. As his mouth met mine, the familiar swooping sensation, the giddy rush of feeling, never came. Instead it was just a mishmash of lips, teeth and tongue. I was too nervous. All I could see when I closed my eyes were those two pink lines.

'Ronnie! Stop being gross and get in the car!' Emily's voice carried across the quad. I yanked myself away from Kevin and ran.

I watched the string of chain stores and fast-food restaurants slide past the smudged back-seat window of Mrs Hennison's minivan. Emily, Jocelyn and Kaylee, my best friends since freshman year, were busy on their phones. We all went to the same church and Mrs Hennison had been driving us to school since the second week of ninth grade, after Joey Mitchell pulled out his penis on the bus and waved it at Jocelyn. Joey got sent to military school shortly after, but the damage had been done. Our parents collectively decided getting driven was the only safe option.

And that's how our little group was formed. I had my driver's licence but no car, and I could count on one hand the number of times my parents had let me borrow theirs. This, along with AP classes, Academic Decathlon, debate team and the school paper, should have killed our social lives, but with Kevin as my boyfriend we were welcome at all the parties. We weren't the coolest kids in school, but everyone knew who we were. And now we were all accepted to good colleges and were getting out of our boring little forgettable town. Assuming we passed our finals. And assuming I . . . My thoughts skittered away from the truth I was going to have to face if I wanted to be ensconced in a dorm room on the East Coast by fall.

Kaylee looked up from her phone. 'It's all set. My dad agreed to move his fishing trip.'

Jocelyn grinned. 'Did you use "puppy eyes" or "lip tremble" to convince him?'

'I used facts. I told him we've been using the cabin every year to cram for finals, and it was our last time so the bass would have to wait. Then I cried a little.' The girls laughed.

Cram weekend. I'd totally forgotten. Every year before finals we spent Friday night through Sunday in Kaylee's dad's fishing cabin studying for our tests. At first, one of our moms went with us, but last year we'd been allowed to go alone. Jocelyn's parents let her borrow their car. Which probably wasn't the best decision on their part. She could barely stay in her own lane. And left turns made her nervous. But we had managed to get there in one piece. We'd gone over our notes, drunk too much soda and watched cheesy romantic movies. It was awesome. Emily nudged me.

'You sure you're gonna be OK?'

I looked at her, startled. How did she know? Did my face look different? Was I fatter already?

'Two whole nights away from Kevin,' she continued. I

relaxed. I was the only one in the group with a boyfriend and they always teased me about it. But I was also their only direct source of sexual information, so they never took the teasing too far.

'You could always bring him with you,' Kaylee suggested innocently.

'Yeah, what exactly are your feelings on polyamory?' Emily asked.

'I bet he could really help us *relax* between study sessions.' Jocelyn grinned and waggled her eyebrows.

'GIRLS!' Mrs Hennison reprimanded from the front seat, and they dissolved into giggles.

A sharp honk startled us. I looked out the window. It was Bailey. One arm dangling out the window of her beat-up Camry, her seat leant way back, she gave me a lazy wave. Emily wrinkled her nose.

'Ugh. What does Walmart Greeter Class of 2020 want with us?'

'Right there's the reason I'm not leaving that cabin until I've got my calculus notes memorized.' Kaylee pulled out her textbook. 'No way am I ending up like that.'

Jocelyn turned to me. 'Weren't you, like, friends with her in junior high or something?'

Emily's eyes widened. 'I totally forgot! Didn't she get arrested on our field trip to the Laura Ingalls Wilder Museum last year?'

'I heard she carved her name on a wagon,' Kaylee added.

'No, she stole a bonnet,' Emily countered.

'Who cares? You were friends, right? She came to your birthday party freshman year.' Jocelyn persisted. I felt my friends' eyes on me, waiting for an answer.

'Only because my mom made me invite her. But we weren't, like, close. Because, you know, she's a total psycho,' I said, making a little twirly gesture with my finger around my ear. The girls laughed.

I immediately regretted my words. There was no good reason I shouldn't have told the truth. My friends wouldn't have cared. So why did I?

Ten minutes later, I climbed out of the back of the van and trudged up the cracked asphalt driveway to my front door. My dad was already home. His Ford was in the drive-way, its bumper plastered with 'My child is an honor student at Jefferson High' stickers.

Carefully opening the front door so it didn't squeak, I tiptoed through the hall and up the stairs to my room. I flipped open my laptop and quickly scanned through every social media platform I could think of, searching for Bailey's profile. But it turned out she really was a rebel. The only thing I found was an old Facebook page, and the only thing on it was a picture of Bailey giving the finger. I sighed, feeling some of the tension in my stomach unspool.

Then, with trembling fingers, I typed the two words I'd known I'd type as soon as I saw those little pink lines.

Abortion. Clinic.

The sun had set and my room was lit only by the glow of my laptop screen, bathing my hands in an eerie blue light. I was limp with exhaustion. Typing those words had been the easiest part of the process. I'd spent the last few hours wading through outdated information and misleading sites. Finally, I had my answer.

There was a clinic two hours away. I was saved.

I could see my future again. Meeting my new roommate at Brown. Studying late in the library. Debating with my professors. An eventual internship. Graduation. A career in a big city. A downtown loft. Fancy shoes. A roomful of people listening to me as I led them through a meeting. Drinks after work. My own Netflix account. But my phone lay beside me untouched. I couldn't seem to type in the number. What would happen if I didn't?

A baby cried. I jerked away from my laptop, startled.

'Ronnie, come down to dinner. Your sister's here,' my mom called. I slammed my laptop closed and hurried downstairs.

At the dinner table I sat in the seat I'd been sitting in since I could remember, right under the sign asking God to 'Bless This Mess', next to my dad. My gingham cushion on the old oak spindle chair was stained and so thin I might as well have been sitting on wood at this point. The room smelt of the thousand casserole dinners that had been served in it over the years. The whiff of chicken and cheese was faintly comforting, especially since at that moment the decibel level in the room was somewhere between rock concert and airport tarmac.

My little brother, Ethan, was on my dad's phone, blasting sounds blaring from its tiny speakers. My five-month-old niece was screaming as Melissa, my sister, tried to shove a bottle in her mouth. Next to her, my two-year-old nephew was throwing goldfish crackers on the floor, yelling, 'Find Nemo! Find Nemo!' My brother-in-law was chasing their oldest kid, Logan, around the table, begging him to sit down. Logan had some sort of robot that was flashing lights and making laser noises. Through all this my dad just sat there, sipping his beer.

My mom entered wearing a bright smile and carrying a creamy chicken noodle bake.

'Shall we say grace?'

We all held hands, my oldest nephew wrangled into his chair by his father threatening to take away Mr Roboto. My dad held my hand firmly. It was big and rough and familiar.

'Dear Lord,' my mom began, 'thank you for this meal—'

'Logan! Get back in your seat!' Melissa screeched. My

nephew had slid under the table. I could feel him playing with the laces of my shoes.

'And thank you, Lord,' my mother continued unperturbed, 'for blessing our daughter Veronica with her acceptance to Brown. The first in our family to go to college.' My dad squeezed my hand, his eyes sliding over to meet mine, a small smile twitching his lips upwards.

'Logan! Right now! One! Two!' my sister counted.

My mom yelped and grabbed her leg. 'Logan, don't bite Grandma. It's not nice.'

'Just give him a kick,' my dad muttered, but I think I was the only one who heard him.

'Pete! Control him!' my sister snapped as the baby took that moment to spit up on herself. My dad laughed, then tried to turn it into a cough.

'Amen,' my mom finished, and dipped a serving spoon into the casserole. 'Who's first?'

The rest of the dinner went reasonably well, with only a minimum amount of noodle bake thrown at the wall by little Logan. We'd moved on to ice cream sundaes when my sister stood, clearing her throat.

'We have a little announcement to make.'

'You're finishing your nursing degree?' I asked.

'No,' my sister giggled, then added, beaming, 'We're pregnant!' My mom immediately jumped to her feet with an ear-piercing screech of joy. My dad exhaled, long and slow, and seemed to sink a little further into his chair. I saw his eyes slide over to my hand, as if reassuring himself my purity ring was still there, before pasting on a smile and managing a hearty 'congratulations' for my sister.

I twisted the ring on my finger, feeling its familiar whorls and grooves. It had been my dad's idea. I'd leapt at it, eager to stand in front of my church and make a promise that had meant next to nothing when I was twelve, just so I could show him I was better than my sister.

I wasn't supposed to know, of course, but I'd heard the arguments. Our house was small and the walls thin. Vision of devoted motherhood that she was now, Melissa got started a little earlier than anyone in my family would care to admit. When she'd cried to my parents that night, she'd only known Pete a few weeks, and she'd just started her nursing degree.

Dad didn't yell. He left that to my mom. No, my dad was calm but immovable. As far as he was concerned, my sister was a parent now, and her needs would always come second to her children's. That's what he and my mother had done for us.

Every argument Melissa made, my dad countered with love. With comfort. He promised help. Money, babysitting, whatever they needed. Finally, he'd begged, his voice thick with tears. By the weekend my sister was engaged and smiling, whatever plans she'd had for her life forgotten.

How can someone's dreams withstand that much love?

I knew mine couldn't.

Of course, my dad probably didn't anticipate my sister's complete lack of parenting skills.

I felt a tug on my jeans and looked down. Logan was under the table, grinning, a baby carrot halfway up his nose. I stood, my chair scraping the wood as I shoved it back.

'May I be excused?'

Five minutes later I was sitting in my closet, my laptop on my knees, phone in hand. A high school career's worth of formal dresses surrounded me like a cocoon, the scratchy lace of my homecoming dress brushing my cheek, the smooth satin of my prom dress sliding against my arm. They still smelt faintly of perfume and hairspray. I breathed in the scent and tried to slow my pounding heart. I was hoping my closet would provide a little extra sound-proofing for the call I was about to make. I pushed the final digit of the number and held the phone to my ear. An automated voice answered. I was relieved. Maybe I wouldn't have to talk to anyone. I selected the appropriate number and waited.

'Planned Parenthood. How may I help you?' My breath caught in my throat. The words wouldn't come. 'Hello?' the voice on the other end of the line asked.

'Hi, I, uh, need to make an appointment.' I cringed at

how small my voice sounded.

'And what is this appointment regarding?'

I squeezed my eyes shut, as if that would somehow keep me from hearing the words I needed to say. 'I need . . .' But I couldn't say it. If I did, it would make it real. 'I'm doing a report on abortion and I, uh, wanted to speak to a doctor.'

There was a pause on the other end of the line. It seemed to go on for ever, but couldn't have lasted more than a second. Within that second I could feel the shame and terror I'd stuffed down deep inside me well up, ready to burst out. Luckily, before I could dissolve into a puddle of choking sobs, the operator spoke.

'Honey, how old are you?'

'Seventeen.' There was another pause. A longer one.

'You can get an appointment to see a doctor for your "report", but in the state of Missouri you need a parent's permission if you're under eighteen. Is that going to be possible for you?' For a long moment all I could do was sit in my cocoon of sequins and satin, taking quick, shallow breaths while something inside me shattered.

'No. I don't think that will be possible. Is there, uh, any way . . .'

'You can petition the court, but that can take a while. And you'll probably need a lawyer.' She said it gently, but I got the sense that she'd had this conversation more than once and knew exactly how laughable her suggestion was.

'Oh. OK. I don't think I'll be doing that. The report's not that important. Um, thanks for your help.' My finger was sliding to the end call button when the operator spoke again.

'There are other places where you don't need parental permission for your . . . report.' My finger froze over the button.

'There are?'

'Yes. Where do you live?'

'Columbia.'

The line went quiet while she accessed something on her computer. 'It looks like the closest place for you is in Albuquerque.'

'There's an Albuquerque in Missouri?' I asked, confused.

'No.'

'Oh.' I cleared my throat, nervous. 'Um, about how far away is that from Columbia?'

'Nine hundred and ninety-four miles.'

Kevin: Three days without you. Not sure I'll survive. 😔

I got the text from Kevin while studying the route from my house to the clinic in Albuquerque. The Planned Parenthood operator had been right. It was the closest location. A mere thousand miles away. I'd been studying the drive since I'd hung up the phone last night. There were a few ways to get there and I'd weighed the advantages of a slightly shorter route versus a longer but faster drive. I'd barely spoken on the way to school, letting the other girls hash out the exact order of the Ryan Gosling movie marathon for our cram weekend while I'd added up the cost of toll roads. I'd taken two bathroom breaks during PE to search for any planned road construction. I'd even risked sneaking a quick glance during physics to rerun my calculations. I had my answer. It wasn't the shortest route, but taking into account all the variables, it was the fastest and it was burnt into my brain. It was lunchtime now, my tray of food sat untouched, but I still couldn't put my phone down.

Kevin: 😟

Kevin: 🙊

Kevin: 😵

Before I'd made that call, I hadn't been sure I was going to tell Kevin. If no one knew, it would be like it didn't happen. I could still go on being me. Veronica. The sort of girl who got straight As and scholarships and didn't get pregnant by accident. But now I needed a ride. And not just into the city. A fourteen-hour drive across state lines, assuming we didn't stop. And another fourteen-hour return trip. Kevin was the obvious choice. He was my boyfriend. He loved me. He was half the reason I needed to do this in the first place. And he was going to have to cover half the cost because it was way more expensive than I thought it would be. I was going to have to tell him. I pieced together a plan. I already had the perfect cover: cram weekend. Seventy-two hours away from my parents. I could tell my friends I wanted a romantic weekend alone with Kevin. They would understand. They were probably half expecting it already. And meanwhile, Kevin and I would be barrelling across four states to get me to an abortion clinic.

With shaking fingers, I typed to Kevin, **Maybe trade cram weekend for a three-day with you?** I took a deep breath, but before I could even exhale . . .

Kevin: 🥒 🥒 🍑 **jk. U sure? I know u love cram weekend with the girls.**

I sighed. He was going to be so disappointed when I told him what this was really about.

Me: I'm sure. ♡

The girls were usually here by now. I scanned the cafeteria, searching for them. Across the room, there was the clatter of a tray hitting the floor. I turned to see a group of freshmen scurrying away from the furthest, darkest corner of the room. Bailey barked loudly at the fleeing boys. Seeing her usual loner routine in full force was a relief. At least she wasn't regaling the cafeteria with tales of my pregnancy.

'Ronnie! Oh my God!' I turned. Emily, Jocelyn and

Kaylee were weaving through the cafeteria tables to get to me. Their eyes were alight with excitement.

'Did you hear?'

'Can you believe it?'

'Are you dying?'

Their questions were flung at me one after another, so fast I couldn't answer.

'Hear what?' I asked with some trepidation. I had to remind myself that if they'd heard about my situation somehow, they wouldn't be vibrating with such gleeful excitement. At least, I didn't think they would.

'Hannah Ballard got caught selling Adderall to some juniors,' Emily blurted, her voice an octave higher than normal from her barely contained delight. The girls clustered around me, eager to give the details.

'She tried to say it was the first time she's ever done something like that –'

'– like it was just the pressure of senior year or something –'

'But, like, please, you know she's probably been dealing her ADHD meds for years –'

'So now she's totally expelled –'

'Which means –'

'You've got valedictorian in the bag!' Kaylee finished, triumphant. The girls bounced up and down, celebrating. Their squeals echoed across the cafeteria. I pasted a smile on my face, but the news left me feeling hollow. As they continued to dance, my eyes scanned the room. From her corner, Bailey sat watching us. Her eyes caught mine and her smile widened. She patted her belly. I looked away.

'Maybe she *was* under a lot of pressure,' I said. The girls stopped dancing and looked at me as if I were speaking Chinese. Not Chinese. I took Mandarin sophomore year. They gaped at me as if I were speaking Finnish.

'We're all under a lot of pressure,' Kaylee sniffed.

'But what if it really was a one-time mistake? What if it was just a stupid impulse? Maybe she was tired of always being so perfect. She messes up once and now her whole life is ruined?' My voice was taking on a tinge of panic. The girls were looking at me, bemused. I forced myself to calm down. 'It hardly seems fair,' I said lamely. There was a beat of silence.

'Ronnie . . .' Emily started.

'You are way too nice,' Jocelyn finished.

'Yeah, can't you sink down to our normal-people level and indulge in some good ol' schadenfreude?' Kaylee added.

'Look at that, German II finally came in handy.' Jocelyn gave Kaylee a no-look high five.

I managed a half smile.

'Is something wrong?' Emily asked. My stomach lurched.

'No. No, of course not.'

'Come on, you've wanted valedictorian since you were a freshman. And now all we're getting is a sad little smile? Something's up. Spill.' I looked at my friends. Maybe I could tell them what was really going on. But then I thought of Hannah Ballard and the looks of glee they wore when they told me what had happened to her. Would they wear those same expressions when they talked about me once they were alone? After all, if I wasn't valedictorian, it would probably be one of them.

'It's . . . Kevin. He wants me to ditch you guys and go away with him this weekend,' I finally said. They didn't need to know I gave him the idea. The girls sagged in relief.

'Oh, thank God.'

'I thought it was something tragic.'

'Like you had brain cancer.'

'Or your scholarship fell through.'

'Or you were pregnant.' My friends dissolved into laughter and I forced myself to chuckle along with them, even though my whole body had gone numb.

'Ha, ha. No way. That's hilarious,' I managed. From the corner of my eye, I saw Bailey approaching. Students scattered out of her way like dried leaves. Was she coming over here? I held my breath. But she stomped past without stopping.

Emily threw her arm over my shoulders and gave me a

squeeze. 'We knew you were gonna bail.'

'Yeah, it's too perfect an opportunity.'

'So, you're not mad?' I asked.

'No way; if any of us had a guy that looked like Kevin we'd be hittin' that as much as possible, too.'

'Seriously. What does he do to his hair to get it to swoop like that?'

'Shhh! Here he comes!' Jocelyn faux-whispered, looking over my shoulder. I turned – and found myself nearly nose-to-nose with my boyfriend. He was so close I could smell the peanut butter and jelly sandwich on his breath. I jerked back.

'Aw, babe. Sorry. I keep scaring you. It's like I'm a bad grade or something.' He stuck his hands out in front of him like Frankenstein's monster and made groaning noises. 'Arrrrg. I'm a C-plus.'

The girls cracked up at his dorky joke. I laughed along but wished he'd lay off teasing me about my grades. Oblivious, Kevin plopped down next to me and offered a pack of Twizzlers. 'Anyone want one?' The girls tittered and each took a piece of candy. He put his arm around me. 'Did you tell them yet?'

'We got your back, bro.' Emily gave him a saucy wink. He indulged her with a lazy smile. She swooned. Kevin turned his attention back to me.

'So check this out. I wanna make it special since you're

giving up your weekend for me. Fancy dinner. A room at the Knights Inn. Chocolate. Hot tub.' He made an explosion with his hand. 'Boom.'

'I think I just ovulated,' Jocelyn sighed.

'Yeah, um, maybe we can just play it by ear?' I squeaked, trying not to think of the conversation we were going to have.

'Spontaneous. I can do that.' Kevin took a bite of Twizzler. 'It's gonna be a weekend we'll never forget.'

He was right about that.

MILE 1

My parents waved to me from the front porch as I threw my duffel bag into the trunk and climbed into Jocelyn's minivan. I tossed my backpack on to the floor and took a seat. The girls were all wearing matching neon-green shirts.

'Look!' Emily squealed. 'I had them made for our last weekend.' They read 'Finals Weekend '20: One Last Cram'. I put mine on over my tank top, feeling a stab of guilt for missing our final cram weekend. But a surge of anger quickly followed. It wasn't fair. Millions of teenage girls had sex and didn't end up pregnant. I followed all the rules. I was safe. So why did I end up punished?

College was just a few months away, and once we were scattered all over the country, the chances of us drifting apart were pretty high. Who knew the next time we would be together? I was realistic. We would all meet new people. Have different interests. This could be our last time together. And now, instead of capping off my senior year with a glorious weekend stuffing my face with Oreos and Red Vines with my best friends, I was going to be . . . again my mind shied away from what was going to actually happen.

For the first time since I'd found out, my emotions overwhelmed the churning panic in my stomach and my eyes pricked with tears. Blinking them back, I made sure my expression was bright and shiny as I returned my parents' waves.

'Study hard, Brown!' my dad called.

'Make sure you text us when you get there!' my mom added. Kaylee leant out the passenger window.

'Mrs Clarke, uh, remember the reception's not so good at the cabin,' she said with a note of aggrieved apology. My mom's face faltered for a moment, then recovered.

'Well, just try, Veronica.'

I nodded. 'OK, Mom. Love you.' I slid the door shut. Jocelyn started the engine and pulled away from the kerb. As we slowly accelerated to the exact speed limit, I could hear my mother's voice call after us.

'We trust you!'

Her favourite line. One she'd been using on me since I was six to guarantee maximum guilt. The woman was good.

Once we rounded the corner, Jocelyn eyed me in the rear-view mirror.

'So where do we drop you?'

'Le Bistro,' I mumbled. Immediately the car was filled with high-pitched squeals. Le Bistro was the nicest restaurant in town. My parents only went there on their anniversary. It was the sort of place where if you went to the bathroom someone would refold your napkin and put it back on the table by the time you returned. It was the sort of place where the whole menu was in French and it was just assumed you knew how to pronounce *haricot vert*. It was also the sort of place that I imagined was very, very quiet. So exactly *not* the sort of place I wanted to have a discussion about the currently occupied state of my uterus. But I hadn't found the right moment to talk to him all week and now I was out of time.

'Uh, you're not wearing that, are you?' Emily asked, looking askance at my T-shirt and jeans.

Kaylee rolled her eyes. 'She couldn't exactly walk out of the house dressed for a date, could she?' She turned to me. 'So let's see what you got.'

Digging into my backpack, I pulled out a floaty floral miniskirt and heels.

'Kevin's favourite skirt,' I explained. I figured I needed every possible advantage tonight and I was not above a miniskirt to soften Kevin up. The outfit earned murmurs of approval from the girls and I proceeded to wiggle out of my jeans. With the camisole I had on under my 'Finals

Weekend' T-shirt, I would look nice enough for Le Bistro. I hoped.

It should have taken ten minutes to get to Le Bistro. And it probably did. But it felt like I blinked and suddenly we were pulling into the parking lot. My heart started to pound. I wasn't ready for this.

'There he is!' Emily squealed.

Kevin was standing on the sidewalk, looking at his phone, the afternoon sun turning his hair an even more impossible shade of gold. At the minivan's approach he looked up and smiled. The girls let out a collective sigh of appreciation. Jocelyn parked and immediately I was being squeezed to death.

'Have fun!'

'We're gonna miss you!'

'I want pics!'

'Yeah, especially of Kevin in the hot tub!'

Eventually the arms hugging me fell away and the girls looked at me, expectant.

'Well?' Kaylee asked. 'Your prince is waiting.' Emily and Jocelyn giggled.

'I . . . don't want to go.' I couldn't believe I'd said those words out loud. And neither could the girls.

'Uh, what?' Jocelyn asked.

'I mean, I know cram weekend is awesome. But that's Kevin Decuziac standing on the sidewalk waiting for you,'

Emily added, not able to suppress another wistful sigh of longing.

'It's just . . . well, Kevin can be . . . a little intense.' It was true. He was intense. Most of the time I thought it was romantic. Like when he did a promposal with the marching band. Or when he set up a scavenger hunt to all the places we'd kissed for Valentine's Day. But now I was going to disappoint him. I wasn't going to be the girl who was so special she made him smile every time he saw her. I could only imagine how he was going to react to the news.

Surrounded by my best friends, a thought flitted across my mind. What if I just told them right now? Maybe I wouldn't have to get out of the van. Maybe Jocelyn could start the engine and we could just drive all the way to New Mexico.

'So, you're saying he's too in love with you,' Jocelyn mocked.

'No. It's just that—'

'Because let me tell you, even with just a few weeks of school left, you let that boy go, someone is gonna snap him right up.'

'Probably one of us,' Emily chimed in.

'He's, like, hands down, the hottest guy in school,' Kaylee reminded me.

'Intense?' Jocelyn scoffed. 'He can "intense" me all night.'

This was not going the way I had hoped. If admitting that I had any doubts about my perfect boyfriend led to this onslaught, there was no way I could tell them the other thing.

I forced myself to smile.

'You're right. I don't know what I was thinking. Probably just nerves. I've never been to a place this nice.' The girls looked visibly relieved at this admission. Suddenly the world made sense again. They were my best friends, but they weren't the sort of friends you told something like this to. Ours was a friendship built on successes, not failures.

I climbed out of the van.

The restaurant was dark. I could barely see the sauce-covered steak on my plate, which was fine with me. Even if I could find my food, I was so nervous there was no way I could force it down my throat. I hadn't told Kevin. I couldn't. Every time I tried, there was another waiter filling my glass of water or asking me if I needed any pepper for my filet. Kevin was almost done with his meal. Only the spinach was untouched.

'Isn't this place romantic?' he asked, stuffing a final wad of beef into his mouth.

'Um . . . yeah.' I was running out of time. And Kevin was starting to notice something was wrong. I'd barely spoken all night. And he was struggling to keep the conversation going.

'I love candles,' he offered.

I had to tell him.

'Yeah. There's something you should know. I . . .' *Come on, Veronica. Just say it.* 'Look, I don't know how it happened . . .' *Just say it and it will be over. Whatever happens can't be worse than this.* 'Statistically it's nearly impossible . . .' *Just don't look at him. Just don't look at him.* 'Try not to be mad when I tell you . . .' My voice had turned into a squeak and I was breathless. I dared a look across the table to gauge Kevin's reaction. But he wasn't there.

Instead he was beside me, down on one knee.

Uh-oh.

'What are you——?' He took a small velvet box from his pocket and opened it to reveal a delicate yellow-gold ring with a princess-cut diamond.

'Marry me, babe.'

I recognized the words individually, but my brain refused to make sense of them.

'I'll try to be the best husband and father ever. I can totally take care of us.'

This was all wrong. I had been preparing for a fight. Accusations. Anger. Not an offer of lifetime commitment. Part of me knew I should be grateful. He wasn't freaking out. But I was thrown. This wasn't what I had planned. I'd planned to confess everything, and then before he got too upset, present him with my solution to drive halfway across the country. I had the route mapped on my phone. I could answer questions about time, distance, rest stops. But this? I wasn't—

My thoughts snagged.

Father. Did he say father? I hadn't said anything about . . .

'Wait . . . you knew I was pregnant?'

But Kevin barrelled forward, words tumbling from his mouth. 'I'll get a job. We'll get a place. You can go to college once the baby is born. Your parents will help. Look what they've done for your sister. And the church has day care. It won't be that bad. We'll still be able to party on weekends.' He waited, hopeful, for my response. But I was still unravelling how he'd discovered my secret.

'Did Bailey tell you?'

Kevin blinked, confused. 'Bailey the boner killer Butler? Why would she—'

'Then how?' None of this made sense.

'Well, you're kind of glowing, and –' he sniffed me – 'you smell different.'

'You know the signs of pregnancy?' A horrible suspicion was beginning to form.

'I . . . did some research?' Kevin shifted uncomfortably on his knee.

'Why?'

'Because . . . I just thought . . . there might be a chance . . .' Dread pounded through me.

'But we used condoms.'

'Yeah, well . . . uh . . .'

I yanked Kevin off his knee and back into the booth. 'Did one break?'

He wouldn't look me in the eye. 'Maybe.'

'Either it did or it didn't.'

'I mean, no. It didn't.'

'But you still suspected I was pregnant. And did research, and even bought a ring.' I managed to keep my voice neutral, with no hint of the rage bubbling up inside. Guilt flickered in Kevin's eyes. A bead of sweat trailed down his temple. And I knew.

This wasn't an accident.

'Say yes, babe.' He took the ring out of the box.

'Did you . . . Did you . . .' As I stuttered, Kevin fumbled with the ring. He was flustered. This obviously wasn't working out quite how he'd imagined it either.

'Here. Try it on.' He shoved the ring on to my finger. I snatched my hand away.

'Did you PLAN this?'

'No! Plan? Babe, that would be crazy!'

'Kevin. Tell me.'

'It wasn't on purpose . . .'

'What wasn't?'

'Nothing! Just . . . the night you got accepted to Brown . . . we drank that six-pack and . . . and I got really sad about you being so far away. I'd always imagined I'd be on the East Coast too. I know my grades suck, but I thought someone would recruit me for soccer. And I knew that once you got to Brown you'd probably find some guy who was smarter and better so I just thought . . . what if there was a reason you had to stay?'

He said it like it was nothing. Like he hadn't taken my life into his hands.

'You did something to the condom!'

'To be fair, I really regretted it the next morning. But I was afraid to tell you because I knew you'd be mad.'

I stood, backing away from the table, not trusting myself to speak, the enormity of what he'd done crushing the air from my lungs. He'd got me pregnant on purpose.

Kevin looked up at me. 'I'm sorry, babe.' I felt something rise up inside me. It was puke.

I barely made it outside before I threw up on the concrete. Flecks of vomit spattered my new strappy heels. I heaved again, surprised that there was anything else to come up since I'd eaten so little at dinner. As I wiped my mouth, I heard Kevin's footsteps as he ran to my side. He examined the mess.

'Hey, I read that means the baby is healthy.'

I spun around to face him. 'How could you do this to me?!' I was shaking. At my words, his expression morphed from concerned to defensive.

'You were leaving and I panicked, OK!'

'So you got me pregnant?! Stuck some holes in a condom?!'

'I didn't think it would work! They were very small holes! My sperm must be, like, super strong.' He couldn't help smiling a bit at this, proud. My stomach heaved. He reached towards me and gently touched my arm. 'Look, you know how much I love you, right?'

A few days ago, I would never have doubted it. Just like I never would have doubted I loved him back. We'd done everything couples were supposed to do: school dances, matching Halloween costumes, holding hands on the way to class, awkward car sex. Was that love? Or just the performance of it?

'How is this happening?'

'Hey, don't worry. I was totally freaked out at first, too. But the more I thought about it, the more I was like, it's not so bad. We won't be the first couple around here to start a family early.'

I could almost see it. There would be backyard barbecues, church on Sundays; everyone would say we were such a beautiful couple. And I would never stop hating him.

Oblivious, Kevin continued, 'It's not ideal, but we'll

make it through. You're smart. You don't need an Ivy League degree to be successful. And I'll be right by your side.' He tried to enfold me in his arms.

It dawned on me, maybe he actually did want this — not a baby, but an easy way out. He wouldn't have to start over in a new place. A place where he wasn't going to be star of the soccer team, a place where the parties were full of strangers, a place where he wasn't king of the campus. He wouldn't have to face being alone. Kevin hated being alone.

I jerked away. 'Don't touch me!'

'I get it. You need your space.' He stepped back.

But I didn't need space. As far as I was concerned, the whole universe was empty. There was nothing but space. I was nothing but space. There were a thousand miles between me and the only thing that could salvage the remnants of my life. What was I going to do?

I paced, my mind scrambling for a solution. What would he do if I told him my plan? He'd already got me pregnant so I wouldn't leave him. Would he even be willing to take me to the clinic? And if he agreed, could I sit next to him in his minivan for three days knowing what he'd done to me?

Then a bright gleam caught my eye: the ring. I examined it as it glittered under the streetlights.

'How much did you spend on this?' I knew I needed at least five hundred dollars. Maybe this ring would be enough.

'I used my lifeguarding money. Is that a yes?' I stared at him, utterly confused. After all this, he still thought we had a future? He sensed he'd said something wrong and quickly added, 'Sorry. Take your time. No pressure.' He paced back and forth a few times and then looked at me again, puppy-dog hopeful. 'So, yes?' I ignored him. A vague sort of plan was forming in my mind.

'I need some time to think.'

'That's cool, babe. You want me to wait in my car for, like, ten minutes?'

'We'll talk Monday.'

'Monday?! But what about the hotel? I already paid!' At my glare, he backed off. 'Monday's good.' Then, as if he couldn't resist, he added, 'I know when we look back on this, we're going to laugh.' He leant in for a kiss, but thought better of it. I realized then we were never going to kiss again.

Five minutes later, he was in his van and I was standing on the kerb, backpack slung over my shoulder, duffel bag in hand.

'You sure you don't want me to drive you to the cabin?'

'No, it's OK. The girls stopped for dinner before they left town, so they decided to just turn around and come get me.'

'OK. But don't tell them anything. I want our engagement

to be a surprise.' He reached out the car window to stroke my arm. I swallowed my revulsion and marvelled at just how obtuse he could be. After being together for years it was like I was seeing him for the first time.

'I'll see you Monday.' I kept my voice firm. Kevin sighed, disappointed.

'Fine.' Resigned, he rolled up the window and drove out of the parking lot. As he pulled away, my phone dinged a few times in rapid succession. It was a group message from the girls.

Emily: Almost to the cabin! Miss u!

Jocelyn: How's the Knights Inn?

Kaylee: In the hot tub yet?

I typed back, **Great! Putting on my bikini!** and added a winky face. Then, making sure Kevin was nowhere in sight, I walked away from the restaurant back towards town.

I'd never been to the bus station before. It was part of a truck stop, attached to a diner and a tattoo parlour, and smelt of old grease and air freshener. As I approached the counter, I could feel truckers' eyes slide over me and I wished I'd thought to change out of my miniskirt.

'Excuse me,' I asked the balding cashier with a wad of tobacco in his lip, 'how much is the seven p.m. to Albuquerque?' The man typed a few words into an ancient computer and grunted.

'Ninety-seven fifty,' he replied, and turned back to the dog race playing on the TV set next to him. I sighed in relief. I had a few hundred dollars of babysitting money that I'd emptied out of my sock drawer before I'd left.

'Great. I'll take it.' I took out my wallet. 'What time does it get there?' The cashier sighed, obviously frustrated at being distracted from his race, and typed a few more words into the computer.

'Nine p.m. Saturday.'

'Saturday night?' I couldn't keep the panic from my voice. 'Do you have anything faster? An express?' The cashier really looked at me for the first time, taking in my age and dress. He smirked.

'Yeah. It's called an airplane.' He spat some juice into a dirty paper cup and turned back to the dogs.

'Oh, never mind then. Thank you.' I was sure he could hear the tears in my voice, but he didn't even glance up as I walked away.

I sat on the hard, graffiti-scored toilet seat in the women's restroom and tried to stifle my tears. No boyfriend, no bus, no hope. I was out of options. I could see my dorm room at Brown fading away. Instead, I was going to be spending my fall putting together a nursery with my sister's second-hand baby gear and being slowly crushed to death by my father's disappointment. At this thought, I let out a fresh sob. In the stall next to me, someone finished their business, washed their hands, and left. Apparently hysterical crying wasn't an unusual feature in truck stop restrooms. My tears turned into a half laugh. I was doing a lot of crying in bathrooms lately. Maybe after this was all over I should rank them. I'd have to put this one below the one at school, because at least Bailey had seemed to care when I started crying. And she hadn't even posted anything about it. My tears stopped completely as I was struck by a new, slightly terrifying, possibly insane thought: Bailey.

The sun was low in the sky by the time the local bus dropped me near Bailey's neighbourhood, but the air was still thick and warm. I'd changed back into my jeans at the bus stop. With my two bags and the heat, I could already feel my clothes starting to stick to me. At least my feet were grateful to be back in my Adidas. I'd tossed the vomit-spattered heels in the trash, never wanting to see them again.

The houses here were all set far back from the street with rolling lush green lawns and perfectly trimmed hedges. Unlike my neighbourhood, no forgotten half-strung Christmas lights or plastic children's toys marred the landscape. Instead, the brick facades loomed, intimidating and stern, ready to judge you for any deviation from the expected. Trudging up Bailey's winding driveway, I felt smaller and smaller as I approached the door. From inside, I could hear the muted sounds of a TV. She was home, probably alone. As far as I knew, Bailey's mom still worked the night shift at the hospital. All I needed to do was press the doorbell.

I really, really did not want to press the doorbell.

I pressed the doorbell.

Footsteps. A shadow crossing the front window. A pause by the front door as someone peeked through the peephole. The sounds of a dead bolt being turned. The door swung open.

Bailey eyed me blearily as she leant on the door frame. She was half dressed in a pair of boxer shorts and an oversized tee featuring a unicorn pooping rainbows. Her relative lack of surprise I attributed to the waft of weed that greeted my nose. 'Wow. What'd I do to deserve a visit from the embryoed one?'

'Sorry to bother you. Are you busy?'

Bailey snorted. 'Super.'

'Look, I know we're not as good friends as we used to be. But you're the only one I know with a car and . . .' I could hear the nerves in my voice. I'd worked out a rough idea of what I was going to say on my way there. But Bailey had a way of ruining any plans I made. However, for once she simply stood there, waiting for me to get to the point, a faint frown creasing her forehead. 'I mean, if I could just go to somewhere in town or even St Louis, I wouldn't ask you, but the closest place is Albuquerque and—' Bailey held up a hand and waved it at me to stop speaking.

'Closest what?' she asked, her voice slow from whatever she'd been smoking. I blushed.

'Place. You know. To get the procedure.' I watched as she mentally put the pieces together. A delighted grin spread across her face.

'Hold on. You want me to be your escort?' Relief rushed through me. The idea was out there.

'Yes. I'll totally pay for gas and food and whatever.' I waited, searching her face for a clue as to her response. She nodded, thoughtful.

'Oh, I get it.'

'Get what?'

'Where are your BFFs, Veronica?'

'It's cram weekend. They have to study—'

'Uh-huh. Sure.' She looked at me knowingly. 'You don't want them to know.'

'No! It's not that!'

'See, everyone has different types of friends. There's your BFFs, and your friends with benefits, and your camp friends, and of course, your druggie friends—'

'That's not—'

'I'm your abortion friend!'

'No! Just listen—' But Bailey wasn't going to let my

53

half-hearted protest stop her.

'Yes! I'm the kind of friend who maybe you don't need for everyday things, not the dress shopping or the weekend getaway kinda girl, but when it comes time to purge the placenta . . . Bam! Call the abortion friend!'

'Shhh!' I frantically waved at Bailey to lower her voice. She had got loud enough that the neighbours could hear. Bailey, however, was now too busy fake crying to pay attention.

'I'm so honoured . . . to be chosen for this . . . honour.'

Frustrated, I yanked Kevin's engagement ring off my finger and shoved it in her face. 'Look, I'm not asking you to do it as a friend. I'm pawning this. It . . . was my grandma's. I'll take what I need for the doctor and you can have the rest, OK? It's a job. That's all.'

Bailey looked at the ring and then back at me. She gave one slow nod of her head.

And slammed the door in my face.

'Bailey?' No. This was my last chance. It needed to work. It had to work. 'Bailey? Please?' But the only thing I could hear from inside the house was the faint drone of the TV.

I didn't remember walking down the driveway, or back to the street. I didn't remember sitting down on the kerb. But that's where I found myself as the day dwindled towards night. Why had I expected Bailey to help? She obviously hated me. And I couldn't stand being around her. We hadn't even spoken in four years until this week. I'd just hoped that the money would be enough to tempt her. There was no way her allowance covered the amount of weed she smoked. But the opportunity to spite me was clearly too tempting to pass up.

Out of ideas, even bad ones, I sat on the hard concrete, staring at my feet, waiting for something to happen. Preferably the end of the world. The rumble of an engine finally shook me back to awareness. It was getting closer. Really close. I looked up.

Bailey was hanging out the driver's-side window of a vintage El Camino, burnt orange with a black racing stripe on its hood.

'One condition. We stop in Roswell.'

'Stop?' I froze midway through standing up and grabbing my bag. She had to be joking. 'I don't know if we're going to have time to sightsee—'

'Veronica. We're talking aliens. Government cover-ups. I've always wanted to go and it's not just your vacation.'

'This is not a vacation!' I spluttered, offended. Bailey rolled her eyes, unimpressed.

'Well, I'm not going to be all tragic about this just because you are.'

'I'm not being tragic, Bailey. This isn't a joke. This last week has been—'

'Blah blah blah. Wah wah wah. I'm Veronica. I'm sooooooo tragic.'

'Stop it, Bailey. I'm serious.'

'So am I. Serious about Roswell.' We glared at each other. Finally, Bailey cocked an eyebrow. 'Why don't I roll this puppy back into the garage? I can hear that *Doctor Who* marathon calling my name.' She put the car in reverse.

'No!' I couldn't get the word out fast enough.

'No, what?'

'No. Don't do that.' I took a deep breath. 'We can stop in Roswell.' She smiled. It wasn't Bailey's normal smirk. It actually seemed genuine. I felt a pang of guilt. I was lying. There was no way we were going to stop in Roswell. We wouldn't have time. But I needed that El Camino. I needed Bailey. I pushed my guilt aside. 'But my stop is first.'

Bailey shrugged, unconcerned. 'No problem, boss. Climb in.'

Knowing this was likely my last, best and only chance, I did.

Taking in the interior of the car, I blinked, unable for a moment to comprehend what I was seeing: black light, smooth, rich leather and a skull on the gearshift.

'Don't you drive a Camry?' It was the first coherent thought that entered my brain. Bailey rolled her eyes.

'Used to. But my mom's boyfriend fixes up cars. He's been teaching me how. We worked on this one together and when we finished he gave it to me for graduation. Sweet, huh?'

'Wow. That's, like, super generous.'

Bailey shrugged. 'We get along. Anyway, who wants to road trip in a Camry?' At this point, I would road trip in anything that got me to Albuquerque on time. Except Kevin's van. Bailey revved the engine. 'All right. Let's do this "procedure"!'

I was slammed against my seat as we peeled out with a squeal of rubber. We rocketed down the quiet suburban street. Dogs barked. Car alarms wailed. Bailey's voice rose above the growl of the engine as she began to sing.

'*Abortion friend, abortion friend. Wouldn't have to do this if you'd let him stick it in your end!*'

I closed my eyes and prayed I'd survive the next nine hundred and ninety-four miles.

MILE 4

We pulled up to a red light. Bailey had cranked the stereo, blasting some sort of angry screaming music, and the El Camino was shaking from the bass. She was screaming along and I was slouched down as low as I could in the seat. In front of us, the entrance to the highway beckoned, the ribbon of roadway quickly disappearing into the distance. In a moment we would be speeding our way across the state, anonymous and safe.

'Can we please be a little more subtle?'

Bailey turned the volume knob up.

'Awesome. Thanks.' I peered over the edge of the window. At least there weren't any other cars stopped at the light. There was a Dairy Queen on the corner, but it looked mostly empty. There was only one customer sitting in a booth, dejectedly eating a banana split. He looked miserable. He looked like Kevin.

He was Kevin.

'Turn off the music! Turn off the music!' I reached for the dial but Bailey batted my hand away.

'No way. It's about to kick in.'

'Just turn it off!' But it was too late. Without even needing to look, I could feel his eyes on me. Dreading what I would see, I turned. Kevin was staring at the El Camino, spoon frozen halfway to his slack-jawed mouth. Ice cream slowly dripped from the spoon back into the bowl. I could see his lips form my name.

'Go,' I begged.

'Chill, Sixteen and Pregnant. I can't. The light's red.'

'Now you're suddenly Miss Law and Order?' Inside the restaurant, I saw Kevin drop his spoon, his ice cream abandoned, and stand.

'I'm not running a light. There could be a cop around.'

He exited the restaurant. 'It's Kevin! He's coming this way!'

Bailey turned to look. He was hurrying towards us. 'Man, that douchebag can run!'

I frantically locked all the doors. 'He doesn't know I'm pregnant,' I lied.

Bailey's eyes swung back to me. 'Shocker.'

Once Kevin was close enough, he called out, 'Veronica? What are you doing?' Then, when he saw who was driving, 'Is that . . . Bailey Butler?' He came to a stop, utterly confused, trying to piece together the puzzle of Bailey, an

El Camino, a highway on-ramp and me.

The light turned.

'It's green. Go!' Bailey slammed her foot down on the gas and we took off with another squeal of rubber. In the side mirror, I could see a confounded Kevin dwindling away.

As we sailed under the sign reading 'US HWY 63 South', my phone pinged.

Kevin: Where are you going?

With shaking fingers, I deleted the text. Then I blocked his number. Bailey glanced over.

'Let me guess. You think he'll dump you if he finds out?'

'Yeah. Stupid, right?'

'Not as stupid as dating him in the first place.'

'You just hate him because he's popular.'

'You're delusional.'

'I'm not delusional! He really loves me. Sophomore year, he asked me out every day for a month before I said yes. There were cute little notes. He literally stood outside my window one night.'

'That's called stalking.'

'It was romantic!' I didn't know why I was defending Kevin – after all, I still wanted to dunk him in the Dairy Queen deep fryer – but I suspected it had something to do with the smug look Bailey was wearing.

'You say, "Romeo". I say, "restraining order".'

'He's devoted to me.'

'Like a stalker.'

'He's not a stalker!'

'Survey says: stalker!'

'Whatever.' I crossed my arms, then sighed. 'It's just, no one ever wanted me like that before, you know?' A look I couldn't quite interpret crossed Bailey's face before she schooled it into blankness.

'No. I don't.' For a moment we drove in silence, but as usual Bailey couldn't let it drop. 'He just really seemed like he wanted to talk to you back there.' I couldn't tell her the truth. It was too humiliating. What sort of idiot would fall for a guy who would do something like this to her? And I wasn't supposed to be an idiot. I was probably the smartest person in school, now that Hannah was out of the way. So what did that say about me? Plus, there was no way I was listening to a thousand miles of Bailey's I-told-you-so's. Bailey looked sceptical. 'Is there something you're not telling me?'

'Look, I'm paying you to drive me, not interrogate me, OK?'

'Touchy, touchy. Fine. Whatever. Let's stick to business. Where are we pawning Grammy's ring?'

'Uh, I figured Albuquerque.'

'Ha ha. No way. What if Gramps was a cheapskate and

got that out of a gumball machine? I'm not waiting until New Mexico to find out if I'm getting paid. That's not how this chauffeur thing works.'

'You're not my chauffeur,' I grumbled.

'Yes, milady. Whatever you say, milady.' Bailey's British accent was appalling. I grabbed my phone and started searching.

'You'll have to wait until Jefferson City.'

MILE 32

I'd been to this town before with my parents, but never this neighbourhood. Streetlights were few and far between. We passed a plumbing supply store and a used car lot before coming to a tiny strip mall. There was a payday loan store, a laundromat and a Chinese restaurant, all closed. The pawnshop was a dingy white stucco building with a blue roof. Behind the large begrimed window were displayed a few faded paintings, dusty guitars and a rocking chair with a hand-painted sign propped on its cushion promising fair prices. The parking lot was empty. We pulled into a space close to the shop's entrance.

'Ever been to one of these before?' I asked.

'Oh yeah, I've got a rewards card,' Bailey replied, rolling her eyes.

'Don't get defensive. It's just a question. I mean, I just thought . . . people say . . .' I watched as Bailey's eyes iced over.

'What? What do they say about me, Veronica?' she challenged me. I blushed.

'Never mind.' I climbed out of the car. Bailey mumbled something under her breath and followed.

Approaching the entrance, we were both bathed in the orange-red glow of the 'Open' sign. I tried the door. It was locked. Confused, I tried the handle again. It jiggled but didn't turn. I started to panic. If I couldn't sell the ring, I couldn't get the procedure. What if we had to drive all over before we found a place that was open? What if pawn-shops weren't open at night? What if we had to wait until tomorrow? We'd never make it to New Mexico in time. I yanked harder on the handle.

'It's not opening. How can they be closed?' Embarrass-ingly, tears sprang to my eyes.

'Ivy League, huh?' I blinked at Bailey, confused. She jerked her thumb towards a small handwritten sign that read, *For entrance, please use buzzer.* 'Application pool must be thin this year.'

Now even more embarrassed, I pressed it and waited. After a moment there was an answering buzz and the door clicked open.

Bailey gestured. 'After you.'

The shop was crammed floor to ceiling with junk. Guitars, drum sets, guns – a lot of guns – and smelt faintly of dust and Elizabeth Taylor's White Diamonds. The source of the perfume scent soon became clear. A sixty-year-old woman with dyed carrot-coloured hair, lime-green eye shadow and an oversized bedazzled flamingo T-shirt lolled behind a glass display counter, idly flipping through an ancient issue of *Good Housekeeping*.

'Yeah?' She didn't bother to glance up from her All Cupcake Detox Diet article.

'I, uh, have something to pawn.' I yanked the ring off my finger. 'This.'

She sighed, carefully folded down her page before closing the magazine, then finally looked up. She squinted at the ring pinched between my fingers. 'Well, I can't see it from there. Put it on the counter, girlie.'

I glanced at Bailey for reassurance, but she had wandered off to play with a baby-blue electric guitar, plugging it into a beat-up amp. I shuffled forward and placed the ring on the glass.

The lady peered at it for a second before pulling back and reopening her magazine. 'Sorry. Not interested.'

'What? What's wrong? Is it a fake?' In light of what Kevin did to our condoms, I didn't know why I was surprised that he might also be a cheapskate fake ring buyer.

'I knew it!' Bailey strummed a triumphant chord on her guitar.

'Bailey! Jeez.' I slapped my hands over my ears. The lady

shot an annoyed glance at her. Bailey mouthed *sorry* and gently put the guitar down.

The lady turned her attention back to me. 'No. It's real.'

I sagged in relief. At least the ring was worth something. 'Then what's wrong?'

She closed her magazine and levelled her gaze at me. 'Well, sweetie, if that ring were really yours, wouldn't you and your friend know if it was real or not?' She smiled at the guilty look on my face.

'It was a gift,' I mumbled.

'Uh-huh. And how old are you?'

'Eighteen.'

'Of course you are. Good night, girls.' She pushed the ring back towards me.

'No. Please . . .' I didn't take it. I couldn't. Already the clock was ticking down. I couldn't waste any more time driving around searching for a place to sell the ring. We still had over 900 miles to cover.

'Come back with your parents.'

'I can't.'

'Exactly.' She had me and she knew it. Reluctantly, I reached for the ring.

'She needs an abortion!'

I whirled around. 'Bailey!' She shrugged, unapologetic. My face was on fire. When I turned back to the woman, I noticed the small gold cross around her neck for the first time. Wonderful. There was a long, uncomfortable silence.

'Is that true?'

I nodded yes, unable to answer. Shrinking, I waited for fire and brimstone to rain down on me.

Instead someone pounded on the door, shaking the glass.

'Babe!'

It was Kevin.

'Stalker!' Bailey thrust both arms into the air in victory.

'Oh God,' I moaned.

'Stop banging on the damn door!' the lady yelled, then turned to me. 'You know this guy?'

'Unfortunately,' I muttered.

'Her impregnator,' Bailey added.

'Well, it looks like you two have something to talk about. Why don't you take your little tea party outside?'

'No!' I yelped before I could stop myself. Then, taking a deep breath, I let it all out. 'See, I got into Brown on a scholarship and he was upset that I wasn't going to go to Missouri State with him so he poked holes in the condoms to get me pregnant and then proposed tonight and my parents think I'm studying for finals with friends all week-end so this is the only chance I have to do it.' When I finally managed to look up, the pawnshop lady's expression hadn't changed.

'Ho. Lee. Shit.' I looked over to Bailey to find her

staring at me, goggle-eyed.

Kevin pounded on the door again.

'What are you doing in there, babe? Come out! I love you!' As he continued to rattle the glass with his fists, I backed as far away from the door as possible. Bailey eyed me.

'Any chance there's a back door?' she mumbled out of the side of her mouth.

There was a buzz and the lock clicked open. My eyes flew to the woman behind the counter in time to see her finger slide off the button. I couldn't hide the look of betrayal that crossed my face. Kevin slid through the door.

'Thanks, ma'am.' He turned to me. 'Veronica, why are you selling . . .' But the words died on his lips.

'Did you get this girl pregnant on purpose?'

I turned to see the pawnshop woman aiming a giant twelve-gauge shotgun at Kevin's face. Her eyes were cool and her hands were rock steady.

'What? I—'

'Did you. Get this girl. Pregnant on purpose?' she repeated.

Kevin swallowed. 'No, ma'am! I was drunk!'

In response she cocked the gun. 'Get the fuck out of here.'

Kevin turned white. 'Leaving, ma'am. Sorry, ma'am.' He backed out the door, hands raised. A moment later, we heard his van sputter to life and zoom off.

The pawnshop lady put the shotgun back under the counter, opened the till, and slapped two hundred-dollar bills on the counter. My heart sank. After all this, it wasn't going to be enough. I needed at least $500 to pay the doctor. Then she reached back into the till.

'You OK with twenties?' she asked, and continued counting. And counting. Soon there was an enormous stack of bills resting on the glass display case. 'Twelve hundred should about do it.' My heart leapt. That was way more than I'd expected.

'Damn, Kevin's a baller,' Bailey said, impressed.

'Please,' the woman said. 'I'm being generous, since you managed to find yourself the biggest asshole in all of Missouri.'

'Right?' Bailey agreed. She reached over the counter to give the lady a fist bump.

A minute later we were pulling out of the parking lot while the pawnshop lady stood on the sidewalk, waving.

'Good luck now! Y'all take care!'

MILE 73

Bailey fanned herself with the wad of bills as she drove. 'This is what Beyoncé must feel like!' I checked behind us for the hundredth time. The strip malls had given way to a dense line of thick green foliage, broken only by telephone poles and the occasional billboard. The four-lane highway rolled gently up and down. The only thing clearly visible was the patch of asphalt illuminated by our headlights.

'Still don't see him.'

'Chill, Veronica. There's no way Crazy Kev's on our tail. Did you see his face when that lady cocked her shotgun? Right now the only thing he's doing is looking for a place to buy new pants.'

I giggled. 'I wish I took a picture.'

'Don't worry. I did.' She tossed me her phone. Kevin stared back at me, eyes wide, mouth open, looking delightfully stupid.

'This is amazing!' I cried. 'Bailey, you're the best.' I went for a high five but Bailey left me hanging. I pulled back, feeling awkward. 'I'm sorry I lied to you about everything,' I mumbled.

'Please. Did you think I was in this for the backstory?'

'Still. I just should have told you.'

'I'll forgive you under one condition: say, "Bailey, you were right. Kevin is a skeezewad."'

'He's not—'

'May I remind you of a certain holey condom?'

I sighed. It wasn't that I didn't know he was awful. But admitting it meant I'd made a mistake in picking him. That I had failed. On the other hand, Bailey was only going to get more annoying if I refused her. It would just be easier to say it and get it over with.

'Bailey, you were right. Kevin is a skeezewad.'

'Louder.'

'Seriously?'

'Louder. I want the whole world to hear this. Roll down your window and stick your head out.' Rolling my eyes, I cranked the glass down. 'Make sure you really scream it,' she added. I leant out the window.

The wind whipped my hair, my eyes teared up, and I screamed into the night, 'BAILEY IS RIGHT! KEVIN IS A SKEEZEWAD!' As I sat back down in my seat, breathless, my hair in tangles, I was surprised to find I had a huge grin on my face.

'See, was that so hard?'

'That felt good. I'm going to do it again.' I leant out my window again. 'KEVIN IS A FUCKING SKEEZEWAD!' The wind ripped the words from my mouth. 'DICKLESS BUTTHOLE FUCKBURGLAR!'

'Woo! Yes! That's my girl. Hold on. I got one.' Bailey rolled down her window and leant out. The car swerved back and forth as she tried to steer with one hand.

'ASSTASTIC DOUCHE-GUZZLER!'

I laughed and shouted out the window. 'URINE-DRIPPING PENIS DRAGGER!'

'UNCONTROLLED SCROTUM FIRE!'

'SPONGEDICK SHITPANTS!'

'SPONGEDICK SHITPANTS . . . THE MOVIE!'

We gulped for air between bursts of silent laughter. 'One more. Together,' Bailey managed to wheeze. We stuck our heads out the windows again.

'SKEEZEWAAAAAAAAAAAAAAAD!' we screamed into the night, then tumbled back inside, laughing like maniacs.

'We need to celebrate,' Bailey said when we'd recovered.

'Celebrate what?'

'Being amazing.'

'OK.'

Bailey's eyes widened in surprise. 'Seriously?'

I nodded. 'Yeah.' I pushed down the part of me that

said to keep driving, to stay on task, to not deviate from the plan. But I was glowing, flush with a warm emotion. I wanted to keep it going. 'Yeah,' I said again.

Bailey grinned. 'I know the perfect place.'

MILE 142

'Not gonna happen.' I crossed my arms. 'Start the car.'

'Heck no. I've driven past this place a hundred times with my mom. I've always wanted to stop. We said we were going to celebrate. What could be more perfect than this?'

We were parked in front of two giant fiberglass statues. At least twelve feet high, they stood on a patch of gravel behind a rusted chain-link fence. One was a pink elephant; the other, a black-and-white cow. Surrounding them, a field of tall grass waved gently in the night breeze. A sign declared, 'Largest Elephant and Third-Largest Cow in the State!'

'OK. We've celebrated. Can we get back on the road?'

'Relax. We'll get back on the road – after we climb them.'

I took a deep, cleansing breath and forced my voice into the sort of reasonable, calming tone I imagined hostage negotiators used. 'I don't know whether you noticed, but it's closed. The animals are behind a locked gate. There's a sign with clearly labelled business hours. We are way beyond them.'

'Come on. Think of the view when we're up there.'

'It's the middle of the night, Bailey. There's nothing to see.'

'There's the stars,' Bailey sniffed.

I shook my head. 'It doesn't even make sense. Why is an elephant hanging out with a cow? An elephant and a lion, sure. A cow and a pig, I get that. But why an elephant and a cow?'

'That's the whole point.' Bailey gestured wildly. Her eyes gleamed with excitement. 'It makes no sense. That's why it's so awesome. Now let's go. I'm taking the elephant.' She unbuckled her seat belt and flung open her door.

'No!' I grabbed her arm as she moved to climb out.

'What?'

'It's trespassing, Bailey. I can't get arrested. I need to make it to Albuquerque, remember?' For a second, I thought Bailey might give in. Then she shrugged.

'So we'll be quiet.' And with a twist, she freed herself from my grasp and slammed the door.

I sat in my seat, frozen. Should I follow her? Tackle her to the ground and drag her back to the car? Should I rev up the engine and drive off, leaving her behind? That last thought was tempting. Bailey's feet sent sprays of gravel into the air as she pounded across the parking lot towards the locked chain-link fence that surrounded the roadside attraction. She stopped when she got to the gate. For a moment I thought she'd changed her mind, but she'd only paused to shrug off her jacket. Tossing it on the ground, she began to climb.

I couldn't let her do this. If she got caught, she'd ruin everything.

Shoving my door open, I tumbled out of the car and ran for the fence.

'Bailey! Get down from there!' I didn't dare yell, so it came out more like an emphatic whisper.

'No problem!' she called back merrily. Swinging over the top of the fence, she dropped to the ground. The chain link rattled loudly.

Now that I was out of the car, I could truly appreciate the scale of the animal statues. They towered over us, looming like two cruise ships on an ocean of grass. I didn't see any steps or ladders, so I wasn't sure how Bailey planned to make her ascent.

It became clear moments later when she began shimmying up the elephant's trunk. Plastered against it, looking like some sort of deranged Spider-Man, she heaved and grunted her way up. I was desperate to look away, but couldn't. Any second I was sure she was going to slip and tumble to the ground.

And then I'd be the one stuck calling 911, explaining to paramedics why we were there. We'd end up in some run-down rural hospital and while I sat in the lobby waiting to hear if Bailey was in a coma or not, some local cops would come and arrest me for trespassing. Then I'd have to call my parents and explain why I was 150 miles from home with a girl I hadn't spoken to in years and not at the cabin with my real friends. I'd spend the night in a cell that stank of urine with a crazy woman called Drunk Marge and then in the morning my parents would show up to bail me out. They'd find out what I'd planned and I'd lose my scholarship and have to live with my parents as an unwed mother for the rest of my life. The highlight of my week would be finding my favourite frozen dinners half off at the grocery store. The grocery store that I probably worked at. And all because Bailey wanted to climb a stupid pink elephant.

'That's it. I'm leaving,' I called, and turned back to the car.

'Ta-da!'

I turned around and stifled a gasp. Somehow when I wasn't paying attention, Bailey had made it all the way to the top of the statue. She stood on the elephant's head, legs spread wide for balance, a black silhouette against an endless grey sky. She looked amazing.

'Get up here,' Bailey demanded. I hesitated. Standing high above me, the wind tousling her hair, Bailey looked ready for adventure. She looked free. I'd never felt the way she looked right then in my entire life. I had too many expectations, too many obligations holding me down. If I climbed that cow next to her, would they suddenly fall away? Standing on its head, surveying the fields and sky around me, would I finally feel free?

I took a step towards the gate, gravel crunching under my heel. My fingers closed over the smooth, cool chain link. The thin metal cut into my hand.

'Oh man! Stupid clouds! I can't see shit!' I looked up. Bailey was jumping up and down on the back of the elephant, waving at the sky. 'Go away, clouds! Move!'

'Bailey! Shhhh!' I cautioned.

'I want to see the stars!' she wailed.

I heard a dog bark. Then another.

'Bailey!' I implored.

'This sucks.'

'Stop yelling at the sky and look down! Do you see dogs?' Bailey swivelled on her elephant perch. She scanned the shadowy field.

'Oh,' was all she said.

'Bailey?' I asked again. My voice was sliding upwards.

'Um, there are maybe some dogs running towards me.' My eyes flew to the signage covering the fence. Below the 'Closed at Dusk' was a 'No Trespassing' warning, and next to that was a sign that read 'Beware of Dogs'. The slavering

Rottweiler image was enough to indicate that it probably wasn't a pair of golden retrievers running towards us.

'Bailey. Get down. Now.'

'I'm trying!' she shouted back. She had already scrambled down the face of the elephant and was sliding down its trunk. Her hands slipped and she skidded a few feet. 'This is harder than climbing up.'

'Faster,' I hissed. I could see the grass parting as the dogs bounded through the field. I could hear the rasp of dirt under their feet now, as well as their barks. They were getting closer.

'Go start the car,' Bailey called. That was actually a great idea. Relief rushed through me. Clearly Bailey had been in situations like this before. I was already halfway to the El Camino when the slight flaw in her plan became clear.

'You have the keys,' I shouted.

'Oh yeah.' Holding on to the trunk with one hand, Bailey dug in her back pocket and emerged with a glittering bunch of silver. She cocked back her arm and threw the keys towards me. They sailed over the fence and landed in the gravel with a puff of dust.

I grabbed them, then realized another flaw in our plan. 'I don't drive stick,' I shouted. I couldn't tell for certain in the dark, but basically felt Bailey roll her eyes.

'Fine. Stick the keys in the ignition. And don't touch

anything else!' she yelled back.

'Hey!' a deep voice boomed from across the field, and the windows of a farmhouse lit up. 'I'm callin' the cops.'

'Shit!' Bailey squealed. 'Time to go.' She swung herself on to the tusk of the elephant, her legs dangling over empty air. It was a solid eight-foot drop to the ground. Unable to look away, I stared at her, mouth agape. This time she definitely rolled her eyes. 'Oh my God. What are you looking at me for? Get in the car!'

I dashed back to the El Camino and threw myself into the front seat, jamming the keys into the ignition. Through the windshield I saw Bailey pick herself up from the ground and scramble towards the fence just as two German shepherds burst from the darkness. She leapt for the chain link and hauled herself up, the dogs snapping at her heels. With a crash, she landed hard on the other side, then sprinted for the car as the shepherds howled their indignation. Her jacket lay forgotten in the dust.

'Move over!' Bailey yelled. I rolled into the passenger seat of the car just as she scrambled inside. Slamming the door, she shifted the car into gear, not bothering to buckle her seat belt. As we thundered back on to the road, I dared a look in the rear-view mirror. The dark figure of a man stood behind the locked gate, shaking his fist. My phone buzzed. I jumped. Was the man calling me? I yanked it out. It was a text.

Mom: You make it to the cabin safely?

I stifled a hysterical giggle.

Bailey looked at me. 'What?' I showed her the text. She snorted. Then hiccupped. And then we were both laughing, tears running down our cheeks.

Eventually we quieted, and for a mile or two the only sound was our breathing. Then suddenly a swell of anger crashed over me, threatening to completely drown me. I turned to Bailey.

'You could have ruined everything!'

MILE 172

Bailey shrugged. 'Come on. It was funny. We laughed.'

'That wasn't laughter! That was hysteria!' I knew I wasn't being rational. But I couldn't help it. And Bailey's nonchalant demeanour was only making it worse.

'Hey, look. I'm disappointed, too. You wimped out on me. And instead of a sky full of stars, all I got were some clouds and a friction burn on my inner thigh.'

'I don't care about your stupid stars!'

'Just admit it, we *were* kind of ninjas back there. Me with the running and the climbing and the jumping. You with the standing and the putting the keys in the ignition. I guess it was mainly me who was the ninja. But still, didn't you have fun?' She frowned, genuinely perplexed.

'Of course n—' But then I stopped. Had I? After all, we'd got away. And Bailey throwing the keys to me had made me feel like the star of an action movie. Did I just not know what fun felt like? I was seventeen. I had friends, a boyfriend who up until recently I'd thought was pretty great. I was decently popular. I checked all the boxes. I did everything I was supposed to in high school. I must have had fun.

Bailey held up her phone. 'Look, I took a selfie of us.' It was taken from the top of the elephant. Bailey gave a toothy grin in the foreground, her face washed out from the flash. Far below, looking small and angry, I stood with my arms crossed. I felt a pang in my chest. I could have been up there smiling beside Bailey. But I'd missed that moment. Instead I was on the ground, worrying.

'Cool shot,' I muttered.

Bailey frowned at something on the dashboard. 'This beast is almost out of juice. We gotta stop for gas.'

I winced at the thought of stopping again already, but pulled out my phone. 'Looks like there's a place a few miles up the road.'

'Think there's a snack shop?'

I sighed. 'I don't know. Probably.'

'Great, because we have, like, twelve hundred bucks in cash that I'm dying to spend. It's time to live large!'

I blinked under the harsh fluorescent lights and looked around. Bailey was grabbing armfuls of chips, cookies and crackers from the aisles of the gas station convenience store, running up to the till, dumping them on the counter, then running back for more.

'This is living large?' I asked.

'I'm a simple girl.' She shrugged, then added, 'Oooh! Pringles!' Taking as many tubes as she could carry, she ran to the counter again. The excitement of our escape from the German shepherds, of screaming my hatred of Kevin into the night, of confronting him in the pawnshop was beginning to wear off. My head started to hurt.

'Come on, Bailey. We have, like, eight hundred and twenty miles to go. Maybe we should get back on the road.'

'Fine. Let me just get one more thing.'

'You bought the whole store. Let's go.'

'No. I just need one more thing to make it really special.' She ran to the back of the store. All of a sudden I knew exactly what she was getting.

'Do not buy that synthetic weed, Bailey. I know what you're thinking. And no. I'm not doing it. Don't you watch the news? It has crazy China chemicals. You may not care about your brain any more, but I am not risking mine.' Bailey returned. She wasn't carrying the bag of fake weed I had expected. Instead she had something else — a pair of giant Slurpees. A wave of guilt washed over me. 'Half blue raspberry, half cherry, with a squirt of Coke on top. You remembered our combo.'

'Yeah. Of course, they're full of crazy chemicals, so you may not want to risk your precious brain.'

'Bailey—'

She shoved one at me. 'Whatever. Let's get back on the road.' I clutched the cup to my chest, feeling the condensation seep through my shirt. I'd ruined the moment. Clearly, I couldn't relax for even one minute.

We drove in silence as the lights of the highway flashed past. Bailey was angrily stuffing Pringles in her mouth. I was staring at the melting Slurpee in between my knees. We used to get them every Thursday after school. And practically every day during the summer. We would race to see who could get the first brain freeze, and take pictures of our blue tongues. It was our thing.

'We can go to Roswell.'

Bailey grabbed another handful of chips and stuffed them into her mouth. 'I know.'

'I was lying before when I said we would. But I mean it now. No matter what, we'll go.'

Bailey's chewing slowed and then stopped as she took this in. She turned to me and grinned. 'Serious?'

I nodded, grinning, too. 'Serious.'

'Hell yeah!' Taking her hands off the wheel, she pumped both fists into the air. The car swerved into the other lane. I grabbed for the wheel and yanked us back.

'Maybe keep at least one hand on the wheel.' But Bailey was too excited.

'You are not going to regret this! After this weekend is

over, it's not going to be the weekend you got an abortion. It'll be the weekend you saw the spot where motherfucking aliens landed on the motherfucking earth!'

'Sounds great.' I couldn't say I had any interest, but I was weirdly charmed by her enthusiasm.

'Shit.'

'What?'

'Nothing.' But Bailey's eyes were glued to the rear-view mirror.

'Is it Kevin?' I sank lower in my seat, afraid to look.

'No way. He's long gone.'

'Then what is it?' I turned around. There was a single set of headlights behind us, fairly far back. At first I couldn't tell what had Bailey spooked until I recognized the car's familiar silhouette. 'Uh, Bailey, there's a cop car behind us.'

'Duh.' At the last possible second she jerked the wheel to the right, just making the exit.

'What are you doing? Why are you getting off the highway?'

'Just stay cool, OK?'

'Not until you tell me what's going on!' Bailey sped on to an unlit street. There was a small public rest stop, but not much else. She slowed and checked the rear-view mirror again.

'Damn. He's getting off. Must have seen us swerve. Hold on, I'm killing the lights.'

'What? What do you mean you're—' Bailey turned off the headlights. We were instantly swallowed by the inky black night. 'Bailey! What are you doing?' My voice cracked as my mind started to tick through all the reasons Bailey might have to fear the police. Bailey scanned the road ahead.

'Come on. There has to be something . . . There!' She jerked the wheel right into a dark corner of the parking lot where there weren't any streetlights and killed the engine. 'Duck.' She pushed my head down below the dashboard.

'Bailey, what is going on?'

'Shhhhhh.' Bailey lifted her head slightly and peered out the window. I did the same. We saw the police car roll past, make a left, and pull back on to the highway. Bailey breathed a sigh of relief. 'Well, I about pooped myself.' She tore open a pack of Nutter Butters and shoved one into her mouth.

'What. The. Hell. Was. That. Bailey?'

Bailey looked at me, bemused. 'Don't know what you're talking about. Back on the road! Abortions and aliens await!' She turned the car on. I turned it off.

'We're not leaving until you tell me why we had to hide from the cops.'

'It's fine. We just need to be careful on the road, that's all.'

'You have a licence, right?' Bailey drove to school every

day, but with Bailey one could hardly take that as proof.

'Please.' Bailey tossed her wallet at me.

I pulled out the licence. 'It says your name is Rhonda and you're twenty-four.'

'Oh, sorry.' She grabbed the wallet back, looked through it, and handed me another ID. I held it up to the light, examining it closely.

'It looks real.'

'Uh, because it is. Can we go now?' Suddenly it all clicked. An icy chill crept down my spine. I opened the glove box. 'What are you doing?' Bailey asked with sudden alarm.

'What does it look like? I'm getting the registration,' I replied coolly. Bailey tried to bat my hand away as I dug through the contents of the box.

'It's not in there.'

'Then what's this?' I waved a slip of paper. Bailey tried to grab it from my hand but I managed to read it before she snatched it away. It confirmed what I already suspected.

'This car is registered to Travis Crawford.'

'Yeah, so? I told you my mom's boyfriend gave it to me. He just hasn't done the paperwork yet.'

'Bailey . . .'

'Fine. So he may not have given it to me. He's letting me borrow it.'

'Bailey . . .'

'Fine. He and my mom broke up. He was creepin' college girls on Tinder. Asshole is on call at the fire department all weekend and hasn't moved his stuff out yet and this is a little payback.'

'You stole his car.'

'Only kinda. We did work on it together. And once after a couple of beers, he did kind of imply he might give it to me someday. And we'll have it back before he's home anyway. But now you see why I didn't want to get pulled over.'

'This is a stolen car!'

'Possession is nine-tenths and all.'

'You made me an accessory to a felony!' I screeched.

'Come on. It's a road trip. We couldn't do this in my shitty Camry.'

'No. No no no no no no.' This was so much worse than just hopping a fence. We had to drive 2000 miles; we were going to pass a cop or two. What if Travis reported the car stolen? I could end up spending my freshman year in an orange jumpsuit. All because Bailey thought a Camry was too lame to take on a road trip. My first instincts about her had been right. It wasn't that I didn't know how to have fun. It was that Bailey was insane. I opened my door and climbed out. Bailey followed.

'Hey, I became a felon for you. A little appreciation

would be nice.'

I paced back and forth, furious. 'I don't know why I'm surprised. I mean, of course you'd steal a car.'

'Whoa! The most I've stolen up until now was a T-shirt. Actually it was the whole mannequin, but it was for the T-shirt.'

'I don't care, Bailey! I'm going to get arrested!'

'No, you're not. Because we're going to go the speed limit and drive safe. And, hey, if we do get arrested, it'll make this whole pregnancy thing seem pretty minor, right?' She stood there, hands in her pockets, totally relaxed.

I had to stop myself from shoving her. Instead I settled for angrily pointing my finger at her. 'This. This is exactly why we're not friends any more.'

Bailey's easy smile faded and she stiffened. 'Um, we're not friends any more because once you stepped foot in high school, suddenly you were too good for me.'

'Not true. I invited you to my birthday party freshman year. You snuck in a bottle of amaretto and puked on my birthday cake.'

Instead of looking remotely sorry, Bailey smirked. 'No one likes carrot cake anyway.'

'I do! You were a mess! You made it impossible to be your friend!'

'My parents were getting a divorce! Sorry I couldn't be

perfect for you any more!' Suddenly Bailey was screaming, too, finally as angry as I was.

'You completely changed!'

'So did you!'

'But I didn't get all dark and weird!' The anger had come upon me so quickly and completely I was out of breath. Bailey was looking at me strangely. 'What?'

'Your jeans.'

'What about them?' I stared at her, confused.

Bailey pointed. 'Look.'

I glanced down. There was something dark and wet on the crotch of my jeans and down one leg. I touched it. My fingers came away red. I stared at them in shock.

'I'm bleeding.'

MILE 192

'I can't believe it! I'm saved!' I ran into the ladies' restroom, momentarily blinded by the bright lights, dove into the closest stall and slammed the door. Bailey followed behind. 'This is the best period ever!' I practically sang as I pulled down my pants.

'Hey, this doesn't have to cut the weekend short, right?' Bailey asked through the stall door. 'You said we could go to Roswell. Mama still wants to see some aliens.'

'Oh no.' I stared at my underwear in disbelief.

'You OK? You need a pad or something?'

'You have got to be kidding me!'

'What?'

I burst out of the stall door and stalked over to the sink, turned on the water, grabbed a handful of paper towels, wet them, and started rubbing. 'It's freakin' Slurpee!'

In the bright lights of the bathroom it was obvious. I'd somehow managed to spill the drink all over myself, probably while Bailey was driving like a maniac to escape the cop. I scrubbed frantically at my jeans, tears in my eyes. Bailey stood to the side, awkward, obviously not knowing what to do.

'Bummer.'

'Yeah. I'm pregnant, stuck in the middle of nowhere with Slurpee on my only pair of pants, with a felon for company.' I blinked back tears.

'Oh, come on. Are we still on that?'

'Yes, we're still on that!' I wadded up the paper towels, slammed them into the trash can, and stomped out of the restroom. I was soaking wet and my pants were still red. This night couldn't get any worse.

'Hey, babe.'

I screamed. Standing in a pool of yellow light from the nearby streetlamp, holding a dozen red roses, was Kevin. Bailey exited the bathroom a few steps behind me and froze.

She thrust both arms into the air again. 'Stalk—' I yanked her arms down.

'He's between us and the car,' I murmured. 'What do we do?'

'So we're back to "we"?' Bailey sounded hopeful.

'You're irresponsible, impulsive, and a criminal. But right now you're also my only option. So yeah. We're back to "we".' Bailey grinned and I barely kept from rolling my eyes. We examined our surroundings. Kevin's van was parked next to the El Camino and he was standing on the sidewalk that led to the parking lot. It was about a fifteen-yard dash to get from the bathrooms to the car.

'I just wanna talk, babe. Look, flowers!' Kevin waved them at me, like he was trying to convince a dog to come eat a treat.

'Even if we make it to the car, he'll just follow us,' Bailey muttered.

'How is he even finding us?' I asked.

'Not important right now. We need to disable his van.'

'How? I don't suppose you still have that pocketknife with Bryant Armstrong's name engraved on it? We could slash his tyres.'

Bailey looked at me, perplexed. 'What are you talking about?'

'Didn't you buy a knife and get the quarterback's name put on it? Because he pissed you off or something?'

'Uh, no. I'm not a psycho.' Then Bailey smiled. 'That's what they say about me? That's pretty badass.'

'Yeah, well, right now I wish you *were* that badass. What are we going to do?'

'Run to the bathroom, lock the door, and keep him talking until I call for you.'

'You have a plan?'

'Nope. Now go.' She took off sprinting for the El

Camino. Kevin whirled as she ran past, then smiled when he saw me standing alone. Before he could get any closer, I backed into the bathroom and slammed the door to the entrance closed. Luckily, it locked from the inside. I slid the bolt home, then leant against the door, panting.

Kevin knocked on the door. 'Hey! I just wanna talk.'

I was trapped, but at least he couldn't get in. 'Go away, Kevin.'

Kevin's muffled voice reasoned from the other side of the door. 'You're panicking, it's understandable. Your hormones are totally out of whack.' A rose slid under the door, its petals bruised and mangled. I stared at it in horror. 'Look, I'm not even mad you sold my ring.' Another rose. 'You are probably pretty pissed, I get that.' Rose. 'I just came out here to apologize.' Two roses this time. 'Look . . . I got you a rose for every hole.' Another rose wiggled its way inside. Then another. I stomped on them as if they were alien tentacles.

'I don't want your roses! Go away!'

'Listen, I know you want to get back at me by blowing all my ring money on a revenge bender with Bailey Butler, but this is serious. We need to work this out.'

I bit my lip trying not to laugh or cry. 'You think I'm using the money to . . . party?'

'Why else would you be with Bailey?' Another rose slid under the door. It was too much.

'I'M GETTING AN ABORTION, KEVIN!'

There was silence on the other side of the door. The roses stopped.

'In New Mexico,' I continued, rushing now that the truth was out. 'So, just go. You're off the hook.' He didn't deserve the reprieve and I swallowed the bitter taste in my mouth from offering it. Why should he spend his weekend at home playing video games while I went through this? But the thought of having him near me was even more repellent.

From the other side of the door, I heard Kevin get up and walk away. Could it have been that easy? Then, a few seconds later, from the other end of the bathroom, I heard the squeal of metal on metal. I looked up. On the far wall, near the top, there was a narrow window for ventilation. And the grate that covered it was sliding open. A rose poked through the crack and fell to the floor. The grate slid all the way open. More roses fell through, flopping on to the dirty concrete. Then a hand appeared, gripping the sill. Then another. I could hear Kevin's feet scrambling against the cinder-block wall and his grunts of effort.

'Bailey?' I shouted. 'Bailey, you about done out there?' But there was no response. To my horror, Kevin managed to pull himself up, his arms, then his head, sliding through the window. Confusion creased his forehead.

'You can't get an abortion, babe. It's my baby, too.'

His . . . baby . . . too? I wanted to scoop up every rose off the floor and hurl them at his face. I wanted to shout that he didn't give me a choice about getting pregnant, so I sure as hell wasn't going to give him a choice about this. But the only thing that came out of my mouth was . . .

'BAILEY!'

There was a pounding on the door.

'Let's go!' Bailey yelled. My heart soared. I slid the bolt back and swung the door open. Bailey stood there, waiting. 'El Camino. Now.' We sprinted towards the car.

'Babe! This is so not fair!' Kevin called after us. I heard him slide out the window and fall roughly to the ground. He charged after us. Reaching the car, I yanked the door open and threw myself into my seat. Bailey did the same and fired up the engine. She threw the El Camino into reverse just as Kevin reached us. His hands slammed against the tailgate of the car as we pulled out. He stumbled and fell to the ground. As Bailey threw the car into gear, his crouching form was illuminated by our tail lights.

'Wait! Does this mean you're breaking up with me?' he wailed. Then, picking himself up, he ran to his van.

Bailey slowed the car and parked it at the exit to the parking lot.

'Why are you stopping?' I asked, not bothering to hide the panic in my voice.

'Watch,' Bailey said. I looked across the dark swath of

asphalt to where Kevin's van was parked. He was in the driver's seat, but hadn't turned on the engine. 'I stuffed gum, M&M's, and Sour Patch Kids into his ignition.' It was then that I noticed that most of the junk food had disappeared from the car. All that was left were a few wrappers. 'I also dumped Slurpee on his seats, then covered them with crumbled-up Pringles and Cheetos. But that was just extra.'

Across the parking lot, Kevin climbed out of his front seat, spotted our car sitting in the shadows, and yelled, 'Bailey Butler, you are such a bitch!'

Bailey cackled, delighted. 'And the legend grows.' But there was a tinge of sadness in her smile. She pulled out of the parking lot.

'I don't understand how he even found us,' I said. My heart was still thumping from the encounter. 'He must have some sort of tracker . . . maybe attached to the car . . . or he's using satellites . . . or . . .'

'Your phone?' My face flushed. I was an idiot. I clicked open Snapchat and turned on Ghost Mode. I'd forgotten I'd shared my location with him.

'Or could be a satellite,' Bailey deadpanned. We drove in silence for a moment, then Bailey spoke. 'Look, if anything happens with the car, I'll take the heat. Promise. Unless you want to turn back and start a registry at Buy Buy Baby?'

'Just keep driving,' I grumbled. But I couldn't help smiling a little.

'Good. Because this is the most fun I've had since I dropped acid on our field trip to the Laura Ingalls Wilder Museum.' Cranking up the music, she floored the gas, and we sped on to the highway.

MILE 193

'Pull over.'

'Why?'

'I forgot to pee when we were at the rest stop.'

MILE 212

'Seriously, Bailey? Kelly Clarkson? What happened to the dark, angry stuff?'

'Shhh. Just let her speak to you.'

MILE 292

'OK. That's enough. We listened to the whole album. Now can we stop with the Kelly Clarkson?'

'I'm never gonna stop with the Kelly Clarkson.'

MILE 331

'I'm just not in a Kelly Clarkson mood.'

'No such thing.'

MILE 344

'Finally. Thank you.'

MILE 345

'BUT SINCE YOU BEEN GONE –
　'I CAN BREATHE FOR THE FIRST TIME –
　'I'M SO MOVING ON –
　'YEAH, YEAH –'

MILE 366

'I have to pee again.'

MILE 518

I woke with a jerk as the car swerved off the shoulder and back on to the highway. I must have nodded off sometime after our last pit stop.

'Sorry,' Bailey said. She rubbed her eyes. 'I think I fell asleep for a second. Need coffee.'

I carefully moved myself back into an upright position. My neck had a kink in it from the way I had been sleeping. I blinked a few times, trying to clear my head. 'Didn't you pound three Rockstars back at the Flying J?'

'Yeah. But that's just, like, a normal Friday for me.'

I took a moment to imagine what Bailey's corroded insides must look like, then pulled out my phone. 'There's a town a little over fifty miles from here that has an all-night diner.'

'Mmm. Pancakes.'

'No. No pancakes. Just coffee. To go.'

Bailey sighed. 'You are a cruel mistress.'

Now that my phone was out, I saw there was a string of texts from the girls. Pics of piles of junk food. A blurry shot of a TV with Ryan Gosling looking incredibly emotional about something. Smiling selfies. They were having a great time at the cabin. Without me. I hadn't expected them to be prostrate with grief that I wasn't there, but seeing them so happy hurt.

I tried to stop the thoughts that piled quickly on top of one another, but it was like an avalanche. Maybe I didn't matter to them as much as I thought I did. They obviously didn't need me to have a good time. I wasn't that important. They only pretended to like me because I was more popular. They were all talking about me. They were actually glad that I wasn't there. Because they were jealous of me. And then an even more terrifying thought: if this was what they were like when they thought I was spending the weekend cuddled up with my boyfriend, what would happen if they found out what I was really doing?

Bailey looked at me, confused. 'Are you OK?'

I smiled brightly. 'Yeah. Of course.' But my voice sounded high and tight. I bent over and pawed through the trash at my feet, searching. I had an idea. Bailey continued to watch me.

'Oh. Because if you need to talk or whatever . . .'

I poked my head up. 'Talk?' It was my turn to be confused.

'Yeah. You know. If you're scared or something.'

Finally everything clicked. She was talking about the procedure. 'Oh. Yeah. Thanks. No. I'm good.' I went back to digging through the trash. Finally I found what I was looking for — a half full bottle of water. Unscrewing the cap, I poured a bit into my hand, then rubbed it on my hairline. Bailey's confusion deepened.

'What are you doing?'

'Nothing.'

I pulled off my shirt. Bailey started. The car jerked.

'This is not a naked car!'

'Relax. This will just take a second.'

I looked around the El Camino for a good angle, something bland and dark. I made sure my flash was on. Then, after adding a few more drops of water to my face and chest, I held the phone as far away from myself as I could and snapped a picture. I took a moment to study the result. The background was black. The water droplets shone on my face and bare shoulders, sparkling from the flash. I looked wet and a bit sweaty. Hardly my best but it would get the job done.

Me: So fun! But do you have a hot tub?? 😊

Immediately my phone chimed with responses.

Emily: Ahhh! Jealous!

Jocelyn: No fair!

Kaylee: Come on! Where's the naked boy pics?? jk. Not really. jk. But if you have any . . .

Bailey leant over and saw the texts on my screen. 'Seriously? You're faking your weekend with Kevin?'

I angled the phone away from her view and thumbed a quick response.

Me: Hahaha! He's just for me, ladies!

Bailey smirked. 'I don't need to see it to know what you wrote. Let me guess. "Ha. Ha. He's all mine"? Did you add in a bunch of hearts, too?'

'No.' My finger was hovering over the pink heart emoji.

'I don't get it. How can you even type that after what he did?'

'Um, I have to keep up appearances. This whole thing is supposed to be secret, remember?'

'Yeah, but couldn't you just, I don't know, not text them for a day or two?'

I stifled a snort of laughter. 'I'm sorry. Are you secretly forty-five? Not text? They'd know for sure something was up. They'd probably send out a search party.' Though I wasn't so sure after seeing all their pictures from the cabin. I quickly squashed that thought. They were still texting me, letting me know what they were up to. It was probably supposed to make me feel like I was part of the group. And so I could keep up my cover story with my parents. They weren't trying to make me feel excluded. If I were with Kevin, this probably wouldn't even be bothering me.

I repeated those thoughts over in my head a few times,

wanting to believe them. Bailey had her eyes on the road but still looked thoughtful.

'But you're supposed to be with Kevin. Don't you guys want, I don't know, a little privacy? Would you really be texting them all the time?'

'Yeah. I would.' Half the fun of being with Kevin was sending updates to my friends. But I didn't say that to Bailey. I sensed she wouldn't understand.

'Seems weird.'

'Um, it's totally, completely normal. Like, billions-of-people normal. And I don't think you're the one to talk about what's weird and what's not.'

'Oooh. Ouch. That stung.' But there was no heat behind the words. Bailey popped a chip in her mouth. 'It's just, like, a lot of work.'

Now that Bailey said it, I realized it did feel like work sometimes. But what was I supposed to do? Not have any friends?

MILE 536

My phone pinged again with more pics from the girls. I flicked through them quickly. Papers were spread all over the rug. I could spot Jocelyn's colour-coded, incredibly tiny writing. Emily had dozed off and the other two had decorated her with Red Vines that spelt out 'B+'. It was looking like an epic cram weekend. Probably the best ever. Which made sense, it was our senior year. It should be the best one. And I wasn't there. I glanced around the car. Bailey gave me the side-eye.

'I think we're out of water if you're looking to do another "Chillin' in the hot tub with Kev" shot.'

'I'm not.' Mainly because realistically we would have got out of the hot tub by now. I needed something new.

'Oh! I know! You could use one of the roses he shoved through the window at the rest stop.'

'Do we have one?' I asked, excited.

'That tone you heard in my voice was sarcasm.'

'Oh.'

'Gross. What were you going to do? Sprinkle rose petals all over yourself?'

'No!' But that would have been good. I definitely needed something romantic. The girls might have *The Notebook*, but I had the real thing. Well, I used to. And as far as they knew, I still did. One more shot would be enough. It was late. They'd go to sleep soon. One more shot just to remind them I was having a good time, too. I studied Bailey's hands as she gripped the wheel.

'Bailey?'

'No.'

'You don't know what I was going to ask.'

'Don't need to. We used to be friends, remember? I learnt my lesson after the sixth-grade talent show.'

'You were great!'

'I was your ventriloquist's dummy.'

'It was postmodern.'

'You made me wear lederhosen.'

'We got third place.'

Bailey groaned. 'Just tell me your evil plan.'

I grinned. 'Well, I noticed your hands were kind of . . . big and—'

'Changed my mind,' Bailey interjected.

'Just let me hold one,' I pleaded. 'I'll cover up your nails with my hand. I think if I angle the shot right, it'll work.'

'What'll happen if I say no?'

I shrugged, then grinned diabolically. 'My backup plan was messing up my hair and pinching my cheeks a lot to fake that post-orgasm glow.'

Bailey made a retching noise, then stuck out her hand. 'Just do it fast. This is way above and beyond the call of duty.'

'Thanks,' I said, taking her hand and wrapping it with my own. I was surprised how familiar it felt. We used to hold hands all the time – crossing the street, running up the stairs to her bedroom, down the hall at school – and somehow my body remembered.

I took the photo quickly and let go. Bailey jerked her hand away. I wondered if holding mine felt familiar to her, too.

After playing with the filters enough to ensure Bailey's hand was unrecognizable, I captioned the photo with 'night night' and hit send.

'Satisfied?' Bailey asked. I was. In some alternate time-line, Veronica Clarke was living the life she should be. The life she worked so hard for. The life she deserved. But I didn't answer Bailey. Instead, I grabbed her phone out of the little cubby in the dashboard.

'Uh, excuse me. Mine?' Bailey made a few ineffectual grabs, sending the car fishtailing, but I darted out of her way, keeping the phone out of reach.

'Sorry, I refuse to believe this whole Luddite thing.' I punched in a few numbers and unlocked her phone.

Bailey frowned. 'How'd you guess my password?'

'Please. You've been using "butt" since third-grade computer lab.'

I flicked through, looking. After a moment, I put the phone down. I didn't know what to say. Bailey kept her eyes on the road.

'Toldja.'

'Bailey, there's nothing on there.'

'What? Just because I don't photograph every meal I eat in the cafeteria, I don't exist?'

'I mean, even in your contacts. There's your mom and an emergency plumber.'

'We have some wonky pipes in our house. Trust me, when the sink's overflowing at three a.m., Demetri is your guy.'

'Bailey . . .'

'What? He's both dependable and affordable.'

'Don't you have any friends?' I blurted. The words sat between us, big, solid and un-take-backable. I felt Bailey stiffen beside me. 'I mean . . .' I started, trying to think of a way to save myself.

'I used to,' Bailey said.

'I'm sorry, I—'

Bailey rolled her eyes. 'Ugh. Just stop. My online life is plenty robust. I moderate a couple of manga forums. And not to toot my own horn, but I've got some pretty popular fanfics. And when I feel like it, there are even a few fellow freaks at school I deign to speak to. I do fine.'

Was she fine? I studied her as she drove. She didn't look upset. She had a slight smile on her lips; her hair was shooting out every which way; she was humming along to the song on the radio. I stopped being her friend because I'd told myself if I wanted to succeed in high school, I couldn't handle that much drama. That it was necessary. That Bailey would drag me down with her. But that empty contact list . . . What would it have looked like if we'd stayed friends?

'Oh my God. Stop with the guilt.'

'I didn't say anything!'

'You didn't need to. I could feel it dripping out of you from here. It was getting all over my leather seats.' Bailey grabbed the phone. 'Will this make you feel better?' She rested it on the steering wheel and tapped on the screen for a minute. Then she handed it back to me. There was a new contact.

'Veronica Clarke. Abortion friend,' I read, unamused.

Bailey cackled loudly, pleased with herself, then pointed.

'Look. I think I see lights up ahead.'

MILE 576

Calling the place a town was pushing it. There were more empty lots than stores lining the two-lane highway and most seemed to be selling something barnyard-related. I looked at the gas gauge. We still had plenty of fuel. 'Maybe we should keep going until the next town.'

Bailey shook her head. 'Nope. It's the middle of the night. Every place is going to look creepy. This one probably has the same amount of serial killers as the next. Which, statistically, is two.'

'Not making me feel better.'

'You promised coffee. And you know what? Now that I know you're feeling a bit guilty over my contact list, I'm going to insist we stop for food.'

'Bailey, we don't have time.'

'You just napped for, like, a hundred miles. You want this car to stay on the road, going in a straight line, I'm going to need more than just coffee.'

'I could drive . . .'

'Stick, remember?'

'I could learn?'

'Not on this baby's transmission, you're not.'

'Maybe—'

Bailey pulled a tragic face. 'But I'm so lonely, Veronica. I have no followers on social media.'

'Stop.'

'No one likes my posts.'

'Seriously.'

'The only thing that could possibly help is a short stack with extra syrup.'

'OK. Fine. We can stop. But chew fast.'

'No problem.' Bailey pointed ahead of us. 'And look, there's our spot.' The brightly lit sign of a roadside diner was a splash of colour in an otherwise empty street. My stomach growled. The promise of pancakes and coffee suddenly sounded amazing.

Bailey pulled into the lot in front of the diner. There were a few empty spaces in the front, but Bailey continued around to the back and parked in the shadows.

'Why are we parking back here?' I asked.

'Because your stalker might eventually get the candy out of the ignition. And since this is the fastest route to Albuquerque, he probably knows we're on it. I get the feeling he's not the quitting type. I don't want him spotting the El Camino again and messing up my breakfast.'

The diner was surprisingly busy for the middle of the night. There was an assortment of old guys who looked like truckers, a couple sucking face over a plate of french fries, and a group of high school guys just finishing up burgers. A lone waitress juggled the various tables. At our entrance the guys looked up, their eyes sparking with interest.

'Hey, girls, looking for some sausage with your pancakes?' one of them drawled, flashing me an easy, confident smile.

'No thanks,' I mumbled, hating how all their eyes were on me. Bailey gave me a nudge.

'Ignore them,' she said under her breath. The guy heard her. A quick flash of displeasure was instantly replaced by another winning grin.

'Aw, don't be like that. Watcha doin' tonight? We can show you the town.'

'No thanks,' I said again, desperately hoping the waitress would notice us.

'Hey, come on. We'd even be nice to your freak friend,' another added.

Bailey stiffened beside me. *Oh no.*

'Bailey . . .' I warned.

Bailey treated the group to a treacly smile. 'Wow. Such a sweet offer, and I *am* super horny, but I'm worried I can't compare to all the livestock you've fucked.' The guys stared, dumbfounded. Bailey called to the waitress cheerily, 'Table for two, please.'

I tried to hide my grin as the waitress walked us over to an empty booth.

'I'll take a coffee and pancakes,' I said as I slid into my seat. 'Bailey, what do you want?'

'Can you give me a minute?' Bailey asked the waitress. The woman grunted and moved off. Bailey flipped open the menu and began perusing it.

'Bailey,' I hissed, 'we can't sit here all night. You said you wanted pancakes. Order them.' Out of the corner of my eye, I saw the group of guys with their heads together whispering about something.

'Yeah . . . but now that I see the menu, I'm torn. Do you think the Denver omelette or biscuits and gravy sound better?' she asked.

'I'm sure they're both great. Just pick one.'

'Maybe I should stick with the short stack . . .' she mused.

'Bailey. We have over four hundred miles to go. We're going to have to maintain a pace of seventy-five miles an hour, assuming we take a fifteen-minute pee break every two hours, to make it there by nine.'

Bailey blinked at me. 'Wow. How'd you do that?'

'Math.'

'Knew I should have gone to that class.' She went back to reading the menu. There was a small commotion at the other end of the restaurant. We both looked up to see that the guys had left, and by the look on the waitress's face, it was without paying. She stomped her way back over to us.

'You know what you want yet?' she asked.

'Pancakes and coffee, please,' I said.

'The biscuits and gravy, the Denver omelette, the mozzarella cheese sticks and the short stack,' Bailey said. 'Oh, and coffee.'

'Bailey!'

'What? You rushed me. I couldn't decide.'

'You kids gonna pay for all that?' The waitress eyed us suspiciously. Bailey took out her wallet. I'd given her all the money I had except for what I needed for the doctor. It was bulging.

'How much did those assholes stiff you for?' she asked.

'Forty-three bucks,' the waitress grumbled. 'Wish we could ban those little shits, but one of them's daddy owns the grain silo.'

Bailey peeled off several bills from her wad. 'Here's for our meal and theirs. Extra's for you.' The waitress's eyes widened, but she took the money.

'Thanks, honey. Food'll be right up.' She walked off. I looked at Bailey. She was playing with the individual packets of jam, stacking them into a pyramid.

'That was really nice,' I said.

Bailey shrugged. 'Whatever. I just wanted my food.'

'Still. You didn't have to.'

Bailey rolled her eyes, clearly uncomfortable. 'Well, didn't want to make you late for the clinic,' she grumbled. 'What time is your appointment, anyway? You haven't told me.' It was my turn to be uncomfortable. Suddenly, the ketchup bottle looked really fascinating. I studied it intently. 'Veronica, what time is it at?' she repeated, suspicion creeping into her voice.

'I don't know yet. They open at nine.'

'You didn't make an appointment?' Bailey practically shouted.

I sank down in my seat. 'I tried to. A couple of times. But every time they answered, I . . . I hung up.'

'Did you think this was like going to McDonald's? Just order an abortion off the value menu and have it served right up? Were you planning to use the drive-through?'

'Bailey! Shhh!' I could feel that my face was bright red. People were starting to stare. 'I hoped we could just show up,' I mumbled.

Bailey snorted. 'You hoped? And you planned to pawn the ring when we got there? That's leaving a lot to chance.' She eyed me sceptically.

'I know.'

'Are you sure you really want this?'

'Yes!' I did.

'Then I don't get it. I've watched you plan your study schedules down to the minute.'

'Making the appointment would make it real, OK?'

Bailey shook her head. 'Guess we finally found the class you failed: common sense.' She grabbed my phone from me and started searching. 'Ah. Here we are. *Duh duh duh DAH!*' she sang as she punched in some numbers. 'It's Abortion Friend to the rescue!'

'Bailey. Stop. They're probably not going to answer. It's the middle of the night.' Bailey held up a single finger to silence me as she listened with the phone pressed against her ear.

'Yes! Hello!' she sang in an extra cheery voice. 'Wow. A twenty-four-hour hotline. So convenient. Anyway, how are you?' She paused for an answer. 'Well, that's great to hear. Sad to say it's not the case for me. You see, I need an abortion.' She enunciated the last word clearly enough for the whole diner to hear. A couple of truckers turned to look at us, disgust and judgement on their faces.

'Please, Bailey . . .' I begged, as I tried to sink even further into the red vinyl booth.

'Thank you. That's so nice of you. My last period? Um . . .' Bailey looked at me, waiting for an answer. I held up some fingers, then shrugged. Her eyes widened slightly. I burnt with shame. My period wasn't super regular, so it took me a while to realize something was wrong. And we *had* used condoms. Or so I had thought. 'Eight weeks. Ish.' Bailey nodded her head as she listened to the person on the other end. 'OK. Yes. That's fine. Say, are there any waxing options? It's like the Amazon jungle down there.' At this, one of the truckers listening to our conversation eyed Bailey with interest. I buried my head in my hands, willing this to be over.

'Right. Sorry,' Bailey continued, 'I'm not making light. I'm just a bit nervous, you know? First time and everything. Not first time having sex. I should've been pregnant like a hundred times by now, just going by the odds. Or maybe my boyfriend's sperm are stalkers, like he is.' I held back a snort of laughter. I hated what she was doing, but I kind of loved it, too. 'So, do you have anything? I'm sorry I didn't call before. I was just really, really nervous. Tomorrow is the only day I can do this. I'm driving from way out of town and my parents can't find out.' She said this last part seriously, putting all the desperation I felt into her voice.

My heart started to pound. What if they couldn't fit me in? What if we had driven this far for nothing? I held my breath waiting to hear Bailey's next words. 'Eleven thirty a.m.? Great. I'll be there. Name? Veronica Clarke. Yes. Yes, I have someone with me. A *friend*. Thank you. Thank you so much. Bye.' I looked up from the table. We locked eyes and grinned. Bailey slid the phone to me, leant back in her seat and crossed her arms behind her head. 'Well?'

'I hate you,' I said.

'I know.'

'That was incredible.'

'I know.' Bailey noticed the older trucker still looking at her. 'That's right, I'm condom-free tonight, sir.' She winked at him. The man turned back to his eggs, embarrassed. I let out a peal of laughter, partly from her audacity and partly from relief.

'You're insane.'

'You're welcome.'

The waitress returned carrying our plates of food and set them down. As she left, she gave Bailey a sympathetic pat on her shoulder.

'I put extra gravy on those biscuits for ya.'

Suddenly feeling better than I had in weeks, I looked at all the food before us. Bailey reached for a plate and I slapped her hand away. 'Hold on. I'm taking a picture of this spread.' I pulled out my phone and snapped the picture.

Bailey rolled her eyes. 'Lame.'

'Go ahead. Judge me. I've never seen pancakes look this good. I want to remember them.' I pulled the plate towards me and started gorging.

Twenty minutes later we were both leaning back in our seats, stuffed and satisfied.

'Do you think Kevin fixed his car yet?' I asked.

'Even if he did, I doubt he'll get far. I wrote "Help Me" in Slurpee on the back window. A cop's probably pulled him over by now.'

I giggled, then slid out of the booth. 'Still, we'd better get going.' Bailey stood as well.

'Sure thing, boss.'

We stared at the spot where the El Camino used to be, stunned.

'The car is not there. How is the car not there?' I asked while Bailey let out a string of curse words.

'My guess is because those dine-and-dash sheep rapers took it for a joyride.' Bailey spat. It was then I noticed the tracks in the gravel, as if someone had done doughnuts before peeling out. There was still the faint smell of burnt rubber. I spun to face Bailey.

'Why did you have to park back here?'

'Hey, you're the one with the demented boyfriend we have to hide from!' Bailey shouted back.

I started pacing. 'Now I have no way to get to Albuquerque!'

'Oh sure, it's always about you and your uterus. I'm the one with the stolen car!'

'That was stolen to begin with!'

'I was borrowing it!'

Another horrifying thought swept over me. 'My duffel bag. My backpack.' My chest constricted. 'My calc notes!'

'Your notes? My phone was in there.'

I stopped and turned to stare. 'What? . . . How?'

Bailey huffed. 'Not all of us are glued to it like you.'

For some reason losing Bailey's phone was making me panic more than losing the car. 'What if your mom calls you? What happens if you don't text her back?'

'My mom's working all weekend. She never checks in. I told her I was at a friend's.'

'And she believed you?'

'Hey. Be grateful the woman is too busy to ask questions.'

I started pacing again. 'If the cops find the car with your phone in it, they'll know you stole it.'

'You have a point there.'

'We are so screwed. My name is on that phone. As "abortion friend"!'

Bailey opened her mouth to respond but whatever she was going to say was drowned out by a loud *boom*, followed by the unmistakable screech of metal crunching. We looked at each other. The sounds had come from well down the road, maybe a quarter of a mile away. Without needing to talk, we both sprinted in that direction.

When we arrived, it was in time to see the tail lights of a pickup truck speeding into the distance. The air was thick with the smell of gasoline and burnt rubber. And in a ditch on the side of the road was our El Camino. Its front was crumpled, and steam, or possibly smoke, was rising from the hood. The shiny paint was scratched. The windshield was shattered. One of its tyres was shredded. It was clear we weren't going any further in it tonight.

Bailey walked over to the car and placed a hand on it, as if it were an injured animal.

'I'm sorry,' I said.

Bailey shrugged. 'My fault. I was the one who decided to take it on this trip.'

Strewn across the road were the contents of my duffel bag and backpack. Everything had obviously been run over several times. My clothes were marked with black tyre tracks; my textbooks' spines lay cracked and broken. A scattering of calc notes flapped dejectedly in the gutter. I rushed over to gather them, desperate to salvage what I could. But as I got closer, I crinkled my nose. So did Bailey.

'Yeah. They peed on it.' Then a glint of moonlight caught Bailey's attention. She waded through my clothes, bent over, and emerged with her phone. The screen was shattered. She pushed the power button. A few bars of colour flashed across the screen before it went black.

'Guess I won't be starting those social media accounts

this weekend.' She shoved it into her pocket. I gathered up what was salvageable of my belongings and stuffed them in my tyre-marked backpack. Then I crawled inside the El Camino and wiped it down with my T-shirt.

We slumped to the kerb.

'Well, bright side, I think that's everything that could incriminate us,' I offered after a moment.

Bailey eyed me, impressed. 'Wow, Veronica, that's very *CSI: Bumblefuck, Texas* of you.'

'We're in Oklahoma. I think.'

'Still Bumblefuck.'

I sighed. 'I guess it's time to find a new ride.'

'Order up an Uber.' We both laughed at the absurdity. Even if my parents had let me have an account, they'd probably wonder why I was ordering up a car in Sayre, Oklahoma. But I pulled out my phone, hoping for reception, and searched for 'taxi'. A second later I had my answer and I couldn't believe our luck.

'There's a cab service!'

'Do we have enough money for that?' Bailey asked.

'Not for the whole way. But maybe enough to get us to a bus stop.' Which put us at the mercy of the bus schedule, but at this point any movement in the right direction was a positive. Then I saw the address. 'Never mind.' I stuffed my phone into my pocket so I didn't throw it into the dirt in frustration.

'What?'

'It's over a hundred miles away. Back towards Oklahoma City.'

Bailey rubbed her hand across the back of her neck, thinking. 'So what do we do?'

We trudged back to the diner. The bright light seared our eyes as we stepped inside.

'Any of you nice people going towards Albuquerque?' Bailey asked the room. The truckers at the counter turned our way, then turned back to their meals. 'Anyone?' Bailey tried again.

'Find Jesus, you devil whores,' one shouted.

'I'll take that as a no.'

A few moments later we stood on the side of the road. It stretched before us hopelessly, an impossible distance from Albuquerque. A car whizzed past, whipping our hair around our faces. We watched as its tail lights disappeared into the darkness. I swallowed.

'I think we do this the old-fashioned way.'

'Our thumbs?' Bailey asked.

I nodded. 'Our thumbs.'

MILE 577

With no better ideas, we began to walk along the side of the road where the grass grew through the gravel. Bailey kept her arm extended, thumb out, waiting for a car to drive past. But whenever one did, the driver never bothered to slow. We kept walking. I swatted a mosquito from my arm. We'd gone at least a couple of miles. The diner was long gone and so was the town. Cell reception was spotty at best. I began to walk faster.

Then faster.

And faster.

I was running. My arms pumped. My feet slammed into the ground. My backpack banged against my back.

'Whoa!' Bailey called. 'What are you . . .? Slow down!'

'Can't.' I pumped my arms faster. Asphalt disappeared beneath my feet.

'You can't run the whole way!' Bailey cried.

'Watch me!' I shouted, but kept my eyes on the horizon.

Somewhere out there was Albuquerque. Behind me I heard Bailey begin to run as well.

'You said this was a road trip, not a marathon,' she panted. I didn't answer. My feet beat a tattoo on the ground. No baby. No baby. No baby.

'Cramp!' I heard Bailey call somewhere far behind me. 'Wait, stop. Don't leave.' But I kept going. 'Seriously, STOP!'

I turned. Bailey was gasping by the side of the road. 'You're . . . pretty speedy . . . but I think . . . this will . . . be faster,' she wheezed. In the distance, a pair of headlights grew brighter. But instead of speeding past us as all the others had, they were slowing down. I trotted back to Bailey. The car was pulling to the shoulder. It was a nondescript saloon. The type I imagined businessmen rented when they had an out-of-town convention. Its tyres crunched the gravel. The warmth of the engine sent a blast of hot air wafting towards us. A window rolled down. The interior of the car was dark, the driver's face lit only from the glow of the console. It was a man, maybe the same age as my dad.

'It's late, girls.' He seemed a little too pleased to find us on the side of the road. I grabbed Bailey's arm, digging my fingers into her flesh. This was a mistake. A big mistake.

'Uh . . .' That was the only sound I could make. Bailey couldn't even manage that. Her mouth was hanging open, but all she seemed able to do was swallow.

'You looking for a ride?' He smiled at us, warm and friendly. When neither of us answered, he leant over and opened the passenger door. 'Hop on in.'

Finally my tongue unfroze. 'No thanks.' It was really more of a squeak than a sentence, but the man must have understood.

'You sure? It's dark out here. Not safe to be walking along the side of the road. Someone might not see you.'

'No, really. We're fine.' I elbowed Bailey.

'Fine,' she echoed.

The man frowned. 'I thought you girls were running away from something dangerous.' He didn't seem so warm and friendly now.

'We were just out for a jog.' My mind was racing. We needed to get out of here. 'My parents are down the road. We're going home. Really. We're fine.'

'I can drop you off.' He was insistent now. With a shaking hand, Bailey reached behind her back to her waistband. My eyes widened at what I saw there – the Taser. Shooting someone on the side of the road would definitely complicate things. We needed to get out of here. I scanned the area around us. There were a few scraggly bushes that bordered the road, a barbed-wire fence and a wide field dotted with dark mounds. It would have to be enough.

'No thanks. Bye!' I said, and ran, yanking Bailey along

behind me.

'Oh thank Christ, I really didn't want to use that.'

'I can't believe you brought the Taser.'

'Now you know why I did.'

'Hey!' the man called behind us. We put on an extra burst of speed.

'The field!' I shouted to Bailey. We dashed towards it. Behind us I heard the car door slam. 'Mom!' I called as we ran. 'There's a man here!' It was an idiotic lie. There was no sign of a house anywhere, but maybe it would be enough to make the man think twice. Ducking under the barbed wire, we scurried into the field. 'Let's hide behind one of those mounds,' I called to Bailey.

We ran towards them. I didn't dare turn around to see if we were being followed. As we neared the shapes, I slowed. So did Bailey.

'Uh, Veronica?'

'I'm sure it's safe.' I wasn't sure at all. My only encounters with livestock up until this moment were in their double cheeseburger state. Which explained why I hadn't recognized the shapes for what they were: cows. The field was full of sleeping cows. Now that we were closer, I could hear their soft snorting and the sporadic swish of a tail. 'Let's get behind that one,' I said, pointing. It looked friendly enough, though I hadn't quite realized how big cows were.

Bailey froze. 'What was that?' she asked, her voice tense.

'What was what?'

'I just stepped in something . . . squishy.' A thick, earthy scent filled our noses.

'Um . . . I think you just stepped in—'

'I figured it out. Thanks.'

We reached the cow and crouched behind it. Sensing our closeness in its sleep, its skin twitched and shuddered. But it didn't wake. Being surrounded by animals, the air was surprisingly warm and cosy. We stilled, listening for any sound of pursuit. There was nothing but the occasional cow fart.

'Ugh,' Bailey said. 'That guy better have been a serial killer, because otherwise this isn't worth it.'

I peered over our cow. It was too dark to see the road clearly. 'I think he's gone,' I said. But I couldn't be sure. I'd heard the car door slam, though not the car driving away.

'We're probably safe,' Bailey agreed.

'Yeah.' But we remained frozen, hidden behind Bessie.

I had no idea how long we crouched there, but my calves were burning and the rest of my body was stiff by the time we gathered the courage to stand up. Upright, we had a clearer view of the highway.

'He's gone,' Bailey said. We were headed towards the highway when Bailey stopped. 'Wait a minute. All those cows were lying down.'

'So?'

'I thought you could tip them over when they were sleeping.'

'I think sometimes they sleep lying down and sometimes they sleep standing up.'

Bailey turned around, a gleam in her eye. 'Let's find a standing one. It'll be awesome.'

'It's not the time to be awesome. It's time to get going.'

Bailey was already trotting back towards the cows. 'I think I see one!' she called.

But just as she neared the edge of the herd, one of the cows lumbered to its feet. It blinked sleepily a few times, then spotted Bailey. It let out a bellowing moo and took a few heavy steps towards her. Bailey froze. She was eye to eye with the animal. It mooed again. Spinning on her heel, Bailey sprinted back towards me.

'Ruuuuuuuuuuuuun!'

I burst out laughing. But her yell woke the other cows. One by one they rose to their feet. The night was filled with a chorus of moos. They all began to follow the lead cow.

'Ruuuuuuuuuuuun!' Bailey's arms were flailing as she scrambled through the field, followed by fifty sleepy cows. I was doubled over, wheezing with laughter.

Bailey pelted past me. I managed to look up. The cows were gaining on her. I had no idea they could move that quickly. My laughter completely silent now, I scrambled after Bailey. The moos were getting louder. I risked a glance over my shoulder. It was a rolling wave of deep sable, with the moonlight adding an occasional highlight of silver to an ear or hipbone. One misstep and we'd drown in a bovine sea. But I still couldn't stop shaking with laughter. Finally we reached the fence, Bailey diving through the barbed wire, me ducking under between gasps for breath. We'd made it back to the road.

I fell to my knees, choking and laughing, tears streaming down my face. Bailey stood next to me, annoyed.

'What's so funny? We almost died.'

'Cows . . . we . . . were . . . chased . . . by . . . cows,' I finally managed. I stood, brushing off my hands, and smiled at Bailey. 'You were right. That was awesome.'

The highway stretched in either direction, blank and empty. There was no sign of the man or the car.

I turned to Bailey. 'I've decided people who offer rides to strangers are not the sort of people I want to get a ride from.'

'In my mind, the person who picked us up was going to be a lot less murdery.' She scratched her head, sending bits of grass floating to her shoulders, then sniffed her shirt. 'Ugh. Cow. So, what do we do now?'

I didn't have an answer. We had no car, no ride, and the

local population was, cows: 102; people: 2. Then something caught my eye. Apparently, we weren't entirely in the middle of nowhere. In the distance I saw the glow of neon. It was flickering in and out, which was why we must have missed it earlier.

'Look,' I said. 'Maybe it's another diner or a gas station, and they can tell us where we can find a bus.'

'Or at least have a place to hang until a nice old grandma with a purse full of butterscotch candies agrees to drive us.'

MILE 578

We stood bathed in flashing pink and blue. It wasn't a diner. Or a gas station.

'Hard pass,' I said, and began to walk away. Where, I didn't care. Any place would be better than this. Bailey grabbed my arm.

'But look at all those cars out front. Someone's got to be going our way.'

I pointed at the buxom neon woman in clamshells shining down on us. 'Maybe you didn't read the sign. Let me help you. It says "Mermaidz – Undersea Grotto and Gentlemen's Lounge".'

'So?'

'It's a strip club, Bailey!'

'I know.'

'There aren't any grandmas with butterscotch candies in there, I promise.'

'Look, we go inside, pick the frailest, most low-tone

139

seed salesman in there and negotiate a ride. It's our best shot at getting to New Mexico. Plus, we still have this.' She pulled the Taser out of her waistband.

'No. No way. You were shaking so hard back there you couldn't get a grip on it. You think you're going to be cool and calm when our seed salesman tries to shove us in a meat locker?'

'That was first-time jitters. Next time, watch out.' Bailey tried to flip the Taser in the air and catch it but nearly dropped it instead.

'Not reassured.'

Bailey stuffed it back in her waistband. 'All I'm saying is, we're two strong young women in control of our destinies. With fifty thousand volts of electricity as backup.'

'That doesn't mean we walk into a situation that's got a ninety-nine per cent chance of going bad. We just escaped death by serial killer and death by cow. Let's not push it.'

'What exactly are our other options? Walking along the side of the road in the middle of the night? How is that better?'

'Because we'll live.'

'I'm going in.'

'In? No! Gross!' I looked around helplessly. 'Can't we just wait in the parking lot?'

But Bailey was already charging towards the entrance. I

caught up to her as she approached the bored-looking bouncer leaning against the cinder-block wall. The closed main door had a half-peeled-off advertisement for Budweiser. A distant thump of bass was coming from somewhere inside. The single lamp providing illumination painted everything a sickly yellow and the ground was littered with cigarette butts. I found myself longing for the diner with its syrup-sticky tables and creepy truckers.

'Hi, is there a cover tonight?' Bailey asked in the friendliest tone of voice I'd ever heard leave her mouth. The bouncer gave us a once-over.

'No one underage allowed in.'

'Oh well. Too bad. Let's go.' I pulled on Bailey's shirt and tried to drag her away. There had to be someplace else we could find a ride. A strip club couldn't be the only thing around here. But Bailey wiggled out of my grasp.

'We're both eighteen. Swear.'

The bouncer crossed his arms. 'Not getting in, little hos.'

At the insult, Bailey's nostrils flared. 'Excuse me? We are two strong young women in control of our destinies.'

The bouncer eyed her up and down. 'Look like little hos to me.'

'I'll have you know, she is a valedictorian and I am a virgin. Hardly ho territory.'

I was momentarily taken aback. 'You're a virgin?' I

blurted before I could stop myself.

The bouncer stood up straighter and stepped towards Bailey. 'I was speaking of hos in the metaphorical sense. And the "ho" is not the problem. The "little" is.'

'And I said, we're eighteen. Hold on. Let me get my wallet.' She reached into her pocket and pulled it out. 'Here's my ID.' She then removed a crisp one-hundred-dollar bill from her wallet. 'And here's hers.' The bouncer blinked. He looked up at Bailey and arched an eyebrow. She gave him an innocent smile. He took the money.

'Welcome to Mermaidz, two strong young women in control of their destinies.' He smiled and opened the door. Thumping bass exploded. Bailey sauntered through the door, then turned.

'You coming?' she asked me.

'What if I say no?'

'Then I'd say, have fun standing in the dark with Bubba there. Mama's gonna make it rain.'

She disappeared inside. The bouncer turned to me.

'My name is Gerard.'

I took in the dark parking lot, the flickering neon sign and the smell of stale cigarettes. No way was I standing here all night with Gerard. And no way was I letting Bailey pick whom we were going to ride with. I braced myself and followed her in.

A narrow, dimly lit entrance led to the main room,

where I found Bailey practically bouncing.

'This is so exciting. I've never been in one of these. Aren't you curious?'

'Nope. Not at all.' I was fighting down a sudden flash of panic, imagining my parents finding out where I was. Of course, if they found out about this, they would have found out about my other thing. And about the stolen car. So compared to a felony and pregnancy, going to a strip club wasn't that bad. Probably. I closed my eyes. Right now at the lake, my friends were dreaming about Ryan Gosling and the second law of thermodynamics. I tried to imagine I was there, too, cuddled under an old quilt. I almost had the image fixed in my mind when someone tapped me on the shoulder.

'AARRGH!' I yelped and leapt away. I turned to see a cocktail waitress smirking at me. She wore a leather miniskirt and a pair of blue clamshell pasties. Momentarily stunned by her nearly naked and very ample chest, I quickly looked for somewhere else to focus. I settled on her earring. This only made the waitress's smile grow wider.

'Amateur night is Tuesdays, girls.'

'We're not here to audition!' I said a little defensively.

'Too bad. Would've been a good laugh.' She sauntered back to the bar. I looked over at Bailey. Her mouth was agape, her eyes slightly glazed as she took in her surroundings.

'This is . . . spectacular.'

'Really? That's the word you're choosing to describe this place?' The decor consisted of neon lights, mirrored walls and cheap turquoise vinyl booths. There was an attempt at an aquatic theme, but at some point someone gave up and settled on trashy. The stage had a pole in the centre where a woman in a nurse's uniform and six-inch Perspex heels was twirling around, to the delight of the few men sitting in front. Cocktail waitresses wiggled their way across the sticky floor to deliver drinks to the handful of customers. The place stank of stale beer with a hint of industrial cleaner. As far as I was concerned, it was very far from spectacular. Bailey tugged at my arm.

'Come on, let's grab a seat and start scoping for our ride.' She dragged us over to one of the turquoise booths. We slid in and I tried not to think of the substances that had been spilt on the cracked vinyl. 'What do you think of him?' Bailey pointed to a man by the stage in a rumpled business suit.

'Potential rapist.'

'OK. What about him?' She pointed to a guy wearing a trucker hat and an American-flag-patterned tank top.

'Patriotic rapist.'

'Come on, Veronica. Now is not the time to be picky. That time was back when you let Kevin slip you the pickle.'

'Look, I let you try your idea. We came in. This place is

filled with creeps. The guy in the saloon is probably a regular. Let's figure something else out before it gets even later.'

'What about that guy?' She tried, pointing to the bar. 'He looks tiny. I bet we could take him if he gets handsy.' I glared at her and crossed my arms. She sighed and rolled her eyes. 'Fine.' I started to slide out of the booth. She grabbed my arm. 'Where do you think you're going?'

'Outside? To start walking to the nearest town?'

'Uh uh uh. You are underage at a strip club. We can't let the story end here.'

'I don't care about the story. I want—'

'Sit. One song.' With a sigh, I plopped back into my seat.

'One song. Then we go.' Nothing too terrible could happen in three minutes, I reasoned. I pulled out my battered macroeconomics textbook and tried to lose myself in endogenous growth theory.

Another cocktail waitress in pasties sidled over to our booth. She had a bunch of tattoos and a nose ring, but her smile was warm and friendly. And once I looked past the heavy make-up and false eyelashes, I realized she was probably only a little older than we were.

'Hey, girls. What can I get you?'

'Nothing. We're leaving after this song,' I answered, being careful to keep my eyes away from her chest.

'Sorry, we have a two-drink minimum.'

'Oh. Really? A Coke? Two Cokes?'

The waitress nodded, unimpressed, and turned to Bailey. 'And you, hon?'

'Uh . . . I . . . uh . . . what do you think I should have?'

I turned to Bailey, surprised. She was blushing, looking away, then directly at the waitress's breasts. I'd seen that expression on Kevin's face the first time I'd taken off my bra. Something clicked in my brain.

'Hmmm.' The waitress pretended to think while leaning closer to Bailey, her boobs nearly grazing her face. 'You look like a Dr Pepper girl to me.' She smiled a flirty smile at Bailey, who had completely stopped breathing.

'Yeah. OK. Good,' she choked out. The waitress's smile grew even bigger at Bailey's reaction. Clearly the woman had the same suspicions I did. She slid into the booth next to Bailey and draped an arm over her.

'Just one song, huh? Better make it a good one. You want a dance?'

'Um, no, thank you,' Bailey managed to sputter while the waitress nuzzled her ear. 'You're very pretty, but, um, no.'

'You sure? I'm good.' The waitress stood reluctantly.

'Yeah. Uh. Thanks, though.'

'Well, think about it. I'll be right back with those drinks.' She walked off. Bailey followed her leather-clad rear end with her eyes.

'Bailey?' I asked. But her eyes were still glued on the waitress. 'Bailey?' No reaction. 'BAILEY!'

Finally she turned to look at me, sheepish. 'You know,' she said, playing it a bit too casual, 'I never thought about it, but I am kind of a Dr Pepper girl. I'd always considered myself a Mountain Dew—'

'You like girls,' I blurted before I could change my mind. 'Like really like girls.'

Bailey jerked back in her seat like I'd slapped her. 'What? No! What?'

'I don't know how I missed it. No wonder you never listened to One Direction.'

'I also didn't listen to chainsaws murdering puppies. That had nothing to do with who I'm into,' Bailey snapped back before she could stop herself, then looked even more uncomfortable at what she'd just inadvertently confirmed. 'We should go.' She started to get up, but I grabbed her arm.

'Nuh-uh. Sit.' She sat down but refused to look at me. Suddenly, I realized something. 'Wait. Am I the first person who knows?'

Bailey snorted. 'Don't flatter yourself. My mom was the first person. Then my aunt, Betsy. You're in, like, the double digits.'

'Oh, right. Sure, I get it,' I stammered. 'But then . . . why didn't you tell me?'

'When? It's not like we've been best buds the last four years. Maybe when we passed each other in the hall? Would that have been a good time to tell you? Or in line in the cafeteria? Right after I got my serving of steamed carrots?'

'OK, fine,' I admitted. 'You didn't exactly have the opportunity. But what about before that? I thought you were, you know, supposed to be born this way.'

'I went to the same youth group you did back then, remember?' she mumbled. I winced, thinking about some of the things we had prayed for. For our representatives to stay strong. For the courts to vote the right way. At the time, I was so sure we were doing good. But thinking of it from Bailey's perspective, it must have felt awful.

'Is that why you stopped going to church?'

'No. I stopped going to church because there is no such thing as God.'

'Hey!'

'Oh, don't act all offended. You must not believe everything they tell you at that church if we're going on this little trip.'

'It's complicated,' I mumbled.

It was. I'd grown up being told what I was planning to do was wrong, and it had seemed so clear-cut and obvious at the time. A test question with an easy answer. But as I grew older, I'd realized so many things they told me were true in church just didn't match up with real life. And now that I was in this situation, nothing seemed as simple as they promised it would be.

We had lapsed into silence. Bailey was staring at the table. When she finally spoke, her voice was barely above a whisper. 'I tried to convince myself for years it wasn't true, you know. Like maybe if I ignored it, it would go away. I already had a hard time fitting in. I didn't need something else to make me even more different. And I didn't tell you because I was worried how you'd react.'

'But we were friends.'

'And would you have stayed my friend?' Bailey wouldn't look at me. Instead she focused on the swirls of the fake wood grain on the table.

'Yes!' I practically shouted the word. 'You're you. Bailey. And if liking girls was what made you you, then I would have liked that part of you, too.'

Bailey finally looked up. 'Really?'

'Yeah.'

Bailey smiled. 'Then yeah. I really like girls. My first crush was on Emma Watson when she was in *Harry Potter*. Actually it's still Emma Watson. Also Ms Poulos has something goin' on.'

I snorted with laughter. 'The school nurse?'

'I faked nosebleeds just so I could hang out in the clinic.'

'Bailey!' I gave her a playful shove. 'So . . .' I said after a moment. 'Do you have a girlfriend?'

Bailey looked away, blushing. 'No.'

We sat in silence for a moment, but I couldn't handle it. I had to know. 'Have you ever?'

'Totally. Oh yeah. So many.' She sighed, then grumbled. 'No.'

'Really? Wait. Have you even kissed a girl?' I asked, incredulous.

'No.' She blushed bright red.

'Really? Nothing? You never made out under the bleachers? Or at any of the school dances? Not even prom?'

'Oh yeah, a big queer girl make-out session in the Radisson ballroom would have gone over really well.'

'Sorry. I'm stupid.'

'Whatever. Prom is for losers.'

A thought occurred to me. 'Well, like, then how do you know . . .?'

Bailey looked at me like I was a moron. 'Uh, you just know. You must have known you liked kissing guys before you tongue danced with Decuziac.' It was my turn to blush. She had a point.

Bailey grabbed a fistful of dollars from her wallet and put it on the table. 'We should go. You were right. This was a dumb place to try to find a ride.' She slid to the edge of the booth, almost knocking into our waitress, who'd returned with the drinks.

'Whoa! Leaving already?'

'We gotta go,' Bailey mumbled, staring at her shoes. I looked at Bailey, then at the waitress. If you squinted, she looked a little bit like Emma Watson. I had an idea.

'How much for a dance for my friend?'

Bailey spun towards me, shocked.

'Veronica!' She was incredulous, but there was a gleam of anticipation in her eye.

The waitress grinned. 'Twenty a song.' I grabbed a bill off the table.

'I thought we had to go,' Bailey reminded me coyly.

'You said you wanted to have an adventure.' I handed the twenty to the dancer. Up close she smelt like vanilla and hairspray. She tucked the money down her skirt.

'Consider the next three and a half minutes the biggest adventure of your life,' she purred. 'The name's Sapphire.' She nudged Bailey's legs apart with her own and stood between them, draping her arms over Bailey's shoulders.

'Hi, Sapphire,' Bailey managed to splutter before the song began and the stripper reached for the zipper of her skirt.

Two seconds in, I dove back into my textbook, knowing down to my bones that I was definitely not a lesbian. But judging by the nervous titters I heard, Bailey was at least enjoying herself a little bit.

The song ended. I looked over at Bailey. Her face had a fine dusting of body glitter and a stunned expression on it.

'Whoa.'

Sapphire smiled and straightened her skirt. 'Aw, thanks. I love first timers. Care for another? I can bring a friend.'

'You can?' Bailey started reaching for her wallet.

'Bailey . . .' I warned.

Bailey reluctantly pulled her hand back. 'She's right. We should go.'

'Aw, where do you need to get to in the middle of the night?' Sapphire pouted. She traced her fingertips along Bailey's shoulder in a lazy figure of eight. Bailey's eyes glazed over.

'My friend's got to get an abortion in Albuquerque and we lost our ride.'

'Bailey!' I shouted. Bailey snapped back to reality.

'Sorry – I . . .' We both looked to Sapphire. She wore a stunned, slightly saddened expression on her face.

'Really?'

I nodded, knowing she had already seen the truth in our eyes.

'I live in that direction. I can get you part of the way there,' she offered gently.

'You can?' I asked, not bothering to hide the desperate hope in my voice.

'Sure. I'm off in half an hour, if you can wait that long.'

I looked to Bailey, who was grinning.

'I think we can find a way to pass the time.'

MILE 584

Nine songs later, Sapphire's shift was over, Bailey had a lot less cash in her wallet and we were speeding down the highway in an aging pickup with a bedazzled licence plate frame proclaiming 'Country Princess'. I was pressed against the window, Bailey was in the middle, and Sapphire had one hand on the steering wheel and the other one dangling out the window. The night air was moist and cool after the suffocating warmth of the club.

'For someone who's never even kissed a girl, you sure caught on to the lap dance thing quick,' I muttered.

Bailey shrugged. 'What can I say? I must be some sort of lady-lovin' genius.'

Sapphire spun towards us, jerking the wheel.

'Hold on. You've never been kissed?'

I was still adjusting to how she looked, now that she wasn't in her work uniform. Dressed in sweats and a tank top, without the layers of make-up, she was less sex goddess and more like a cool older sister type. At least how I imagined a cool older sister to look. Mine never had a cool moment in her life. She went straight from choirgirl to mom.

Bailey was blushing again. She mumbled something that sounded like 'haven't had a lot of opportunities' and 'I think you look like Emma Watson'.

Sapphire guided the pickup over to the shoulder of the road, the tyres crunching on the gravel as they rolled to a stop. She shifted it into park and killed the lights. Now the only illumination was the faint glow of the dashboard and a hint of moonlight. She turned to Bailey.

'Well, we are gonna have to fix that right now. A person who's willing to do what you're doing? Driving a friend halfway across the country? That's a special sort of person. That's a person who deserves to be kissed.'

Bailey was frozen, her eyes wide. She looked ready to run, but being in the middle seat of a pickup, had nowhere to go. She opened her mouth to speak.

'Grrhuuuugh.'

Sapphire smiled, as if she was totally used to people losing the ability to speak when they were around her.

'Also, I thought you were cute since the moment you walked in tonight.'

'Eeeerp,' Bailey responded.

'I'm gonna take that as "I thought you were cute, too."'

Unbuckling her seat belt, she leant over, gently placing her hands on Bailey's thighs. I looked away to give them privacy, though out of the corner of my eye I could still see Bailey and Sapphire dimly reflected in the glass of the windshield. Bailey was doing her best impression of a goldfish out of water, but that didn't seem to bother Sapphire. She parted her lips and softly placed them on Bailey's. At the contact, Bailey's eyes closed. She shuddered. And then her whole body sort of melted. Sapphire pulled back. Bailey's lips were shiny with the gloss from Sapphire's and she wore a dazed expression. Sapphire wore a satisfied one.

'You were right.'

'I was?' Bailey asked, confused.

'Yep. You are a lady-lovin' genius.' And with that, Sapphire flipped the headlights back on, threw the truck into gear and pulled back on to the road.

We barrelled down the highway, mile markers flying past. Bailey and Sapphire kept making googly eyes at each other. I was becoming faintly nauseated.

'I love your hair,' Sapphire purred, playing with a strand of turquoise.

'Thanks,' Bailey replied. 'I do it myself. Your eyes are really sparkly.'

'Thanks. And you have the cutest lips—'

I couldn't take it any more. 'So, Sapphire, is that your real name?' I blurted. For the first time in what seemed like hours, the other two people in the cab noticed I was there.

'Yeah. Can you believe it? It's like my mom wanted me to grind on truckers for a living,' she laughed.

'Well, you're good at it. Really good at it,' Bailey breathed. I barely kept my eyes from rolling out of my head.

'Thanks, babe,' Sapphire said, rubbing Bailey's thigh. 'Where are your parents? You still live with them?'

'My parents think I'm studying for finals at my friend's lake house,' I answered.

'My mom's at the hospital all weekend,' Bailey said. 'And I haven't heard from my dad since December, when he sent a happy Hanukkah email and a coupon for his lawn and garden centre. His new wife is Jewish,' she explained. 'He converted when he moved to Albuquerque.'

'Are there a lot of Jewish people in New Mexico?' Sapphire looked mildly confused. I was confused, too. But for an entirely different reason.

'Your dad's in Albuquerque?' I blurted, a little louder than I intended. I'd known her parents had divorced. And I had heard her dad remarried, but I'd always assumed he'd stayed in town. That he and Bailey still saw each other. Bailey had always worshipped her dad. They shared a love of obscure British TV shows and artificially coloured junk food. It was hard to imagine Bailey without him.

Bailey had drawn away from Sapphire and was staring hard at the road in front of us.

'Yeah. He's there. But we're not popping in to say hi, if that's what you're wondering.' I wanted to ask why not. Ask what had happened. But I didn't. Because if I had been a better friend, I wouldn't have to. If I'd been a better friend, Bailey would have told me who her crush was. But I hadn't. I'd only been worried about myself. And all those years of not asking, not being there, were now a gulf between us that I couldn't cross. Not in the middle of nowhere in a pickup truck driven by a stranger. So, I too stared straight ahead, watching the road slip beneath our wheels.

MILE 636

We had both dozed off, the monotonous drive lulling us to sleep. By the time Sapphire rolled the truck to a stop outside a single-level house with a sagging front porch and a faded recliner in the yard, it was just before dawn.

'Home sweet home,' she said, unbuckling.

I nudged Bailey. She mumbled incoherently and wiped a line of drool from her chin. She quickly glanced at Sapphire to see if she had noticed, but the stripper was already climbing down from the truck.

'I thought you were going to drop us at the bus station,' I said blearily. The scattering of houses in this neighbourhood were all on big lots and backed on to a cluster of scraggly trees. There was no sign of a town.

'I thought you might like a bite to eat before I took you. I make a mean ham and cheese omelette.'

I looked at Bailey, then darted my eyes to the road, trying to convey that we needed to keep moving. Bailey nodded imperceptibly. I felt a glow of warmth. We still understood each other without speaking. Maybe our friendship wasn't beyond repair.

'Sure!' she chirped. 'I'm starving!'

My glow extinguished.

'Great!' Sapphire said, clapping her hands together, her eyes alight with satisfaction. I glared at Bailey. She shrugged. I groaned, grabbed my backpack, and followed her into the house.

We stepped into a small, dark living room, but down the hall I could see a yellow light coming from the kitchen.

'In here!' Sapphire called. 'Come have a seat at the table while I crack these eggs.' We walked down the hall. There was the faint odour of wood chips in the house, along with something musky. I blinked when we finally entered the kitchen. Sapphire wasn't alone. Two sets of eyes gave me a once-over. One set belonged to a guy with a patchy goatee, wearing a stained muscle tee and a backwards trucker hat. The other belonged to the ferret perched on his shoulder. Bailey stopped short when she saw the man.

''Sup,' he drawled, exhaling a cloud of pot smoke as he spoke. 'Name's Dwayne. You must be Sapphire's new little buddies.' He stroked the ferret on his shoulder and grinned. 'So glad you could dine with us in our humble abode. Ganja?' He offered his joint, thick smoke wafting towards us from its smouldering tip. Bailey looked from

Dwayne to Sapphire then back, confused.

I could see whatever fantasy Bailey had constructed of Sapphire was crumbling under the combined weight of the dingy, smelly house and Dwayne's poor dental hygiene. 'Are you guys . . . together?'

'Can anyone really be together in this world? We all walk alone, little one.'

'We've been with each other since high school,' Sapphire added from where she was stirring the eggs, 'but we've evolved past labelling ourselves.'

'Oh.' That single syllable was all Bailey could manage. She sat down heavily on one of the cheap plastic chairs around the kitchen table. I wanted to get out of this place for Bailey's sake, but suddenly the combined smell of cooking eggs, weed and ferret was too much. A wave of nausea washed over me.

'Is there a bathroom?' I asked weakly.

'Sure, hon. Down the hall to the left,' Sapphire answered.

I stumbled down the hall, trying to keep the contents of my stomach where they belonged. Finding a small door on the left, I pushed it open and ran to the toilet, not bothering to turn on the light.

A few moments later, I flushed, feeling slightly better. Flipping on the lights, I went to the sink to wash my hands and rinse out my mouth. After letting the tap run for a second or two, I took a few gulps of water and then froze.

Behind me, reflected in the mirror, there was a large framed painting of a crying Jesus holding an armful of babies. He stared at the viewer with eyes full of sorrowful accusation. My stomach flip-flopped. I knew this image. I'd seen it at my sister's house. I then noted the other items in the bathroom I'd missed in my rush to the toilet: a votive candle with an image of a pregnant Virgin Mary, a collection of baby angel figurines balanced on the top of the medicine cabinet, a tissue box cover cross-stitched with the verse 'Before I formed thee in the belly I knew thee.' My heart started to pound. Then I saw something that sent me into full panic mode.

'We need to go!' I practically shouted as I rushed into the kitchen. Bailey looked up at me from her seat at the kitchen table, a joint pressed between her lips. I skidded to a halt. 'I left you alone for two minutes and you're already high?' I couldn't believe I'd been worried about her feelings. She clearly didn't have any.

'Dwayne's cousin just gave him a bunch of Blackberry Kush from California. You can't pass that up,' a now very relaxed Bailey said after a long exhale.

'Yeah, my cousin's got terminal brain cancer, so I'm selling off his scrip so he can pay for his medical bills,' Dwayne explained proudly.

'You are so noble, baby,' Sapphire added, coming over

to rub his shoulders, her breasts pressed against the back of his head. She eyed me warily. 'Why you in such a hurry to leave? You haven't had my eggs yet.'

I started to back out of the kitchen. 'Oh, you know, it's getting late. Or early. However you want to put it. We should get on the road.'

Bailey looked at me blearily. 'Isn't Sapphire supposed to take us to the bus station?'

'We can walk—'

Bailey started giggling. 'But . . . I can't feel my feet—'

'Or get a taxi . . .'

Bailey laughed harder. 'Yellow is a funny colour.'

'We don't want to be a bother. Let's go.' I stepped into the kitchen and tugged on her arm. Bailey looked at me, then at her joint.

'But I want more.'

'We can get more later. Lots more,' I promised desperately. Dwayne stood up, gathering his ferret off the table, stroking it gently. 'You two ain't a bother.' Dwayne's friendly voice sent shivers down my spine.

Sapphire nodded, agreeing. 'Not a bother at all.'

'See. They say we aren't a bother,' Bailey whined.

I bent down and whispered into her ear. 'Ook-lay in the allway-hay.'

'You know I suck at pig Latin,' she complained.

'Look in the hallway,' I repeated through gritted teeth.

163

Her eyes drifted to the hall, which was now lit by the light spilling from the bathroom, and widened slightly at what she saw – a pile of handmade protest signs that read, Stop the Baby Holocaust. Abortion is Murder.

'Ohhh. That's not good.' I yanked Bailey out of her seat.

We hurried towards the living room. Bailey giggled nervously.

'It just makes no sense. She grinded in my face.' I jerked on her arm, pulling her along faster. 'I'm horrified right now, but I can't stop laughing.'

'I hate you.'

'So funny!'

'This is all your fault.'

'You say that all the time!' We reached the front door.

'Don't go. I'll let you hold Malachi.' Dwayne and Sapphire stood in the entrance to the living room, haloed by the golden kitchen light. Dwayne stroked his struggling ferret.

'Not right now. Thank you so much for the ride.' I put my hand on the doorknob, half expecting one of them to dart forward and yank me away. But they just stood there, smiling. I opened the door.

And immediately closed it again.

'How . . .?' Stunned, I turned to stare at Sapphire. She wore a pleased smile.

'What?' Bailey asked, looking back and forth between us, uncomprehending. 'What's out there?' She opened the door.

'Babe!'

Bailey slammed the door shut. 'Oh my God. I'm so high. I just saw Kevin.'

Kevin pounded on the door. 'Babe? Babe? Open up.'

Sapphire walked towards us. 'Go ahead, sweetie. Let him in. He wants to talk to you.'

Bailey looked from Sapphire to me, confused. She opened the door again.

Kevin. Still there.

'Holy snarks!' Bailey slammed the door in his face. 'He's real!'

I tried to piece together what had happened. 'Did you go through my phone when we were asleep?'

Sapphire was unapologetic. 'I had to find someone who cared about you. When I saw that boy on your lock screen, I knew Jesus wanted me to reach out to him.'

'How? Did you watch me type in my code? Use my thumb?'

Bailey screwed up her face. 'That's your top concern right now?'

'He sent you so many loving texts,' Sapphire continued. 'We had a real nice conversation. Did you know he's been chasing after you all night? You're so blessed.'

Bailey gasped as a new realization hit her. 'Wait . . . is that why you gave us the ride? I thought it was because of my cute lips!'

Sapphire shrugged. 'It was kinda for both.' Then she turned back to me. 'I had to save that little angel growing in your belly.'

Next to her, Dwayne nodded sagely. 'You do what you're planning on doing, you're gonna burn in hell for all eternity.'

Bailey was looking at me, panicked, waiting for me to do something, to shout, to run. But I couldn't move. They were saying everything I'd been afraid to even think since this whole thing started. Damned. Hell. Eternity. Fiery lakes and burning brimstone. Tears pricked my eyes. Sapphire's smile softened.

'It's OK, hon. There's a centre right here in town that can help you. You can still do the right thing. Let him in.'

From the porch, Kevin shouted, 'Babe, you can't do this! Sapphire told me abortions are super dangerous!'

Dwayne gestured to the couch. 'Sit down. We can talk about your options.'

'Jesus gave you this baby for a reason,' Sapphire added.

I began to shake. It was too much. Part of me wanted to give up. All I had to do was open the door and let Kevin in. It would be so easy. My hand twitched towards the door-knob. Sapphire's eyes glowed.

Bailey started to giggle. 'Sorry. Sorry. Serious moment. But I'm just so confused – is Jesus down with stripping now?'

It was like the time Bailey shocked me awake by pouring a cup of ice water down my pyjamas after I'd fallen asleep during her favourite episode of *Ancient Aliens*. Suddenly, I could move. I jerked away from the doorknob.

Sapphire rounded on Bailey. 'I am saved by Jesus the Lord. And he forgives me!'

Bailey smirked. 'Is that, like, after each dance? Or do you save it up for one big giant forgiveness at the end of the night?' Sapphire gave a yowl of rage.

Dwayne put a calming hand on her shoulder. 'Things are getting tense. I think we should all pray.'

Sapphire gave a tight nod. 'You're right, honey.' Together, they walked to the couch and sat down. She took his hand and bowed her head. Dwayne turned to me.

'Join us.' He carefully placed Malachi on the floor and extended his hand. I stared at it like it was a viper.

'Babe,' Kevin called into the silence, 'you could get breast cancer!'

I glanced towards Bailey, then to the hallway leading to the kitchen. 'Back door.'

We ran.

Whirling around, we fled across the living room. I leapt over the coffee table while Bailey skirted around an aging recliner. Dwayne rose from the couch.

'Wait.' For the first time I noticed how big he was, his tank top showing off surprisingly ripped arms. We dashed into the kitchen.

'We want to help!' Sapphire called. Over my shoulder I could see the hulking figure of Dwayne catching up to us. Luckily, he was super high, so he wasn't exactly moving at light speed.

'There!' I pointed to the other side of the kitchen. There was a door at the far end with a window in it. I could see the glow of a porch light through the glass. We ran for it. Bailey knocked into the dining room table, sending paraphernalia flying. Dwayne staggered into view, looking at the mess.

'Not cool!' He stopped chasing us, dropped to his knees, and began to scrape up the scattered leaves of cannabis.

'Dwayne!' I heard Sapphire shriek from behind him. Bailey paused, distracted by the joints rolling on the linoleum. She bent down to reach for one.

'Come on!' I shouted, and yanked her towards our escape.

A moment later we burst through the back door. But the steps were broken and we tumbled into the backyard. The overgrown grass was slick with dew and it quickly seeped through my jeans.

'Oh man, my high is totally gone,' Bailey panted.

'Sorry if I don't feel too bad,' I shot back, 'considering you're why we're here.'

'Still might be worth it if we don't get murdered,' she gasped. 'Saw . . . some . . . boobies . . .'

I was gathering my strength to run again when two scuffed Nikes stepped into my field of vision.

'Babe.'

Scrambling to my feet, I came face to face with Kevin. Behind me, I heard Bailey stand.

'Move, asswipe,' she growled.

'Get out of here, freak,' he spat, then turned to me, his expression earnest. 'If you do this, you may not be able to have babies, babe.'

I stared at him, transfixed by the horrible absurdity of it all. 'What are you talking about?'

'Are you seriously getting medical advice from Dr Stripper and Nurse Ferret?' Bailey asked. But Kevin ignored her.

'I'm here to save you, Veronica.' He opened his arms. He was so proud of himself. So confident. I took a step back to stand beside Bailey.

'Bailey's the one that's saving me, you idiot.' From beside me, I felt Bailey's smile.

'Awww,' she said. Then she pushed me to the side. 'To the rescue!' And she swung her combat boot into his groin. Kevin crumpled, clutching his balls and mewling like a kitten. She held out her hand to me. 'Let's go, Veronica.'

We jogged to the front yard.

'I've been wanting to do that all night,' Bailey said. 'Actually, to be honest, ever since I saw his stupid face. God, did you have to keep your eyes shut when you slept with—'

'Bailey!' I warned. 'I kinda love you for destroying Kevin's nuts right now. Don't ruin it.'

'Point taken.' Bailey nodded. 'Let's get out of here.'

'How?' I asked. I could detect rustling in the backyard that could only be Kevin getting himself back into a standing position. From inside the house, I could hear Sapphire and Dwayne arguing about the weed, but I doubted they would be distracted for long. Bailey ran over to Sapphire's pickup truck. It was locked.

'Try Kevin's van,' she called. I ran to the kerb where it was parked.

'All locked,' I shouted back. 'Can't you break in or something?'

'Um, do I look like a professional car thief?'

'What about the El Camino?'

'Trav left his keys at our house.'

'Well, what are we going to do?' I was starting to panic.

'I don't know. But I'm really regretting not grabbing that weed when we ran through the kitchen. That was the best stuff I've ever had.'

'I don't really care about the weed right now.'

'That's because you didn't have it.'

'Bailey, we need to get out of here.'

But Bailey was looking past me, over my shoulder. 'Too late.'

I turned. Sapphire emerged from the backyard with a limping Kevin. Dwayne approached from the other direction. With our backs against the truck, we were trapped.

'No! It's not too late! It's never too late with Jesus!' Sapphire called. 'This boy is ready to be a father!' Beside her, Kevin made an affirmative groan.

Dwayne held up a piece of paper that looked like some sort of certificate printed off a computer. 'And I'm a minister in training at the LifeSong Pentecostal Church. I can marry you right now!'

I tried to step backwards but felt the cold metal of the pickup truck against my spine. I turned to Bailey.

'Do something.' But Bailey didn't seem to hear me. She was focused on the house, a dreamy look on her face. 'Bailey,' I hissed. 'Do—'

She took off running, dashing between the trio in the front yard, leaping up the front steps and through the front door. My mouth dropped. I knew exactly where she was headed.

'Are you kidding me?' I shouted. 'You're abandoning me to these lunatics for some weed?'

Seeing me alone, Sapphire smiled, the light of fanaticism in her eyes. 'Go to her.' She shoved Kevin forward.

'Hey, relax, lady.'

'Jesus is on your side,' Dwayne said encouragingly. Looking hesitant at first, but with growing confidence now that I was on my own, Kevin walked towards me.

'Babe, what's the harm in checking out the pregnancy centre? It might help you figure some stuff out. You don't want to rush into this and do something you'll regret. Plus, Sapphire said they'll give us lots of free baby supplies. That's pretty cool, right?' His shoes crunched on the dead grass as each step brought him closer. I pressed myself against the pickup truck and screwed my eyes shut, wishing it could swallow me. Just a foot away now, I could feel the heat radiate from his body. He reached towards me. 'We'll go together.'

'Step the fuck back, crunch nuts.'

Kevin jerked his hand away. I opened my eyes to find Bailey standing on the front porch of the house. In one hand she held the ferret by the scruff of its neck, its tiny legs kicking ineffectually. In the other hand she held her mom's Taser.

'Malachi!' Dwayne wailed. Bailey's smile bordered on feral.

'That's right,' she confirmed. 'Now everyone needs to step away from my friend, or the ferret gets it.' No one on the lawn moved. We were rooted to the spot as we stared at Bailey in astonishment. She glared at us all. With a flick of her finger, she turned on the Taser, letting it spark. That warm glow I'd felt towards her when we arrived reignited.

'Do what the crazy chick says!' Dwayne shouted, and stepped away. Sapphire rolled her eyes but moved back. 'Now!' he shouted at Kevin. Kevin looked from me to Sapphire and Dwayne, to Bailey and the ferret, then back to me. His chin lifted in rebellion, but Dwayne cracked his knuckles. Kevin eyed his two hundred pounds of muscle and reconsidered. Walking backwards, he stood beside them on the lawn, hands raised in surrender. Dwayne nodded. 'Wise decision, my man. I raised Malachi from a baby. Bottle-fed him and everything.'

My body sagged against the truck once I was freed from Kevin's proximity. Still holding the ferret in front of her, Bailey stepped down the front porch and made her way to me, keeping her eyes trained on the trio the whole time.

'Now, here's what's going to happen,' she continued, emphasizing each word with a stab of her Taser. 'You're going to give us the keys to the truck.'

Sapphire snorted. 'Like hell we are. Go ahead and fry the rodent.'

'Baby, no!' Dwayne exclaimed.

'We are not giving her the truck,' she hissed. 'It's mine.' They began arguing in a series of whispers.

Bailey turned the Taser towards Kevin. 'Fine. We'll take the keys to the van.'

Kevin looked at his shoes, his cheeks stained red. 'IthinkImightalockedeminside,' he mumbled.

'What?' Bailey asked.

'I think I mighta locked them inside,' he repeated. Everyone looked at him.

'Seriously?' Sapphire asked.

Kevin shrank, embarrassed. 'I was gonna ask if you could call AAA.'

Bailey leant over and whispered in my ear, 'Got any other ideas on how to get out of here?' I gave her the tiniest shake of my head. She sighed. 'This would have been a lot cooler if we could have stolen a car. Oh well.' She turned back to Sapphire, Dwayne, and Kevin. 'Fine. Plan C.'

Bailey launched Malachi towards the group on the lawn. The ferret soared through the air, its tiny feet flailing, its back arching, before landing with a thump on the grass and tumbling right to Dwayne's feet. 'Go!' Bailey shouted at me, and took off towards the patch of wilderness at the end of the road.

I ran. 'Where are we going?' I asked when I caught up to her.

'No idea!' Bailey replied. 'But our best chance of losing them is in those woods.'

'They look a little murdery.'

'The people behind us look murdery!' We were both terrified, out of breath and running into a wood that looked like it came straight out of a horror movie, but the gleam in Bailey's eye told me something.

'Oh my God. You're enjoying this!'

'Please. You are too.'

That was ridiculous. But I couldn't ignore the fact that my endorphins were flowing and I felt totally, completely . . . alive. I put on an extra burst of speed and crossed into the safety of the trees.

MILE 637

Dry leaves crunched under our feet as we crashed through the undergrowth, running blindly. Behind us I could hear our pursuers.

'Y'all are only running towards hell,' Sapphire called, almost lazily.

I leapt over a fallen log, darted around a half-dead juniper and scanned the area ahead of me, looking for some clue on which way to run. Instead I realized why Sapphire had sounded so unconcerned.

'Bailey?'

'Yeah?'

'You seeing what I'm seeing?'

'If you're seeing a cliff, then yeah.'

'I'm seeing a cliff,' I confirmed. Ahead of us the trees ended abruptly, falling off into the unknown. It was impossible to tell how big the drop was. We both kept running.

'We're still running,' I observed.

'Yeah,' Bailey agreed, her breath coming in short gasps, creating a counterpoint to the rhythm of her feet hitting the ground. I could hear Dwayne and Kevin closing in on us, branches cracking and leaves scattering as they forced their way through the woods. The cliff grew closer.

'We're not stopping.'

'We're not stopping,' Bailey agreed.

'This could really hurt.'

'Yep.'

I could see the muddy edge of the drop now. The undergrowth had faded away, leaving only a few bedraggled, half-grown plants between us and whatever lay beyond. I looked over at Bailey. Her tangled, multicoloured hair was sprinkled with dead leaves; her black eyeliner had smudged until there was more under her eyes than on them. Her shirt was riding up and her skinny jeans were slipping down. She was panting like a dog and her eyes were sparkling like the stars. And I felt something with more certainty than I'd ever felt with Kevin — bone deep, like when I nailed the Writing and Language portion of the SAT.

'Bailey? I know I've been terrible . . . but you're the best friend I've ever had.'

Bailey looked at me through the tangle of her hair. She wiped a strand out of her mouth and grinned as we neared the edge. 'Me too.'

I reached my hand towards hers. She took it. And hand in hand, with one final burst of speed, we launched ourselves into the air.

And landed in a muddy drainage ditch five feet below.

'Owwwweeeee,' Bailey moaned, clutching her shin. I rolled on to my hands and knees, checking to see if any part of me was injured. My whole body hurt from the impact, but as far as I could tell, nothing was seriously wrong. I searched for my cell phone, finding it covered in slime, and shoved it in my pocket. Somewhere above us I heard Kevin.

'Baaaaaabe?'

'Quick,' I whispered. 'In there.' I gestured to a storm drain a few feet away. The smell emanating from it was eye searing, but it was so dark inside no one would be able to see us. We climbed in. Huddled together, we could hear our pursuers trampling through the undergrowth above us.

'Babe, come back. You don't know what you're doing.'

'Ugh. My shoes are getting muddy. This is lame. Let's go.'

'I'm hungry. Does anyone want to go to Denny's?'

'Babe, abortion regret is real!'

'Screw it. I need a Grand Slam.'

'Babe? . . . Babe?! . . . Babe.' The sound of hurried footsteps. 'Hey, before you go, can you call AAA?'

We waited for the footsteps to fade away entirely. And then waited some more. I pulled out my phone and tapped the screen. Completely dead.

'No.' I tapped it again, then tried the power button. It remained stubbornly dark. 'No no no no no.'

Bailey leant over. 'Damn.'

'This is a disaster.'

'Yeah. No shit.'

'My parents . . . My friends . . .'

Bailey blinked, confused. 'Wait. That's what you're worried about? Not losing our only map?'

'You don't understand. They expect . . . They want . . . They always . . .' I was shaking.

Bailey wrapped an arm around my shoulders. 'That's a lot of "theys".' Feeling her arm around me, I relaxed.

'Yeah. You're right.'

We both stared at the blank screen in my hand. After a moment Bailey said, 'It was a good phone.' I snorted with laughter and leant my head against hers. We listened to the birds and watched as the sun chased away the morning mist. Finally, crawling on our hands and knees through the mud, we emerged from the storm drain and stood.

'Any idea where we are?' I asked.

Bailey shook her head. 'Nope.'

We looked around the little wilderness. The gauzy light had tipped the leaves with silver and the air was fresh and sharp.

'But I have a good feeling.'

I breathed in the air, letting it fill my lungs, then let it out with a whoosh. I smiled at Bailey. 'Actually, I do, too.'

Bailey grinned, threw her arms wide, and spun around. 'Pick a direction, any direction!'

I pointed. 'That way.'

Bailey stuck out her hand. 'We walk?'

I grabbed it. It felt warm and familiar in my own. 'We walk.' And we tramped off through the fallen leaves hand in hand.

MILE 637.5

'Walking sucks.'

MILE 639

Bailey and I sat at the edge of a field, our shoes off, our feet dangling in a tiny stream. Bailey was making moaning sounds that bordered on obscene as the water washed over her feet.

I examined the red and raw patches on my own feet. 'I don't think Adidas were made for hiking.'

The optimism I'd felt initially was fading. We were running out of time and there was still no hint of civilization. Then the distant whistle of a train broke through the morning birdsong. Bailey stopped her orgasmic performance.

'Did you hear that?' she asked. 'I think our problem is solved. Look.'

A ribbon of train track bisected the fields of grass.

'I don't see a train depot anywhere.'

Bailey raised her eyebrows. 'Who said we need one?' My face must have looked sceptical because she added, 'Look, we still probably have at least three hundred miles to go and the tracks are heading west.'

She was right. The sky was lighter behind us than in front of us. The train was heading in the right direction. But getting on it was another matter entirely. 'I don't know, Bailey.'

Bailey stood and grinned. 'You still have that good feeling, right?'

I held on to it desperately. Without another word, I grabbed my shoes from the side of the bank and stood.

A few moments later we were scrambling up the slight embankment that separated the tracks from the fields. I squinted into the distance. I couldn't see the train yet.

'So we just run alongside and jump in?' I asked.

'Yep. Like old-timey hoboes.'

The train appeared, a black smudge on the horizon. Bailey crouched, readying herself. I followed her lead and dropped into position. The train whistled again, its piercing shriek louder as it approached. Through my sneakers I felt the rumble of the engine as it shook the tracks. As the train neared, the vibrations spread through the bones of my feet to my legs.

'OK,' Bailey said, a little breathless, her eyes locked on the train, 'When it gets here, we look for an open-sided car and hop on. Follow my lead.' I nodded my agreement, my throat too tight to speak.

The engine was twenty yards away, eating up the rails as it thundered forward. It was enormous, almost as tall as my house. Its silver sides gleamed. Another blast of the horn ripped through the air. Bailey looked over her shoulder and shouted something.

'What?' I screamed, but my voice was swallowed by the sound of a hundred tons of steel barrelling towards us.

Bailey tried again. This time I could just make out, 'This is a terrible idea!' Then, grabbing my hand, she jerked me off the embankment and we tumbled down into the field.

Sitting up, we watched as the train snaked past us.

Bailey cocked her head. 'Damn. Those old-timey hoboes must have had some legs on them.'

I barely heard Bailey. Instead, I watched the train dwindle into the distance, disappearing like my chance of making it to New Mexico. The good feeling I'd had was gone. It was replaced by something uncontrollable. Something primal. Something I'd been refusing to feel up until now.

Rage.

'I should not be here.' I stood and kicked the embankment. 'I . . .' Kick. '. . . SHOULD . . .' Kick. '. . . NOT . . .' Kick. 'BE HERE!' I stopped kicking and began to pace, arms flailing wildly. 'I should be able to just walk down the street and say, "Hello, my name is Veronica, my boyfriend is an asshole, here is my five hundred dollars, oh yes, I'd love a cup of water, thanks so much, ten-minute wait? No problem."' I spun around to face Bailey. 'But nooooooooooo! I have to drive one thooooooousand miles, have my ride stolen, have a stripper kidnap me, lose my homework, and now I'm in the middle of a fuuuuucking field and the fuuuucking train won't fuuuuucking slow down . . . so FUUUUUUUUCK YOUUUU, MISSOURI STATE LEGISLATURE!' I rushed up the embankment to the tracks and tried to pry them up with my bare hands. 'ARRRRRGGGGGGHHHH!'

Bailey calmly walked over and stood beside me. 'Well, I still have a good feeling.'

'HOOOOOOOOWWWWW?' I wailed.

'Look.' Bailey pointed across the tracks. In the distance was a scattering of boxy buildings. A town.

MILE 640

We walked across the cracked asphalt of a middle school basketball court, the hoop with its frayed net blowing in the breeze. After my freak-out, I felt better. The good feeling had come back. But that could just be because I had Bailey beside me. We'd finally reached the outskirts of the town. It was quiet and empty in the early morning. Bailey inhaled deeply.

'Ah, the sweet smell of angst and body spray. Can't say I miss it.'

We passed a tetherball pole, a scuffed yellow ball dangling from its chain. I gave it a tap and it swung around.

'Bet I can still beat you.'

Bailey narrowed her eyes.

Two minutes later our laughter rang out across the empty playground as we each tried to wrap a sad, deflated ball around a pole.

MILE 641

'I still say you cheated,' Bailey grumbled.

'That wasn't cheating. That was strategy.'

'Yeah. Well, rematch at the next junior high we find in the middle of nowhere.'

I laughed. 'Deal.' We walked down the deserted main street. Most of the businesses were boarded up. It was the sort of town no one lived in any more. Or if they did, they left as soon as they could. I pulled out my phone and tapped the screen hopefully. It was still dead. No chance of finding a ride that way.

'Maybe we should try hitching again.'

Bailey cocked an eyebrow at me. 'I'm not a third-time's-the-charm sort of girl.'

'We need to be in New Mexico in a couple of hours.' Panic was beginning to creep its way in.

'No way. We tried twice. Not worth the risk. The only thing I want to die on this road trip is your—'

'Ugh! Bailey!'

Bailey tried to feign innocence. 'What? Too far?'

'Yes!' I shouted, appalled.

'Shut up,' she said.

'Um, you shut up. You're the offensive one here. It's really not funny.'

'No. Shut the fuck up.'

I saw then that she was looking past me and pointing at something across the street. A storefront had a large poster in the window that read: Mitch's Elegant Evening Limo Rental. There was a picture of a white stretch limo, a smiling man with a comb-over whom I could only assume was Mitch, and a phone number.

'It's, like, maybe six a.m. They're not open yet and we don't have a phone.'

But Bailey was already running across the street. 'This is what we've been waiting for! Can't you feel it?' She practically sang the last sentence. She was pounding on the door by the time I caught up with her.

'Bailey, how much is this gonna cost? A limo to New Mexico? We can't afford that.'

'Veronica, if you want to make it to New Mexico, we can't afford not to.' She continued to bang on the door. I winced as the sound punctuated the peaceful early morning quiet.

'Look, the hours are posted on the door. They don't

open until nine.'

But Bailey kept hammering. 'I feel like Mitch is the kind of guy who sleeps in the office.'

'Bailey . . .'

She stopped her pounding and turned to look at me, serene and utterly certain. 'Veronica, this is our destiny.'

Then, to my surprise, the door opened.

Ten minutes later we were climbing into the back of the oldest limo I'd ever seen. The leather seats were mauve and there was stained purple carpeting running down the middle of the floor. An ancient CRT TV hung in a corner and a couple of dusty champagne glasses sat in the built-in minibar. It smelt faintly of mint and disappointment. Bailey practically vibrated with excitement.

'Yes! This is how you do an abortion road trip! Why didn't we think of this earlier?' She started pressing buttons on her armrest. The sunroof opened a crack and then stopped. Bailey harrumphed in frustration and tried again. The sunroof made a whining sound but didn't move an inch. She crawled forward and banged on the smoked glass dividing window. After a moment it rolled down. An old Latino man wearing a white cowboy hat turned around to stare at us.

'Yes?'

'Oh. Hey. We met a minute ago. By the way, you're not

Mitch, are you?'

The driver shook his head. 'Mitch is my brother-in-law.'

'Oh. That's cool. What's your name?'

'Bob.'

'Hi, Bob. Nice to meet you. Anyway, I was wondering if you could help us. You see, the sunroof isn't opening.' Bob turned further around in his seat to get a look at the sunroof. After a moment, he nodded.

'Yes. That's as far as it goes.'

'Really?'

'Yes.'

'Because I was kinda hoping for a sunroof. This is my first time in a limo, and I wanted to get the full experience. Is there another limo somewhere? With a sunroof?'

'No.'

'Really?'

'Yes.' And with that, he rolled the divider up and started the engine. Bailey flopped back in her seat.

'Can you believe that?'

'That at six a.m. in a town with maybe two hundred people there's no other limo available? Yeah. I'm with Bob on this one,' I said.

MILE 682

Cutting through empty rolling plains dotted with lazily spinning white windmills, our limo raced down the highway. Bailey had quickly abandoned her seat and now stood in the middle of the limo, defiantly squeezing her arms through the small crack in the dust-covered sunroof and raising her middle fingers to the sky.

'WOOOOOOOOOOOOOO-HOOOOOOOOOOOO!' She turned to me, a wild, triumphant look on her face. 'Veronica, get up here.'

I shook my head. 'No. I can't do it.'

'Are you kidding me? This is what limos were made for.' Her smile flickered a little as I sat there, refusing to stand.

I grinned. 'No. I can't do it until I get some party music on!' I shouted. Bailey's smile returned full force when she realized I'd been teasing her. I dove for the radio and pushed the power button. And as if God Himself was controlling the airwaves, 'We Are Young' blasted through the speakers. Soon we were standing side by side, heads squished against the ceiling, arms thrust into the air, howling the lyrics. Bailey smiled.

'Limos are the best! Let's ride in one always!'

'OK!' I agreed, unable to get the stupid smile off my face. The song over, we sank back into our seats, breathless.

'You really should have got pregnant earlier,' Bailey said.

I groaned. 'You really should know when to stop.'

Bailey reached for the TV remote and pressed power. A morning talk show lit up the screen. The well-coiffed hosts chatted over cups of coffee. 'Oh good. Let's see if the blond one's drunk again. Watch her. She'll start leaning to the left.' I studied my friend while her eyes were glued to the screen. She'd travelled nearly 700 miles for me. She'd called the clinic when I was too scared to. She'd kicked my ex-boyfriend in the nuts. She'd done all this for someone who hadn't spoken to her since freshman year. For the first time on this trip, I wondered . . .

'Why?'

Bailey didn't even bother to look away from the screen. 'Because, stupid.'

'But I was horrible to you.'

'Yeah.'

'And you still came.'

'Uh, you offered me cash.'

'You didn't need it. Not really.'

'I was bored.'

'Your dream weekend involves Netflix and a never-ending bowl of Doritos.' But Bailey just kept studying the screen. 'Bailey . . .'

'Maybe it was because I didn't want to graduate without giving you one last chance. Or maybe it was just because.' Suddenly she pointed to the screen. 'Did you see that? She just leant!'

'You're saving my life,' I whispered.

'There she goes again! Ohhh, girl's had her chardonnay today!' Bailey crowed.

'Bailey.'

'Yeah. I heard you. Whatever. I'm in a limo watching my favourite morning show. Things are good.' She wouldn't look at me, but a moment later she sniffed loudly and surreptitiously rubbed her nose. I watched her for another minute, but Bailey kept her eyes fixed on the screen. She still didn't understand. I had to do something for her, something to show her I was there for her, too.

'You know, once we're done with my . . . thing, we can go to see your dad—'

'I'd rather dig my eyeballs out with a fork.'

I sighed. Bailey never made things easy. 'Just think about it—'

'I did. And I'd rather dig my eyeballs out with a fork.' She turned to me, finally looking away from the TV.

'Look, you're already doing enough to "prove" your friendship and wash away those four years of guilt. You're taking me to the greatest historic site in the country: Roswell. I'm going to get to see aliens.'

She was right. Of course she was. Offering to take her to see her dad was just an easy way to absolve myself of all the wrongs I'd done. And Bailey wasn't easy. She never was. It was why I'd rushed into the arms of new friends once we entered high school. Friends whom everyone liked. Friends who did what was expected. Friends who didn't question. Friends who didn't push. Friends who didn't ask for anything. Simple friends. Empty friends. But Roswell . . . I'd assumed once we lost the car Bailey had realized it would be nearly impossible to make the side trip. It was hundreds of miles out of our way. I wasn't even sure how we would get there, much less leave enough time to catch a bus back home. If we made the trip, there was a good chance my parents would find out what I'd done. But I had told Bailey I'd take her.

'You're right, taking you to see your dad wouldn't make up for the last four years. Roswell can't either. Nothing can. Still, I'm going to try. So, if it's really aliens you want to see, Roswell it is.'

Bailey blinked as if she was surprised at my response, then nodded. 'There's a tour that leaves from Old Town. Eleven a.m., one p.m. and three p.m. I looked it up when my dad moved to Albuquerque. It's thirty-five dollars each.'

I nodded. 'Great.'

She clapped her hands. 'Holy crap! We're gonna see Hangar 84! That's where they kept the bodies!'

'You know that whole alien thing was a long time ago. It's not like they just keep showing up there. So don't get disappointed if we don't see anything.'

Bailey rolled her eyes. 'Duh. I know how aliens work.'

I shook my head. *How aliens work?* Then another horrifying thought occurred to me. 'And I'm not going to break into any government areas.'

Bailey huffed. 'Fine.'

'Just tourist stuff.'

'Just tourist stuff.'

I stuck out my hand. 'Deal?'

She took it, grinning. 'Deal.' We shook. Bailey's eyes took on a devilish gleam. 'There's one section of this limo we have not explored.' She opened the minifridge with a flourish. It was empty except for a lone bottle of water. Bailey's eyes narrowed. 'This will not stand!' She pounded the intercom button. 'Bob!'

Five minutes later, Bailey was running out of a liquor store, paper-bag-wrapped bottle in hand and huge smile on her face. She climbed into the limo and tossed me the bag. I pulled out the bottle.

'Peach schnapps?'

'What? Funds are running low.' She grabbed a smudged champagne glass from the bar. 'Now, drink up!' She splashed some of the sticky-sweet drink into the glass and handed it to me.

I stared at it for a moment, then put it down. 'I can't.'

Bailey cocked an eyebrow. 'Um . . . I hope this isn't about protecting whatever's going on in there, because . . .'

'It's not,' I insisted. Still, it felt wrong, as though taking a drink would make my decision real. Bailey frowned, studying me. I quickly smiled and handed the glass back to her. 'Anyway, they aren't going to let a drunk teenager get an abortion. I kinda think they prefer you sober.'

Bailey shrugged. 'Didn't say anything about escorts.' She slammed it back, then hissed, 'Burns so good!' Bailey pulled a magazine out of the bag. 'OK! Quiz time! Let's discover what sexual position matches our zodiac signs!' I laughed. We quizzed each other while Bailey continued taking swigs from the bottle. Soon her words were slurring and I was yawning. Bailey laid her head down on my lap.

'Just gonna closemyeyesforasec . . .' she mumbled. I didn't bother to respond. The magazine slipped from my fingers and I too closed my eyes. The gentle rocking of the limo and the whine of the motor made an irresistible lullaby and I fell asleep.

MILE 983

An insistent buzzing against my thigh broke through my hazy dreams. I opened my eyes and looked down. My phone. I'd been charging it in the vain hope of reviving it. But the drainpipe muck must have evaporated and by some miracle of Apple engineering, it was working again. All of a sudden there was a flurry of notifications – including a text from my mom.

'Shoot!' I frantically started typing a response assuring her that I was safe and having a good time (all true, actually). She asked when I would be home. I told her I wasn't sure yet. It would depend on how studying went. I would probably miss church. She sent me an OK, a winky face, a palm tree and a bowling ball. She'd never got the hang of emojis, but I took it to mean that was acceptable and possibly that she and Dad were going bowling. Or to Hawaii. I breathed a sigh of relief. All that trust I'd built up over four years of being a perfect daughter and student was paying off. Not in her wildest nightmares would my mother suspect why I needed to get home as late as possible on Sunday.

The rest of my messages were from the girls. There was speculation about what Kevin wore to sleep in, a couple of calculus questions, a long debate about which nickname was funnier: 'Hannarall Ballard' or 'Hadderall Ballard', then more questions about Kevin. I quickly scrolled through the conversation and tapped a few vague responses, grateful Bailey was asleep. Hopefully that would keep them satisfied for a while.

I turned my attention to another problem that had been niggling at a back corner of my mind. The return trip. I pulled up a Greyhound schedule. There was a bus home from Roswell, New Mexico, that left at eight p.m. Roswell was three hours from Albuquerque. We could take the tour bus down to Roswell after my appointment and catch the Greyhound that night. We'd be back home by late afternoon Sunday. I put two tickets on hold and felt another rush of relief wash through me. I hardly dared to let myself think it, but everything was working out.

Just as I looked up from my phone, a sign flew past. I nudged Bailey. She grumbled and burrowed deeper into my lap. I nudged her again.

'Bailey!' I whisper-shouted.

'Whaaaaaaa,' she moaned.

'Wake up!'

'No. Uggghhhh. Sleep more.'

'Bailey! We're here! We made it.' Bailey sat up with a jerk and looked out the window. We were whipping past low-slung sun-baked buildings. Red mountains rose in the distance. I pointed to a green road sign.

'Albuquerque, eleven miles,' Bailey read. She turned to me, eyes wide in surprise. 'Holy shit, we did it!'

'I know!'

'I can't believe it!'

'Neither can I!'

Bailey started counting on her fingers. 'I mean, we were robbed, chased, stalked –'

'We jumped off a cliff –'

'Hid in a ditch –'

'Hid behind cows –'

'Threw a weasel –'

'Ferret, but close enough.'

'Saw boobies.'

'I don't think that was an obstacle.'

'I know. I just wanted to mention it again.'

'Whatever. We made it.' I was practically breathless with excitement and smiling so hard my face hurt. Bailey was, too. We hugged. 'Uh, Bailey?' I said with my nose in her hair.

'Yeah?'

'You really stink.'

'Well, you're no bouquet of daffodils either.'

For the first time since our trip had begun, I realized what we must look like to strangers. Our clothes were mud-stained. I had a faded splotch of Slurpee on my thigh. Bailey still had leaves in her hair. What was left of her make-up was smudged down her cheeks. There was a hole in my shirt I didn't remember getting. 'We need to clean up,' I said, and grabbed the bottle of water from the minibar. Splashing it on my hands, I began to scrub my face. Bailey began to comb her hair with her fingers and pick out the leaves. Five minutes later we were marginally more presentable and slightly better smelling. Bailey had me turn around to ensure I'd got all the dirt off.

'So?' I asked. 'How do I look?'

'Like someone who drove nine hundred miles in one night.'

I sighed, disappointed.

Bailey laughed. 'What? You thought a half bottle of water was going to restore you to prom princess? Sorry, girlie. You're just going to have to look average.'

I wrinkled my nose in mock disgust, but inside there was a little prickle of irritation. I hated looking less than my best. In my mind, I'd imagined coming into the clinic, my hair shiny, my clothes neat, so that anyone who saw me would have a moment of surprise that *that* sort of girl would need an abortion. But coming in looking like this? Messy, smelly and sleep deprived? Looking *average*? How would people know I was better than this?

My phone buzzed. Bailey clapped her hands together, excited.

'Dude, your phone works again! Sweet. Let's order a pizza.'

'No pizza. And yeah, I know. I reserved two seats on the bus home while you were sleeping. As long as we are out of the clinic by two thirty, we can catch your tour bus down to Roswell and then go home from there.'

Bailey settled back in her seat. 'Piece of cake.' My phone buzzed again. 'You gonna check that?' I glanced at the screen.

Emily: Um really? That's all we get?

Jocelyn: Yeah more deets lovebird

Kaylee: Or we're driving down from cabin 2 find u

Answering them had been a mistake. I needed to quickly shut them down.

Me: Jeez calm down. Can't a girl get some private time?

Jocelyn: Not when ur man looks like Kevin. Spill

Emily: Calc is boring need boy

Bailey's eyes narrowed as my thumbs flew over the screen. 'Is that Kevin text-assaulting you?'

'Blocked him, remember?'

Me: Not sharing. Shy.

Kaylee: Liar! Give up the good stuff! What happened in the hot tub?

Bailey edged towards me, trying to see the screen. 'Who is it, then?'

'No one.'

Me: None of ur business. Get back 2 studying. Emily ur in danger of a B+ unless u nail this.

Emily: Nope. Not leaving you alone till we get a pic. What are you doing right now?

Kaylee: Show us!!

Jocelyn: Now or face our wrath!!

Bailey peered over my shoulder. 'Are you cheating on me?'

'Cheating?'

'With your real friends.'

'What? No!' I laughed half-heartedly. Angling away from Bailey, I scrolled through my phone.

Me: Fine. Here.

I loaded up a photo and tapped send.

Jocelyn: NOT GOOD ENOUGH!!!!!!!!!!!!!

Bailey leant over and peered at my screen. She looked up, stricken. 'You sent our pancakes.'

I had sent the girls the photo I'd taken of the short stack I'd ordered at the diner. They were big and fluffy. The scoop of butter shone as it slid off to one side. Syrup pooled along the edges of the plate in sticky deliciousness.

They were perfect. And until a moment ago, they were a memory that belonged only to Bailey and me.

We stared at each other, her mouth settling into a firm line, my mouth slightly agape as I searched frantically for something to say.

My phone began to ring. Emily's name flashed on the screen. Bailey eyed me, arms crossed.

'Answer it.'

'I don't want to talk.'

The phone continued to ring. Bailey cocked an eyebrow. 'You gotta keep your cover.'

'No. I'm not playing their games. I told them I was busy.' Bailey continued to glare at me. The phone continued to ring. Suddenly, Bailey whipped the phone out of my hand and pressed accept.

'Bail—' I screeched before I caught myself. Grabbing the phone back from her, I pressed it to my ear. 'Hey, girls . . . Nothing. No. We're just mellow . . . Totally not! No. Just a little breakfast break between study sessions.' I hated each word as it slid from my mouth. I hunched away from the heat of Bailey's gaze and continued. 'Kev? Of course not. He's helping me prep. What? Now that Hannah Ballard is out of the way, I can't let one of you nab valedictorian at the last second.'

As I spoke, a tiny fissure cracked my heart. Why couldn't my fake conversation be real? Studying in a hotel room with my boyfriend was the sort of rule breaking I was comfortable with. Not whatever these last sixteen hours were. As I babbled meaningless nothings to my friends, Bailey continued to watch me, arms crossed, expression unreadable. 'No . . . that's just the air conditioning. I know, it's loud. Right? It totally sounds like I'm in a car.' I laughed to cover my nervousness and attempted to ignore Bailey. 'How was the movie binge? I know! I wish I was there!' My voice was getting higher and higher as I spoke. 'Well, yeah. He's great. But you're my besties! Oh, he ran to the bathroom. Right? He's incredible.'

Out of the corner of my eye, I saw Bailey open the bottle of schnapps, take a swig, and give me a thumbs-up. A very sarcastic thumbs-up. *What?* I mouthed. Bailey just rolled her eyes. Emily was speaking, but I couldn't follow what she was saying. 'Oh! Hey, I hear the door,' I blurted. 'He's back. Gotta go! Bye!' I hung up and flopped back on the seat. 'Oh wow. They almost had me with the car noise. Good thing I thought of the air-conditioner, right?'

'Sure. I wouldn't expect any less from perfect Veronica Clarke,' Bailey muttered.

'OK, I'm sorry I used the photo, but what was I supposed to do? They wouldn't leave me alone.'

'Don't act like this is just about the pancakes.'

'Hey, you're the one who answered the call. I was just going to let it go to voicemail. You forced me into that conversation. You don't get to be angry about anything I said to get out of it.'

'I'm not angry.'

'You broke out the schnapps and you're glaring at that stain on the carpet like it did something to you.'

'I'm thirsty. And it's interesting. It looks like Totoro.'

'You made me talk to them.' I was indignant. Bailey continued to study the floor and drink. Finally . . .

'You wish you were there, huh?'

'Not pregnant and studying for finals? I don't know, Bailey, that seems pretty good right now.'

'With your besties?' Bailey spat the word out.

'I was covering! You told me to cover.' This really wasn't fair. She'd made me do this and now she was angry.

Bailey took another swig and shrugged. 'I guess I forgot how good you were at it.'

At her words, anger sliced through me, sharp and clean. 'What is that supposed to mean?'

'You always cover, don't you? This whole trip is a cover.'

'Why are you being such a jerk all of a sudden?'

Bailey spun around to glare at me. 'Why can't you just tell them? Huh? If you're such besties? Why can't you tell your *besties* about your little problem?'

'They wouldn't understand!' I shouted.

Bailey's eyes lit up like she'd just caught me in a trap. 'Ha! Liar! They would totally understand. I bet they'd cry and hug you and make you freakin' tea. No. No, it's that if you told them, you wouldn't be Perfect Veronica Clarke any more. You're a fucking coward.' Bitterness dripped from every syllable of her speech.

'I am not,' I sputtered. But the pit of my stomach felt like ice.

'You run away every time shit happens because you're terrified it might make you look bad. Because you need everyone to think you're perfect. Get a B on a test? Claim you had a cold and ask to take it again. Boyfriend's a creep-tastic asshole? Fake an entire weekend lovefest with pictures so your friends don't suspect. Best friend's parents are going through a divorce and she's a little messed up? Ditch her for some stuck-up Mensa clones!'

'I already said I was sorry—'

'Whatever. My asshole dad said he was sorry. It didn't change anything.'

'Look, you're drunk—'

'Ha! There it is. I'm the crazy one,' Bailey crowed, wiggling her fingers in the air and making a face. 'Don't listen to Bailey. She's sooooo screwed up.'

'I never said—'

'But who's the one getting the abortion? Not Crazy Bailey!' Bailey's arms stopped waving wildly and dropped abruptly into her lap. There was a moment of silence in the limo where the only sound was the tyres coasting over the road as we both absorbed what she'd just said.

'Are you judging me?' I managed to ask. Bailey crossed her arms and jerked her chin up a fraction.

'So what if I am. Am I not worthy to judge Perfect Veronica? We both know why you're doing this. Not because you don't want to raise a baby. Not because you couldn't support it. Because you're embarrassed what other people would think about you.' Waves of heat and ice were rolling through my body. Was she right? Was that what all this was about? Embarrassment? I looked away so I could piece my fractured thoughts back together, but Bailey held my gaze. She smiled ruefully when she read the emotions in my eyes. 'Not so perfect, are you, Veronica?'

Fury flashed through me. 'You've been waiting for this for years, haven't you? A chance to feel superior to me. That's why you agreed to drive. So you could secretly gloat. That whole "last chance to be friends again" thing was bullshit.'

Bailey crossed her arms. 'Go ahead, try to make yourself feel better by thinking I'm an evil asshole with secret motives. But I meant what I said last night. All of it. Remember, I don't need perfect friends. Just one who's there.'

'You're infuriating.'

'You're a slut who should have kept your pants on.'

'I can't believe you're judging me for this! You're a

lesbian!' Even as I said the words I wanted to take them back. I needed to explain—

Bailey smacked me. Hard. I'd never been hit before. It took me a minute to process the pain, to register the heat on the side of my face. My eyes welled up and a cold tear traced a path down my burning cheek. I touched my fingers to my face and stared stupidly at Bailey. She stared back, equally surprised, but then her eyes hardened and her mouth quirked into a smile of smug satisfaction.

'I knew it.'

'That's not what I meant . . .' It wasn't. I didn't care that she was a lesbian. It wasn't a sin. Or whatever my church said. I didn't believe any of that. I'd just thought because she was one, she'd be supportive of my choice. The words had come out wrong. But even if they had, was what I'd meant really any better? I was still judging her. Still making an assumption.

A new thought hit, one that made the pit of my stomach once again turn to ice. When I'd told her I didn't care if she was a lesbian, was I thinking of her sexuality as some kind of flaw? Something to be looked past? Something that made her less than perfect? Did it make me feel better that I was straight and she wasn't? Where did I start with my apology?

'I'm sorry, I—'

But Bailey was pounding on the partition window.

'Pull over!' The glass was shaking in its frame. 'Pull the fuck over!'

The car coasted to a stop in front of a strip mall. We were somewhere in Albuquerque, or maybe its suburbs. 'Bailey . . . don't.' But it was a half-hearted protest. I didn't try to stop her, to reach out and grab her. It was too late for that.

She opened the car door and climbed out. She took a wad of cash from her wallet, all that was left over, and threw it at my face. As the bills floated to the floor of the limo, she stepped away from the car. 'Have an awesome abortion, you fucking baby killer,' she said, and slammed the door.

MILE 990

For a moment I simply sat there, staring at the money scattered around my feet, not really seeing it.

I was a horrible person. I'd claimed to be friends with Bailey, but even back in middle school, part of the reason I'd liked hanging out with her was that I thought I was just a little bit better. That I had it more together. That my hair was shinier. That my clothes were cuter. That my grades were higher. That I wasn't weird like her. Even with Emily, Kaylee and Jocelyn, I wasn't friends with them just because I liked them; I was friends with them because I was the smartest. I had the cutest boyfriend. I was friends with them because I knew I could always be just a little bit more successful than they were. What sort of person did that?

But now, I wasn't. Better. More successful. Perfect. I'd lost my claim to that title because I was getting an abortion. And no one gets an abortion because everything is going swimmingly. Perfect people don't need to get abortions. And the worst part was, Bailey was right. My friends would hug me and make me tea if they knew. They would support me. But I couldn't stand to let them. Because then I couldn't feel superior to them.

The squeak of the partition lowering snapped me out of my spiral of self-hatred. Bob looked over his shoulder, his expression carefully neutral.

'Still going to the same place?'

I couldn't answer. I just jerked my head up and down and turned to stare at the sidewalk. The early morning sun bounced harshly off the bits of glass in the concrete, making everything seem to sparkle. There was no sign of Bailey. I wasn't surprised. She knew how to get by without anyone's help. I'd made sure of that.

MILE 994

The abortion clinic was not what I'd expected. A single-storey stucco building with freshly painted trim, it looked no different from any of the other beige stucco buildings surrounding it. There were trees shading the parking lot and a neatly trimmed hedge under the window. Somehow I'd expected it to be dirty, run-down, or maybe just have a giant neon sign proclaiming 'Get Your Abortions Here' with orange and red blinking flames of hell surrounding it. If I hadn't double-checked the address, I could have imagined the people inside were getting their teeth cleaned.

It looked like any other building until I noticed the scattering of people on the sidewalk. People with signs. Protesters. Why hadn't I realized they would be there?

CHOOSE LIFE

ABORTION IS MURDER

PRAY TO END THE KILLINGS

CHOP SHOP

This last one was done in bloody red letters like a horror movie poster. One girl, who was probably my age or a little younger, held up a giant poster of what looked like mutilated body parts with the words '12 Weeks'.

It wasn't like I hadn't seen all this before. I'd even helped make some similar, if not quite as bloody, posters in my youth group. As I read the ones outside my window, I waited for the stab of guilt. When I'd painted the signs in church, I'd imagined some woman reading them and suddenly having a soul-shattering moment of realization. She'd turn her car around and go on to raise her baby and live happily ever after. But instead, there was nothing. No guilt. No moment of awakening. No tearful repentance. My eyes slid over the signs and my heart remained unaffected. I'd made my decision long before we arrived. Those signs were just words.

And then, almost as one, the protesters noticed the limo. Every eye turned towards me, trying to pierce the tinted windows. They flocked forward right to the edge of the kerb. Their chants intensified, rising to a guttural roar. Faces twisted into anger. A man my father's age shook his fist, nearly pounding on the limo as we slowed to make the turn into the driveway, spittle flying from his mouth and slapping the dusty window. The protesters surrounded us, getting as close as they dared, not allowed to block us with their bodies, but trying to do so with their screams.

They weren't trying to help me. This wasn't a prayer. This was hate. Even though they couldn't see me through the tinted windows, I covered my ears and rolled myself into a ball, feeling their shrieks like slaps.

The limo had stopped. Bob had pulled into a parking spot as far as possible from the sidewalk under one of the green shade trees. He sat staring straight ahead, waiting. I slowly uncurled and found my hands trembling slightly. I could still hear the faint sounds of protests from the sidewalk.

I peered out the window, locating the entrance to the building. A vast expanse of asphalt separated me from the door. But the protesters weren't allowed on the property. All they could do was hurl shame. I steeled myself, reached for the door handle and—

'Oh no.' The words slipped from my mouth as a horrible realization hit me. In the rear-view mirror, Bob's eyes flicked to mine.

'You OK?' he asked.

I had no escort. No one to drive me after the operation. I'd come all this way, but without Bailey, they would turn me away. I shook my head, embarrassed.

'Um, I need someone to go with me. They need to know I have a ride and my friend . . .' My face burnt. 'Is there any way you could come?' My voice sounded pathetic even to my own ears and I cringed waiting for his response.

Bob was old enough to be my grandpa. There was no way he approved of what I was doing. He rubbed the stubble on his cheeks, thinking. I could sense the no forming on his lips. I willed myself not to cry. 'Please,' I whispered.

He slumped a bit in his seat and sighed. 'It's seventy-five an hour.' I counted the cash that I had left. I was pretty sure there was enough to cover Bob, the abortion, and the bus fare home. I nodded.

'OK.'

With that Bob opened his door and strode around to my side of the limo. Opening the side door, he stood, waiting for me to climb out, just as if we were at prom. My heart pounded. I stepped into the dappled sunlight of the parking lot. The dry air sucked the moisture from my skin. I was desperate for a drink of water. The protesters quieted at my appearance, straining to see me.

I heard the familiar click of a camera phone and flinched. Someone had taken a picture. Before I could react to it, Bob had swooped around to the other side of me, blocking me from the protesters' view. I melted a little in gratitude. But denied a view of their quarry, the protesters chants soon resumed with renewed vitriol. I shrank against the assault, but Bob firmly took my arm in his and hurried me along. The door was drawing nearer. I could see the neat letters of the clinic's name labelled beneath a small, probably bulletproof frosted-glass window. We were almost there.

Suddenly one of the protesters broke loose from the pack and came tearing across the parking lot, darting in front of us and blocking our path. I stifled a yelp as Bob shoved me to the side to protect me. But the protester continued to advance.

'Babe!'

Babe? I looked more closely at the approaching figure and felt a burst of fiery anger.

Kevin.

'You can't stop me.' And taking Bob's arm, I resumed my walk towards the entrance. Kevin rushed in front of us again. The protesters' chants petered off as they strained to see the drama unfolding before them.

'I'm not trying to stop you,' Kevin said. 'I know words can't really fix anything, but don't run away.'

'I have to go. Goodbye, Kevin.' And I strode forward, not bothering to take Bob's arm this time. I heard Bob mutter what I could only assume were Spanish curse words at Kevin as he hurried to catch up with me. We reached the deep shade of the awning that stretched over the entrance. The immediate drop in temperature helped me to relax a bit as I reached for the door handle.

'Please.' His voice cracked on the word. 'I was wrong.'

I froze, my fingers inches from the door. He sounded so broken. Wanting to confirm the remorse I heard in his voice, I turned. He stood, shoulders slumped, the hard, bright sun beating down on him.

'I, um, googled some stuff,' he began tentatively. 'It turns out that a lot of the things Sapphire told me might not be true. I don't know why I listened to her. This whole thing spiralled way out of control. I wasn't thinking for myself. I was doing whatever everyone else said was the right thing. What our parents would want. What our church would want. I was on autopilot. But this is real life stuff and we need to make real life choices, right?' I blinked, too surprised to answer. He continued, 'I support whatever you want to do. I know you've thought a lot about it. I'm sorry. I've been an asshole.'

I didn't know what to say. Kevin didn't sound like Kevin. This wasn't the high school boy who called me 'babe' and sometimes forgot to chew with his mouth closed. This was someone else. Maybe the Kevin he was going to be. Uncertainty pooled in the pit of my stomach. Kevin, still waiting for my response, seemed to notice Bob for the first time.

'Where's Bailey?'

'Not here.' It was all I could manage to say. But it seemed to be enough. Understanding sparked in Kevin's eyes. His face softened.

'Oh, I'm sorry. I know you thought she was your friend.'

I had to swallow my tears. I didn't know what Bailey was

now. Or who I was to her. Or if we had ever really been friends at all. 'It's OK,' I managed to choke out, hating the emotion that thickened my voice.

'No, it's not.' And Kevin opened his arms. When I didn't move into them, he stepped towards me. I didn't move away, and taking that for consent, he enfolded me in his arms. My body was stiff under his. I couldn't yield to his embrace, but even so, comfort washed through me. I closed my eyes. He smelt like he always did, and right now the familiarity felt like safety. 'It's OK. It's OK,' he murmured, stroking my tangled hair. We stood there, him in the sun, me still in the shade.

'I know this has been a nightmare. And I know it will take a lot for me to earn your trust back,' he said. 'But I realized on the drive here, this sort of thing could really bond us together.' I pulled away slightly. He was looking off into the distance, lost in thought. He continued, 'Me holding your hand in the waiting room, filling out forms, getting a big bowl of ice cream after. In the end, I think it's gonna make us stronger as a couple. We'll always have this memory, you know? And since we'll probably have a lot to work through, I've been thinking, I don't need to go to Missouri State. I could just get a job in Rhode Island near campus. We could move in together!'

I leapt back in horror. Kevin was smiling benignly, pleased with his plan.

'Ugh! Your DNA is inside me!' I felt sick. Dirty.

'Is something wrong, babe?' His perfect eyebrows were drawn into a frown; his golden hair flopped gently over his confused blue eyes. He was a monster.

'You think my abortion is going to bring us closer together?' My screech rang out across the parking lot. The protesters began to whisper among themselves. I didn't care. I pointed back towards Missouri. 'Go.'

Finally, Kevin's placating smile slipped. He didn't look confused now. He looked angry. 'Oh, so now you don't want this, either? What do you want, Veronica? I apologized. I offered to marry you. I offered to go to the clinic. I was willing to do whatever you wanted. But none of it's good enough for you, is it?'

'For me?' I echoed. Suddenly, everything was blindingly clear. 'None of this has been about me. This has all been about you. You being sad everyone was leaving. You being scared if I went away to college you would lose me. You afraid of being alone. Of being left behind. Marriage? Abortion? You don't care as long as it means I'll take you back. Because if I do, if I stay with you, that means you aren't a shrivelled, rotten pestilence of a human being who peaked in high school.'

Kevin gaped.

'Go or I'm calling the police.'

'But—'

I stepped towards him. 'I'll tell them everything,' I promised, enunciating every syllable. I didn't know if what he'd done was illegal, but obviously Kevin didn't know either. And he wasn't willing to find out. He nodded, raising his hands in submission, and my three-year-long mistake began to back away. It was over. I turned to the entrance of the clinic, feeling emptier than ever.

'Fucking cunt.'

The words were quiet, but I was meant to hear them. I whirled around, closing the space between us in a few quick steps, my right arm already pulling back. Kevin didn't even give me the dignity of looking alarmed. There was merely mild confusion. I took one final step and, putting my whole body behind it, sent my fist flying into his jaw. It landed with a knuckle-numbing thud. Kevin's head snapped back. It was just like the movies. I could have sworn the skin where my fist met his cheek even undulated in slow motion. Adrenaline and joy burnt through me as I watched him stagger a few steps before crumpling to the ground, dazed.

I started to lunge towards him, ready to aim a solid kick to the part of his body that had caused me all this trouble, when Bob gripped my arm. His eyes flicked to the crowd of protesters. Some of their signs had been lowered and I thought maybe one woman had a glint of satisfaction in her eye, but most remained stone-faced. Explaining assault to a police officer with twenty unfriendly witnesses wasn't what I needed. I nodded and let myself be led inside, leaving the moaning heap that was my ex-boyfriend to the New Mexican sun.

I was here. This was real. I was doing this. The thought echoed in my head. The inside of the clinic was clean and spare, a few chairs lined up along a wall, a reception desk, some vaguely soothing art and old magazines scattered on end tables. A few women sat waiting quietly, paging through back issues of *People* or flipping idly through their phones.

I was doing this. I was in an abortion clinic. Everything was too bright, yet hazy all at once. People spoke, but the sound was muted by the blood thundering through my veins. My palms were slick with perspiration. This was real. This was real. This was real. I approached the reception desk on unfeeling feet as Bob trailed along behind. The middle-aged woman looked up from her paperwork.

'Welcome. Do you have an appointment with us today?' Her eyes flicked to Bob, likely curious at the pairing of a scruffy teenager and an old man dressed like a cowboy, but her voice remained warm and her eyes held no judgement. I relaxed a fraction, though my heart was still in my throat. I nodded.

'Veronica Clarke,' I managed, pleased no tremor entered

my voice. She looked to her computer and typed a couple of lines before nodding.

'OK, there are just a few forms you'll have to fill out before we can have a nurse take your vitals. Have you been to us before?' I shook my head. 'Well, let me know if you have any questions.' She handed me a thick stack of papers attached to a clipboard and a ballpoint pen.

I am sitting in a chair. Words in black ink. Check boxes. Middle initials. Allergies. My last meal. My last drink. Medical history. How many pregnancies have I had? I scratch out zero and write in 'one'.

Bob, paging through a *Cooking Light*, reading up on slow cooker recipes.

Me handing the sheaf of papers back. A polite request for money. Scrambling to find my wallet and produce the sticky, crumpled wad of cash. Counting it out carefully, seeing flashes of Bailey with every bill hitting the counter. The pawnshop. Pancakes. Slurpees. Strippers. I count the twenties, fives and tens faster and push them towards the woman. This time she isn't able to completely hide the flash of pity. I smile to tell her it's OK. She takes the money.

More waiting. Women are called and disappear, summoned by anonymous numbers rather than their names. Their partners, friends and mothers read magazines. On my phone, I find a new bus ride home. One that leaves from Albuquerque instead of Roswell. Because I don't need to go to Roswell any more. There's only one. It leaves at three thirty. I make the reservation.

A number.

My number.

They are calling me. I stand. A nurse holds open a door. I cross through.

A scale. It rocks slightly as I stand on it. The scrape of metal as fingers delicately push it into perfect balance. The squeeze of a blood pressure cuff. Quietly given directions. Answers written down on a clipboard. A prick of needle. Blood drawn. A small plastic cup and packets of baby wipes.

I carefully crouch over a toilet and clean myself, the wipes cold on the folds of my skin. I empty my bladder into the cup. I place it on a counter with other yellow-filled cups.

I wait.

A nurse approaches. She explains to me in a pleasant but emotionless voice that I will need an ultrasound. On the form they gave me I marked the date of my last period with a question mark. I explain that I know basically when it was. She says they have to be sure. I'm led into a darkened room and handed a paper gown. Have I ever had a vaginal ultrasound before?

Vaginal?

Of course not, I want to shout, but instead I shake my head. She explains I might feel a little discomfort but it is nothing to worry about. She leaves me alone in the dark room to change. I'm worried.

I'm splayed open on a table, my feet in stirrups. The technician tells me to scoot lower. Lower. I'm shown the equipment that will be inside me. Told there will be some pressure. It's bigger than I expected. All the monitors are turned away from me, their beeps and whirs muted. I stare at the ceiling, counting the tiles. A cold squirt of gel and it begins. The ultrasound hurts less and more than I was expecting. Stretching and pressure and invasion. I keep counting tiles. I breathe. I'm told I'm doing well, that it's almost over, but it keeps going. I lose track of my counting. I start over. My eyes sting with tears.

It's finished. I'm given tissues to wipe myself. Told again I did well. I'm left alone to dress.

Emerging into the hallway, I blink at the bright lights. A new nurse waits for me. I'm led to another room. Given a chair. I'm asked if I need anything. I shake my head. I wait again. The walls have pictures of oceans and trees. Bland beautiful things. When the door finally opens, I start. A soft, small woman with short hair and tired eyes enters and sits.

*

'Hello, Veronica. I'm Dr Rivera. There are just a few questions we have to go over before we can do your procedure.' As she said this she rifled through the papers on her desk, brisk and businesslike.

'OK.' My voice was raspy. I cleared my throat and tried again. 'OK,' I repeated, this time with more confidence. The doctor smiled at me, but there was little warmth.

'First, is this your decision? Have you been coerced in any way?' She looked me in the eye as she asked this, searching for any hint of emotion on my face.

'No. No, I want this,' I said, making my voice sound as firm as possible. There was a beat as Dr Rivera continued to study me. Finally, she gave a quick nod and turned back to her papers.

'How do you feel about terminating your pregnancy today?' The first word that popped into my mind was *ecstatic*. It was almost over. Then I remembered Bailey's words in the limo. Was I really doing this just because I was embarrassed? Because I didn't want people to know I'd made a mistake? And if I was, was that reason enough to go through with this? I took a breath and let it out. If I was going to do this, I had to know exactly how I felt. No more hiding from the thought. No more running away from the word, even in my mind. Abortion. I was going to get an abortion.

I waited. I let every emotion surface. Examined every

belief I'd been taught. I didn't flinch away or try to stuff anything down.

Parents.

Church.

Hell.

Friends.

Shame.

Failure.

College.

Judgement.

Life.

Honesty.

Responsibility.

Love.

And I had my answer.

Bailey was right. I was embarrassed. But not at my choice. I may not have wanted my friends to know about this, but I was going to get an abortion no matter what. At my core I knew, and I'd known since I first suspected it was a possibility, that a baby was not right for me, not now. Every cell of my being rebelled against the idea. There was no question. I looked Dr Rivera in the eye.

'It's the right choice for me.'

She nodded. In the rush of emotion following my response, I half wanted a pleased smile from Dr Rivera, but her expression remained carefully neutral. Still, my body sang with relief. I was doing the right thing.

The doctor continued, brisk and businesslike. 'So, I want to talk to you about your options. There's the medical abortion, using pills, but you're from out of state, correct?'

'Yes.'

Dr Rivera smiled gently. 'I'm assuming you'd have trouble returning to us for another visit?'

I nodded. 'Yes.'

'Then I'm going to recommended doing an in-clinic surgical abortion.'

And just like that my sense of calm evaporated. I'd spent so much energy just trying to get here, I'd forgotten what would actually happen when I did. But that word made it real.

Surgical.

It brought to mind images of gleaming scalpels. Bright lights. Blood. I knew it was the plan all along, but hearing it come out of the doctor's mouth, in this office – as comforting and friendly as they'd tried to make it – a nerve tightened in my legs and my chest contracted. I'd never been to so much as a check-up alone before, and now I was getting surgery.

Dr Rivera's voice broke through my panic. 'Do you have any questions?'

Yes. Why was I sweating? I had spent hours researching

the procedure, reading countless accounts and articles, even diving deep into the online Yale School of Medicine library. I should be ready for this. But there it was, sweat. On my neck. Down my back. No matter how much I'd prepared in my head, my body was nervous.

'Is it going to hurt?' I asked before I could stop myself.

'There will be some discomfort, but we have medication that will help you relax. Afterwards you'll likely feel something similar to strong menstrual cramps.'

OK. I can handle cramps, I thought. But there was still that trickle of sweat down my neck.

'You'll need to wear a pad and can expect something like a heavy period for up to three weeks. If you experience more severe bleeding, you will need to go to a doctor.'

Severe bleeding. I'd forgotten about that. What if it happened?

Dr Rivera noticed the frantic look on my face. She smiled. 'Don't worry. We'll give you a printout with all this information. It's normal to be nervous right now. We don't expect you to remember everything.'

But my nervousness didn't feel normal. It wasn't like the morning before a big speech or the day I took the SATs or right before I was about to tell Kevin I was pregnant (which felt like a million years ago). It felt like running towards a cliff and not knowing how far the drop would be. Like I needed to reach out and grab someone's hand.

I smiled back to let her know everything was OK. It was a lie. She continued with her speech. 'Now, the actual procedure will only last a few minutes, but after, you will need to wait in the recovery room for an hour or so. The medication we will give you will make it unsafe to drive. Do you have someone to take you home?'

The answer was no. I had someone to take me from this place. Someone to take me to a bus station. But home? I didn't have that. I visualized the waiting room, with Bob sitting in his chair, flipping through diet advice or fifteen-minute recipes. It should be Bailey out there. Bailey should be taking me home. But Bailey was gone.

'Yes,' I said.

Dr Rivera nodded and continued speaking, but I couldn't hear her. All I could think of was Bailey. We hadn't spoken for four years, but suddenly she was the only one I wanted – needed – waiting for me at the end of all this. Bailey was gone because of me. I'd screwed everything up, I'd judged her, and now I was alone in an abortion clinic.

But then anger blossomed. Anger I hadn't let myself feel until now. Bailey had judged me, too. And she was the one who'd left. After everything she had said to me about friends being there for each other, she had left. If she were here, if she had stayed, I could tell her she was wrong, that I wasn't doing this out of embarrassment; I could tell her I was sorry, not just for what I'd said, but for everything; for every time she'd been alone when I should have been by her side; I could tell her . . . I could tell her . . . The anger faded away, leaving only a numb, hollow space where it had been. She wasn't here now. I hadn't been there for her before. It didn't matter. We weren't friends.

'Well, OK. That's about it, if you don't have any more questions.' Dr Rivera's voice wrenched me from my thoughts. She looked at me expectantly.

'No. No more questions.' But my certainty had cracked and I felt adrift.

'OK, then I'll have the nurse take you to the waiting room until an exam room is ready.' The doctor stood. I stood as well. And then a tiny spark of an idea ignited in a back corner of my brain. Quickly, I tried to douse it. I followed the doctor from her office and into a hallway. A nurse introduced herself and led me towards the waiting room.

As we went down the hallway, the idea refused to be ignored. It grew, its wild flames burning away any other thoughts. We passed the other side of the reception desk, the side the doctors and nurses used to speak to the receptionist. The woman was filing some paperwork. I veered away from my nurse and over to the window and then the idea leapt out.

'Excuse me, are there any other appointments today? Later ones?' The receptionist looked up from her papers.

'Well, I'd have to check.' She turned to her computer, a slightly confused expression on her face as she typed.

'My ride situation has changed,' I explained. *Hopefully.*

'We have a spot available at three thirty p.m. It's our last of the day. You'll be finished around five thirty.'

And just like that, the fire inside me went out. 'Oh, um, is there anything earlier? My bus home leaves at three thirty, and if I miss it I won't make it home in time.' *And my parents will find out what I'm doing* remained unspoken, but the receptionist seemed to hear it all the same. She looked again at her computer and clucked her tongue sympathetically.

'I'm sorry, but that's the only appointment we have left.' Was it worth it? Risking everything? For once in my life I couldn't weigh the pros and cons, couldn't play out all the consequences, couldn't keep the cool, rational, logical facts ordered neatly in my head. Because in the end, it wasn't even a choice. The thought of going back into that exam room without Bailey waiting for me on the other side was impossible. I'd thought I'd only needed a ride, but now I realized I needed much, much more. A friend. Not one who I only let see the best parts of me. A real one. And if I wanted a friend – if I wanted someone there for me – I needed to be there for her too. I had to fix this.

'I'll take it.'

There was some brief confusion as I explained to the

231

nurses that I was coming back later. I tried to assure them that I wasn't changing my mind, but *I have to save a friendship* probably wasn't an excuse they heard very often. I ignored the doubt in their eyes and made my way back to the reception area, where Bob was waiting. He looked up from his magazine.

'Already?'

'Change of plans, Bob. Let's go.'

MILE 995

With one last glance at 'Laser, Botox, Both? Lift Your Face, Lift Your Spirits', Bob put down *Glamour* and followed me out the door. I could see a thousand questions in his eyes, but was grateful that he left them unspoken.

The protesters barely registered as I marched across the parking lot. Once at the limo, rather than climbing into the back seat, I opened the passenger door and slid in next to Bob.

'We're coming back here at three thirty. I haven't changed my mind. I'm still getting the abortion. I just need to find Bailey first.' I waited for Bob's reaction. He looked thoughtful as he stared at the dancing patterns of light the leaves made as they moved in the warm New Mexican air. I bit my lip. Bob's support was by no means assured and it was absolutely necessary. And as he rarely said more than a word at a time, I still had no real idea what he thought about all this. Finally, Bob nodded.

'Good.' The single syllable sang through me and I grinned.

'I have money to cover you for a couple more hours.'

Bob shook his head. 'No need.'

I found tears leaking from my eyes for what seemed like the hundredth time in the last hour. But at least these were tears of happiness.

'Thanks, Bob.'

A grunt was all I got in return. But now I knew enough to realize that meant 'You're welcome', and maybe even 'I'm proud of you'. He turned the key in the ignition and looked at me enquiringly.

I fastened my seat belt. 'I have an idea.'

MILE 997

Bob weaved between lanes of traffic like Vin Diesel in one of those fast-car movies that Kevin always made me watch. Bailey had said the Roswell tour left from Old Town at eleven a.m., one p.m. and three p.m. That was likely where she was headed. It was around eleven when we'd had our fight, so I didn't think she'd had time to catch the earlier bus. And it wasn't quite one now, so as long as we got there soon, we could stop her. The problem was, if she wasn't there waiting at the depot, I'd have no idea where to look for her. My only option would be to scour the city searching for my teal-haired friend and hope that I could find her, apologize to her, and convince her to return to the clinic with me before time ran out.

There were a thousand variables that could send this plan careening into disaster, but adrenaline was coursing through me and I was determined to make this happen by sheer force of will. I ran through ways to apologize to

Bailey, to push the fractured pieces of our friendship back together, to make her understand how much she meant to me. But no matter what, three-thirty p.m. kept creeping into my thoughts. I had to find Bailey. There was no other alternative.

My phone buzzed.

Emily: Call us between D.

I ignored it and wished for the millionth time that Bailey's phone wasn't broken. At least then I could send her a text. Right now, even getting an 'F off' from Bailey would have made me feel better. I'd have had a glimmer of hope that we could repair this. But instead I was flying blind. She could be fuming with anger, sobbing her eyes out (though I found that hard to imagine), or worse, she could be on a bus home to Missouri, her face turned towards the sunlight streaming through the window, blissfully at peace, having completely forgotten about me. About us.

Bob pulled up across from a tired-looking bus depot. It was done in a traditional adobe style and needed a fresh coat of paint. A sun-faded sign over a ticket booth proclaimed: 'Fastest Way to Roswell – A Galaxy of Fun Awaits!' I didn't see a bus waiting. Had it already left? But then I saw a few people walking around with tie-dyed shirts or carrying tote bags that read, 'My other car is a flying saucer', so perhaps we were still in time.

'Do you see her?' Bob asked. I scanned the crowd again and shook my head. There was no flash of teal hair among the milling tourists.

'No,' I sighed, trying to contain a mounting sense of dread. This had to work. 'I'm gonna ask around,' I said to Bob, pocketing my phone. I climbed out of the limo and walked to the ticket booth.

'Welcome. How many tickets to uncover the true story of aliens right here on Earth?' a bored woman intoned from behind a Plexiglas partition. I held up my phone and pushed it against the window.

'Have you seen this girl?' I asked. The lady squinted, trying to peer through the thick plastic that separated us to see the image on my phone. It was a picture of Bailey from the diner. She was flipping off the camera with one hand and holding a pancake in the other. After a moment the lady shook her head.

'Nope.'

It took me a moment to process her answer. Somehow I hadn't anticipated a negative.

'Are you sure? Did the one o'clock bus leave already?'

'Nope. No buses have left yet. Roy's hungover again.'

'Maybe she had her hair pulled back?' I tried desperately, my brain refusing to accept such a definitive answer. The woman sighed, but more with pity than frustration.

'Look, she's under forty, not wearing crystals or a tinfoil

hat, and looks like she showers on a semi-regular basis. I haven't seen her. Trust me. I'd remember.'

I looked around at the crowd. The woman was right. There was no way she would have missed Bailey. I turned back to the ticket seller, feeling suddenly very small. I grabbed a brochure and scribbled my number on it. 'Well, if she turns up, maybe you could call this—' Before I could finish, a pair of lady retirees in matching muumuus and wearing copious amounts of jewellery walked up to the counter and pushed in front of me.

'Excuse me. If we don't leave soon, I will be demanding a refund. I didn't pay thirty-five dollars to miss out on my full two hours at the museum. There is a lot of material there to cover and I'm a meticulous reader.'

The woman standing next to her pushed her face right to the Plexiglas. 'I bet the bus isn't coming. I bet the government shut it down. But you can't hide the truth!' I slid away from the counter, leaving the ticket seller to deal with her customers.

Maybe Bailey was still on her way here. Maybe she couldn't find a ride. Should I wait? I'd felt so certain this was her destination. I'd already played the whole scene out in my head. We'd pull up to the kerb with a screech. I'd see Bailey gripping her ticket in her hand, waiting in a long line of tourists about to board the bus. I would push through the crowd, shouting her name. She'd turn, surprised, but a fleeting smile would cross her face before she forced it into a frown. I'd apologize. And her frown would soften. The other tourists would surge around us, stepping on to the bus as we stood staring at each other. The bus driver would lean out the door and ask if Bailey was still coming. She'd shake her head. The door would close with a hiss and the bus would pull away. We'd watch it together as it disappeared into the traffic. Then Bailey and I would climb into the limo, hand in hand.

But Bailey wasn't here. So none of that would happen. Once again, my knowledge of Bailey proved faulty. And now I was alone in a sea of strangers – a sea of very peculiar strangers. And one of those strangers, a man dressed in an army jacket and silver lamé sweatpants, clutching a grimy teddy bear in one hand, was inching closer, eyeing me with suspicion. Mistakenly, my eyes briefly met his. His face split into a wild-eyed smile.

'Haven't seen you on the tour before!' He took a lurching step towards me. With a yelp I hurried back to the limo and slammed the door.

'Drive.'

Bob took one look at the man shuffling towards us and floored it.

MILE 999

I slumped against the fake leather seat with a sigh. 'She wasn't there. I . . . don't understand.'

'Clinic?' Bob queried.

'No. Drive back to where we dropped her off, using the easiest route from here. Maybe she's still on her way. If we don't find her, we'll . . . just drive around town.' Bob raised a single sceptical eyebrow. 'I know,' I replied. 'It's not much of a plan, but it's all I've got.' I ignored the clock in my head that was rapidly ticking its way to three-thirty p.m.

MILE 1001

We saw a girl in ripped jeans, but her hair was just an ordinary brown.

MILE 1004

A police car was pulled over on the side of the road, lights flashing. The officer was writing a ticket for a pedestrian. I saw a flash of teal. My heart stuttered.

But it was just a hipster with a turquoise knit hat and a handlebar moustache.

MILE 1008

I hissed in frustration as we waited at yet another light. There was way more traffic in Albuquerque than I'd expected. I scanned the sidewalks, but there were only a few people and none of them remotely resembled Bailey.

'Come on. Where is she?' The possibility that I wasn't going to find Bailey was rapidly changing to certainty. We'd driven almost the entire route, with no sign of her. The only option left was to just randomly drive the city, and finding Bailey in that scenario was about as likely as finding evidence of alien life on earth.

Bob pointed to a 7-Eleven across the street.

I grinned wildly as hope surged through me. Of course. Snacks.

'Bob! You're a genius!'

MILE 1009

I clambered out of the limo and ran to the entrance of the 7-Eleven. I dashed to the counter, my phone out and ready, the silver bells on the door still tinkling as it swung closed behind me.

'Have you seen this girl?' I panted. As the sleepy-eyed cashier leant forward to squint at the photo, I caught a faint whiff of an earthy, herbal smell: weed. My hope for his powers of observation plummeted. He blinked as he looked at the picture. He blinked again. He chewed on the corner of his lip.

He nodded.

'Yes?' I squeaked, hardly daring to believe.

'Yeah,' he confirmed.

'When?' The word was more breath than question.

The cashier looked thoughtful. 'Maybe like a half hour ago?' My heart began to thump. Finally, something. Wherever she was, she couldn't be more than a half hour away.

'Did she say where she was going?'

'No. She just, like, bought Pringles. And thought about stealing a lighter. But she put it back.' He smiled, proud of Bailey.

'Did you . . . did you see which way she went?'

The cashier shook his head. 'Nah.' My heart sank. I suppose expecting the high cashier of a 7-Eleven to notice where a customer went was a bit of a stretch, but I'd still hoped. 'She sat on that bus bench outside for a while,' he added suddenly. 'I was going to tell her the bus doesn't stop there any more. But then the hot-dog cooker started smoking again and when I came back, she was gone.'

I raced back to the limo. 'She was here!' I threw open the door, slid into my seat, leant over, and hugged Bob. He grunted. I sat back, still grinning.

'So?' he asked.

I ran my hand through my hair. 'I don't exactly know where she is right now. But she was on that bench half an hour ago.' I pointed to the bench and gasped. For the first time I noticed the advertisement on the backrest. The image was faded and parts were peeling off, but I could just make out a man in a yellow polo shirt sporting shoulder-length hair despite a violently receding hairline. He had a plastic smile and a garden gnome under one arm. 'Loco Larry's Lawn and Garden Emporium,' I whispered. 'Of freakin' course.'

MILE 1010

We pulled up to the front of Loco Larry's, aka the business of Bailey's estranged father, whom she swore she didn't want to see, which I should have realized in Bailey speak meant, 'I really, really want to see my dad, even more than I want to go to Roswell.' Because the less Bailey wanted to talk about something, the more it meant to her.

The building was on the corner of the street, a wrought-iron fence encircling an outside area with an assortment of terracotta pottery. The actual store was painted a baby blue with a mural of dancing cacti on its front wall. There was more wrought iron over the windows and the dusty front doors could have used a good squeegee. I wasn't sure about the local Albuquerqueans, but I wouldn't have wanted to buy a plant there.

'Drive the limo around the corner. I don't want her to look outside and see us.' I wasn't planning on surprising Bailey, but I didn't want her spotting me and running out the back door. Once Bob had parked, I climbed out of the limo and cautiously made my way to the front door. The windows were too high for me to peer into, so the front door was my only option. I approached it carefully. It was tinted, and it was too bright outside for me to clearly see the interior of the store. I stepped to the side and listened. I couldn't hear Bailey or her father. All I could hear was the faint sound of soft rock playing over the store's speakers. Maybe Bailey and her father were already in the back somewhere having a heart to heart. But even as the thought crossed my mind, I knew it wasn't true.

Bailey was angry at her father. And Bailey pissed at anything was never quiet. If she and her dad were talking, I'd be able to hear her. The whole block would probably be able to hear her.

Just then, a young mom wearing yoga pants and jogging shoes brushed past me and entered the store, towing her toddler along behind. I wouldn't learn anything more by waiting outside. I took a deep breath and followed her in.

The interior smelt faintly of dirt and damp. Large bags of soil were piled in high stacks. Wind chimes tinkled in the air conditioning. A few tropical plants hung from a trellis. The woman in the yoga pants was talking to a man at the counter, asking about organic seeds while her kid played with her iPhone at her feet. As the man turned to search the ancient computer attached to the till, I saw his face, or more accurately his hair. It was Bailey's dad, no question. His hairline was even further back than in the picture on the bus bench, but it was him. His smile to the woman seemed placid; there were no lines of tension around his eyes. Obviously Bailey hadn't made her appearance.

I turned down the first aisle before Mr Butler could spot me. I wasn't sure if he remembered me from four years ago, but I didn't want to risk it. I trod softly down a row filled with various types of natural pesticides, listening for any hint of movement. It was quiet except for the conversation at the counter. Unease flickered. What if Bailey wasn't coming here? What if she'd gone to his house? Or hitched a ride to Roswell? But before my doubts could fully bloom, I saw her.

She was hiding amid the lawn art, at the very back of the store, crouching next to a large ceramic goose, her eyes glued to the cashier. It looked like she'd been there a while, just watching him. I peered through a crack in the shelf back towards the till. Bailey's dad was just finishing with the yoga mom, handing her a few packets of seeds. As the woman searched for her credit card, Bailey's dad made silly faces at the toddler, who burst into giggles.

I glanced back to Bailey and almost turned away again immediately. Her face shone with such naked longing that just looking at her was an intrusion. I waited for her to get herself back under control, to put the spiky, snarky mask she normally wore back in place – the one that was so gloriously, completely, singularly Bailey – but instead it was like the years were falling away. Her whole posture shifted; her perma-sneer melted into a soft, eager smile. She might as well have been eight years old. And she was going to face her dad like that – a dad who, as far as I could tell, hadn't really spoken to her in years.

'Bailey,' I whispered, trying to get her attention. But she was already standing. I peered again through the shelves to the counter. The mom and her kid were leaving, the toddler clutching a lime lollipop in his sticky hand. Her dad had picked up a feather duster and was idly trailing it over the cluttered shelves behind the counter. 'Bailey! Don't!' My whisper was harsh as I tried to get it to carry to her hiding place. But if Bailey heard me, she gave no indication. She was staring fixedly at her father as she began to walk to the front of the store.

There was no way to stop her. Interrupting her at this point would undoubtedly be worse than whatever scene was going to unfold – I hoped. I pushed myself up against the shelf again, inhaling dust and fertilizer and a hint of mould, and peered through the crack just in time to see Bailey approach the counter. She didn't say anything. She just stood there, waiting, one foot sliding on to its side, bending her ankle at an awkward angle.

Her father's back was to Bailey as he tended to the shelves, but I saw the moment he realized someone was there. His shoulders straightened. He put the duster down and turned, a warm salesman smile plastered across his face — a smile that flickered and faded when he saw the girl standing on the other side of the counter. A new one quickly replaced the lost one, warm and almost as friendly as the first. But in the space between the smiles I saw fear and guilt and a hint of frustration, and there was no way Bailey didn't see it, too.

She must have greeted him but I was too far away to hear the words, because I saw her father's lips form her name in return. But that was it. That was all he said. 'Bailey.' And then a silence stretched between them.

Bailey started talking, her body animated and eager. As the words spilt from her mouth, I could see the smile slip further and further off her father's face. Soon there wasn't even a shadow of it, and all that was left were his terrified, slightly trapped eyes. But Bailey didn't see, or wouldn't, because she kept talking.

I had to get closer. I needed to hear what she was divulging at such a remarkable, desperate speed. And I needed to stop it. Before she eviscerated herself on her father's empty eyes.

I crept along the shelves, darting from aisle to aisle, slowly making my way to the front of the store. Luckily they were too focused on each other to notice the soft falls of my footsteps. Finally I was close enough to hear Bailey's manic rambling.

'. . . and I thought that maybe I could just hang out here?' Her voice lilted upwards in a question, unsure and very unBailey-like, as she finally ended her monologue.

Her father ran his hand through what was left of his hair, causing a few wiry strands to shoot out in all directions. He let out a breath that he seemed to have been holding since he'd first turned and saw his daughter.

'Now's not really the best time, Bailey girl. It's . . . uh, my busy season.' The lie wasn't even said with conviction; it just trickled from his lips, half-hearted and limp. I waited for Bailey to snap in her usual acerbic way that the store was obviously empty. Instead, she let out a tiny, disappointed sigh.

'Oh. Yeah. Of course.' *Of course, Bailey? Come on, tell him that there's more garden gnomes in here than customers; tell him you can pitch in if there's a sudden rush on cactus-shaped planters. Tell him —* 'How 'bout dinner, maybe? I could even cook?'

Noooooooooooo! You're better than this, Bailey!

Her father's face tightened. His eyes sharpened. The fear and guilt were gone. Now there was just frustration.

'I'm not sure . . . you really should have called.' A flicker of hurt chased across Bailey's face before she replaced it with an even brighter, more brittle smile.

'I know. But it was kinda spur of the moment. You know me!' She added a fake little laugh, like they were both sharing a fond remembrance. Her father didn't join in.

'You've always been too impulsive.'

This time the hurt on Bailey's face stayed. 'I know. I'm sorry, Dad.' I waited for her father to soften. To see his daughter breaking into a million pieces and catch her before she fell apart.

He sighed. 'Do you want some money to get home?'

A look of incomprehension on Bailey's face. And probably mine as well. That was it? A thousand miles for a two-minute conversation and bus fare home?

I waited. Here it came. The anger. Bailey's fists would clench. She'd shout. She'd snarl. Probably throw a rake. Tell her father exactly where he could shove a ceramic sundial.

'No. I'm OK. I'll just . . . go.'

No. No, Bailey. No. I looked to her father. Relief. The only expression on his face was relief. His daughter was shattering and he was already thinking about organic squash seeds. And once she was broken, once every last piece of her was scattered on the floor, what would be left?

I was moving before I was aware I'd made the decision.

'You've got to be fucking kidding me!' Bailey and her father jerked around at the sound of my voice. It was a lot louder than I had intended. Mr Butler looked confused

252

and Bailey . . . I couldn't tell. Possibly she was furious. Or thrilled.

'Veronica! What the hell?' she spat. Definitely furious.

Bailey's dad's brows shifted from confusion to comprehension as my name clicked with my face.

'Veronica Clarke?' He put on his salesman smile. 'What a surprise!'

'She drove almost a thousand miles to see you and you can't even have dinner with her?' I was still shouting. I didn't mean to be, but a normal tone of voice was impossible at the moment. Mr Butler took a step back from the till and looked like he wished he could take a few more.

'Veronica, stop,' Bailey hissed. But I didn't. I couldn't. Not when Bailey was in pieces. I kept on walking, right up to the counter. I slammed my fist down. The service bell next to the till gave a faint ring.

'You think a Hanukkah card somehow covers your parenting duties for the year?'

Bailey's dad made a tiny noise that was somewhere between a whine and choking. Bailey grabbed at my arm, trying to pull me away.

'Shut up, Veronica. Just forget it, OK?' The expression on Bailey's face was so unfamiliar, it took me a minute to place it. She was embarrassed.

Bailey's dad looked from her to me and smiled. 'I don't think this is any of your business, young lady. Why don't you run along while I finish with Bailey here.'

'No.'

He blinked, clearly not having expected a seventeen-year-old to flat-out ignore him — making it more obvious than ever that he didn't have much experience with seventeen-year-olds.

'No? I'll have you know this is my property and I can call the police if need be.' He extended his hand towards a grimy cordless phone resting by the till. Instead of backing away, I leant forward, looking straight into his eyes. His hand stilled halfway to the phone.

'I'm Bailey's friend. I'm staying right here.' Out of the corner of my eye, I saw Bailey flinch. 'I wasn't there for her when you bailed. But I'm not abandoning her now that you're breaking her heart again.'

Bailey's father's eyes flared with anger, then settled into a determined indifference. He looked away from me, from Bailey, and stared unseeingly at a garden hose hanging on the wall. Finally he shrugged and ran his hand through his thinning hair again, suddenly looking shrunken, small and unsure.

'Look, when you get older you'll understand these things. I mean . . . Bailey's mom knew I never wanted kids.'

There was a sharp intake of breath. Panic flashed across Mr Butler's face as he mentally replayed the words he'd just said. Panic followed by relief that the truth was out. I turned. Bailey. Bailey was crying. She hadn't made a sound other than that first sharp breath. But tears were pouring down her face and her whole body trembled as she tried to keep her feelings inside.

'I mean . . . you're a great kid, Bailey,' Mr Butler continued, looking like he thought maybe he should pat her on the shoulder or something. 'But' — he looked me in the eye now, no hint of remorse, only deep, placid indifference — 'some people aren't parent material.' I stared at him, my mouth likely open in shock. He picked up his feather duster and went back to his shelves as his daughter's body shook silently from the hurt he'd inflicted.

We had to get out of here.

'Bailey?'

My voice snapped her back into herself. Bailey glared at me with unrestrained loathing.

'Get the fuck away from me.'

Wiping her eyes with the back of her hand, she stormed out, shoving the door open with both hands, sending a wave of hot New Mexican air through the store. I sprinted after her.

'Bailey!' I grabbed her shoulder roughly and spun her around.

'What? What can you possibly want now, Veronica?' she asked, her voice breaking. I ignored her and reached behind to stick my hand into her waistband. 'What the—'

she started, but I'd already headed back to the store – her Taser gripped in my hand.

The door chimed and the chilled air washed over me. Mr Butler whipped around, feather duster drooping, his defensive expression melting into confusion as I barrelled towards him. I think I was screaming. Someone was – an angry karate-chop yell. I saw the exact moment he noticed the Taser in my hand.

I never hesitated. With one fluid movement I raised the Taser and squeezed.

Everything went out of order.

The crackle of electricity.

The hum of the machine, warm in my hand.

His body dropping.

Twin thin wires, arcing gracefully through the air, a nearly invisible promise of pain.

His jaw clenching, muscles standing out on his neck.

Probes piercing his polo shirt, two sharp little kisses.

The jerk of the Taser.

Mr Butler on the floor, his eyes wide and staring.

Then it was over. The B-52s played over the store's sound system, mingling with Mr Butler's groans.

I waited for regret. For a sense of horror at the crime I'd just committed. It didn't come.

I stepped closer and leant over him as he flopped on the ground like a balding, pathetic fish. I pulled the probes from his chest.

'Having a kid makes you "parent material", asshole.'

I stumbled outside on numb legs, the rush of adrenaline dissipated. My whole body was bathed in a clammy sheen of sweat and my hands wouldn't stop shaking. I wasn't sure if I was going to throw up or start laughing. I bent over and tried to do both but only a weird choking sound came out. When I finally stood back up, Bailey was staring at me, her eyes wide and a little frightened.

'Ho. Lee. Shit,' she whispered. I looked away, suddenly embarrassed.

'Sorry, I, uh, don't know what came over me—'

'You tased my dad.'

'Yeah.'

I tensed, preparing myself for more of Bailey's anger. If she didn't like me defending her to her father, assaulting him probably wasn't going to win me any points. What I did was rash, stupid, impulsive, unasked for, could definitely get me arrested, and worst, kicked out of Brown, and I still couldn't bring myself to regret it.

'For me.' The words were so quiet I almost couldn't hear them over the noise of the cars passing us by.

'Yeah.'

Bailey's smile lit up her whole face. 'That was . . . awesome.'

I managed to give her a shaky one in return. 'Well, he deserved it. And it was the least I could do.' She snorted and I giggled a little more than I should have.

'We should probably, uh, go. I doubt he's gonna call the police. He's way behind on child support, but . . .'

'Yeah. We should . . .' We both started walking in different directions. We stopped. Giggled again. I jerked my head towards the corner. 'Our ride is that way.'

'Wait. You still have Bob?'

'Just for a little bit longer. He's got a quinceañera tonight.'

'No way. What about paying him?'

'He's doing it for free.'

'Good guy, Bob.'

'The best.' And suddenly it was awkward. We were almost to the limo. I could hear Mexican pop music playing intermittently from behind the tinted windows. I took a breath. 'Bailey, about what I said – '

'I said some stuff, too. We're good.'

'– about you being a lesbian –'

'I said we're good.'

'No, we're not.' I stopped, planting my feet. Bailey took a few steps, sighed, and stopped too. I waited for her to turn around, but she didn't. 'Fine. I'll say this to your back, then.' All I got in response was a grunt and what I was fairly certain was an eye roll. But she didn't keep walking.

And she didn't tell me to shut up. So I continued. 'Look, I know this isn't something that can be covered with an "I'm sorry". I was really, really mad. Which made me not think. And I said some stuff I didn't mean . . . well, I did, but not like it sounded. Which isn't the point. The point is, I was stupid and blind . . . and now I'm going to try not to be. I hurt you. Again. And nothing can fix it. But I'm . . . I'm going to do better, OK? You can still be mad at me. You should be. For ever. I—'

'Dude. Just stop.' My mouth closed with a snap. Bailey turned, a weird half smile on her face. 'Thanks. For saying that. I didn't think I needed to hear it, but . . . I did. And, um, you should hear this. I didn't mean it either. About you deserving it, or being a slut, or . . . the other thing I said. I was angry and trying to think of any way I could to hurt you. Even if it wasn't true. It was cruel. And horrible. And . . . I'm sorry.'

We stood for a moment in silence. 'So . . . we're OK?'

'Um, you *tased* my dad. We're cool. We're . . . more than cool.' Bailey sniffed. She was smiling through tears. Immediately, tears sprang to my own eyes, answering hers.

'More than cool?'

Bailey nodded. She wiped her nose with the back of her hand and scratched the back of her neck. Her eyes darted everywhere but my face. She seemed awkward and angry and vulnerable all at the same time.

And I had to ask, just to confirm, just to make sure the wild surge of emotion beating through my veins wasn't misplaced, 'More than cool? Like . . . friends?'

'More than friends.'

'Like best . . .?'

'Maybe not quite there yet,' she quickly corrected me.

I nodded, my throat almost too tight to get the words out. 'More than friends is good.' We exchanged watery smiles and scrubbed at our eyes, suddenly embarrassed to be standing on a street corner baring our souls. Bailey let out a deep breath.

'Great. Glad that's sorted. Now can I have my mom's Taser back?'

MILE 1011

Bailey and I tumbled into the limo.

'Bob! I found Bailey!'

Bob grunted.

Bailey grinned. 'Good to see you, too, Bob.' Bob started the limo and pulled into traffic. Bailey settled into her seat. She gave me a once-over, taking in my appearance. 'So, you were moving pretty spryly back there for a girl who, you know, got the ol' . . .'

My cheeks warmed. 'I . . . didn't get it.'

Bailey jerked up. 'What? Why? Did you change your mind?'

I shook my head. 'No. I moved my appointment to three thirty . . . I had to find you first. I wanted you there.'

Bailey looked away from me, hiding her face. 'You're crazy.'

'Bob just wasn't a good replacement.'

'I don't know. I think Bob's kind of amazing.' From the

front seat, Bob held his hand up for a high five. Bailey leant forward and slapped it.

'And . . . Kevin showed up,' I continued.

Bailey whipped around with a look somewhere between horror and amazement. 'No! Please tell me you ran over him with the limo!'

'Close. I decked him.'

She groaned. 'Now I'm really pissed I left. What I would pay to see Kev's face splattered on asphalt.'

But a moment later, Bailey's delighted grin faltered. She turned to stare out the window, quiet and withdrawn.

'I wish you hadn't left, too,' I said. 'We could have avoided your dad altogether.'

Bailey sighed and turned to face me. 'No. It's good that we went. I needed to be reminded what an asshole he is.'

'He could at least have had dinner with you.'

'Why should I even want to?' Bailey burst out, suddenly angry. 'I mean, seriously, all he would do is microwave a couple of Hot Pockets and sit us down in front of *Doctor Who*. And you know what? Can I just tell you? I fucking hate *Doctor Who*!'

'Really? I thought—'

'I keep watching it hoping I'll discover some hidden secret that will explain him. Something that will show me what I can fix about myself to make him like me. But you know what? There's no secret! It's just someone in a stupid coat with a stupid blue police-box spaceship!'

Bailey blinked hard, refusing to cry. I tried to think of something to say, but came up empty. So I sat there, dumb, as she continued.

'And my dad doesn't care. And he never will, no matter what I do. When I was six he was all bummed out because my mom wouldn't let him go to Burning Man. So what did I do? I spent a week constructing a giant man out of cardboard. I dragged all our house lamps into the backyard and covered them with scarves and stuff to make a light show. And did I get a "Thanks, Bailey", or even a thumbs-up? No! Granted . . . there was some fire damage to the house, and he ended up with some second-degree burns, but how was I supposed to know that that much lighter fluid would be a problem? I was six! And the important thing was that his daughter was doing everything she could to try to make him happy. And he never noticed. And I'm so tired of it. I'm so tired of being a stupid, sad, scared six-year-old, for fuck's sake.'

Bailey curled into a ball. And since I still couldn't think of anything to say, I put my arm around her instead. It seemed to be enough. I felt her shoulders relax.

With a sniff, Bailey wiped her eyes. 'I know right now I'm saying I'm never going to see him again, and I hate everything about him, but in a few months I'll probably suddenly decide I'm super into lawn art or Judaism or something and you just need to remind me my dad is a dick. Promise me. I can't keep going through this.'

'Only if you promise me you'll never let me date another douchebag.'

'I can't promise that.'

'Why?'

'All men are douchebags.' Bailey leant forward and called out, 'Except you, Bob!'

From the front seat of the limo, Bob shrugged.

MILE 1013

The clock on my phone ticked over to read 3.15. I looked out the window. We were surrounded by cars, harsh afternoon sun glinting off their windshields. None of them were moving. Ahead of us the freeway stretched into the distance, a seemingly unending river of traffic.

'Bob?' Bailey asked, her voice strained. 'How we doin'?'

'One more exit,' he grunted. 'Sorry.'

I studied my friend as she craned her neck to see the road ahead, her brow creasing. She was worried for me. I felt a glow of warmth and smiled. 'You know, I still have a good feeling about this.'

Bailey groaned. 'Did tasing my dad magically turn you into an optimist?'

No. But having Bailey next to me did.

MILE 1017

With a screech of tyres, Bob pulled into the parking lot. Before we were even fully stopped, I had my hand on the door handle. But seeing the clinic in front of me again, I paused.

'You don't have to come with me,' I said.

I felt Bailey's reaction, rather than saw it. I wasn't ready to look at her.

'Why wouldn't I come?'

I forced myself to face her. 'I get it that you might not want to. I know I said I wanted you with me, but you don't have to come. It's not that important.'

'Uh, it's totally important.'

'It's important to *me*. But I don't want you to do something you're not . . . you're not comfortable with.' Even though Bailey had apologized, I was still worried there may have been some truth to what she said, deep down. But I wasn't sure how to ask. I was dancing around the issue, not trusting the strength of our newly re-forged friendship to withstand bluntness. But Bailey had no such qualms.

'You're worried I still think you're wrong for getting an abortion,' she stated.

I nodded. 'You can be. That's fine. But I don't think I am. And I'm going to do it. And . . . I'm hoping we'll still be friends after.' I looked her full in the face, my chin lifting in a hint of challenge.

Bailey smiled. 'I don't think you're wrong. You're making the right choice for you. That's what's important. Anyway' – her smile faltered – 'no one should be forced to be a parent if they don't want to be one.' Bailey looked different. Her hair was still a mess, her clothes still rumpled; probably no one else would have noticed the change. But I did. And I wondered if she could see the same thing in me. I nodded, unable for the moment to speak.

'So you'll come?' I finally managed to ask.

Bailey slung her arm around me. 'Wouldn't miss it for the world.' I leant my head on her shoulder and smiled, my lips trembling. 'Don't,' Bailey said.

'Don't what?'

'Don't start crying again. 'Cause I'll start crying and I'm done with that. This limo ride has been intense.'

I laughed.

In the rear-view mirror, I saw Bob wipe his eye. I leant

over the partition and threw my arms around his neck.

'Thank you,' I whispered.

'Anytime.'

A moment later, we burst from the back of the limo, hand in hand.

The protesters barely had time to register our presence before we were safely indoors. I heard a half shouted, 'Shame on—' before the door swung shut behind us.

I hurried to the receptionist, out of breath. 'Hi, I'm back.' The receptionist gave me a small smile.

'Glad you made it.'

It was so different. The clinic, the doctors, the nurses were all exactly the same, but nevertheless the colours seemed brighter, the people warmer, the shadows softer. There was no flicker of nerves dancing in my stomach, no shallow, tight breaths. And I knew why. She was sitting beside me, so close our shoulders almost touched, waiting with me for my number to be called. We didn't speak. We didn't need to.

'Patient seventy-six?' a nurse called. I stood.

'That's me.'

Bailey smiled. 'Go get 'em, tiger.' I rolled my eyes. 'What? Not right?'

'Stop. Just stop,' I managed. Then suddenly, she was there, pressed up against me, her arms encircling me in a long, tight hug. I squeezed back, crumpling her T-shirt under my fingers, burying my face in her hair. And then, since we couldn't stand like that for ever, we let go.

I walked to the nurse. She opened the door.

'Follow me.'

I did.

MILE 1018

The sun was getting lower when we emerged from the clinic. The sidewalk was empty, the protesters gone for the night.

'So?' Bailey asked. 'How are you feeling?'

I looked at the buildings tinted gold and pink, the empty street, the trees, leaves still without the day's warm breeze. I looked up, up, up to the sky, a soft clear blue. I grinned. 'I feel . . . like me.'

'I meant more, "Are you sore?" Or "Can you walk OK?"'

'Oh, yeah,' I answered, a little embarrassed. 'I can walk.'

'Good. 'Cause I'm starving and I see a Tex-Mex place down the street. Nachos?'

'Nachos.'

The restaurant was a labyrinth of different rooms decorated in Mexican flags and faded piñatas. Filled with families out for a Saturday night meal, it was colourful, noisy, and seemed to go on for ever. We sat across from each other, a mountain of nachos between us dripping in golden cheese and greasy meat. Shoving one chip after another into our mouths, we barely paused to speak except to mutter a 'So good', or an 'I wanna marry these chips'. Bailey took an enormous gulp of soda and sighed with satisfaction.

'So, what time's the bus?'

'We missed the bus. There's not another one until tomorrow morning.' I saw comprehension dawn on Bailey's face.

'When you changed your appointment to go look for me, you knew it meant you wouldn't be able to make it home in time.'

I shrugged. 'Finding you seemed more important.'

'But your parents. They'll know.' I shrugged again, surprised at how upset Bailey seemed. 'And people at school. They'll find out.'

'Yeah. I know.' I couldn't hide that I wasn't thrilled.

'That was stupid.'

'No. It wasn't.' My eyes flashed. 'And I'm not saying I'm expecting thanks or anything, but you don't have to be so pissed about it.'

'I'm not pissed!' Bailey snapped.

'Then why are you practically yelling at me?'

Bailey sighed, frustrated. 'Sorry. It's just . . . I didn't realize everything until right now. It's kinda huge. I mean, we did all this so people *wouldn't* know.' She pulled out her wallet. 'I have seven dollars. How much do you have?'

'Two hundred and eighty.' I didn't need to look. I'd already counted.

'Think anyone will sell us a car for two hundred and eighty-seven bucks?'

'Not one that will get us out of town.'

Bailey ran her fingers through her hair. 'I don't think you realize how bad it's gonna be. Trust me. I know what it's like to feel the whole school against you.' She grabbed another chip and shoved it into her mouth. Then she mumbled something that sounded a lot like, 'I'm not worth it.'

I blinked in surprise. 'Of course you are.'

Bailey snorted. 'Say that again once you have half the football team chanting "slut" as you walk down the hall. Or whispering that you're some sort of devil worshipper because you don't wear pink. Say that when the teachers pretend not to see people jostling you as you walk to class because you're just that weird girl.' The bitterness dripped from every syllable. Seeing the expression on my face, she cocked an eyebrow. 'What? You think I liked sitting alone at lunch for the last four years? Like that was some sort of choice?'

'You always made it seem like it was.'

She rolled her eyes. 'No one makes that choice.'

'Well, you've got someone to sit with now.' I smiled, attempting levity, but the expression felt watery at best. Bailey just huffed. 'You're worth it,' I repeated, strong and certain.

Bailey's face split into a grin. 'You know, it'll be kinda fun, having another weirdo to sit with.'

'You gonna teach me to bark at people when they pass by?'

'Oh yeah. And I'll lend you my old combat boots. You gotta look the part.'

I giggled. 'Maybe I should dye my hair green.'

'Totally. And get your nose pierced or something.' We both dissolved into helpless giggles. Bailey looked up, her eyes shining. 'I know it's kind of horrible, but I'm not gonna lie, I'm a little excited. It's what I always imagined high school was going to be like. Just us against the world.'

I sobered, the giggles replaced by guilt. 'I'm sorry, we should have had years of this.' I cracked a half smile. 'At least you'll get a few weeks.'

Bailey's smiles were gone now, too. She shook her head. 'Look, you've always got a spot at my table, but . . . it really sucks that you'll have to sit there.'

I nodded. I couldn't pretend it didn't. I'd liked my life. It was amazing. I was one of those annoying people who was going to look back on high school with fondness. But that was over. My parents, my friends, they would all know. The shiny, perfect Veronica Clarke would be obliterated. The years of debate team, straight As, student council would mean nothing. All anyone would remember about me now was that I was the girl who got an abortion.

Kevin was probably halfway to Missouri, texting all his friends as he went. I'd punched him, refused his marriage proposal and aborted the baby he'd tried to force me to have. He didn't have any reason to stay silent. It was possible the whole school already knew. My phone had been ominously quiet all afternoon. I'd tried to convince myself that was a positive sign, that the girls were just busy studying, but there was still a little niggle of doubt. What if they were too horrified to speak to me? But I knew . . . I knew I'd made the right choice. I could feel that still, a warm, steady flame burning deep inside. I just hadn't fully calculated the costs.

I swallowed a gulp of soda, as if I could drown my panic in a wash of syrupy carbonation. I would just have to bear it. School was almost over. It was only one final summer with my parents. I could get through it. I'd got this far. I'd sit with Bailey at lunch and we'd have each other. I looked down to see my hands trembling slightly. Bailey merely raised a single, knowing eyebrow and went back to the nachos.

The plate was empty. I carefully counted out the money for the bill while trying to breathe through a wave of cramps. They'd been building slowly during the meal and had reached 'curl up in a ball and beg for deliverance' intensity. The ibuprofen I'd swallowed hadn't kicked in yet. Bailey had gone to the bathroom — I really needed her to get back so we could leave and I could find somewhere private to bellow out my pain like a wounded moose.

A waitress paused, noticing me with a little frown. I smiled brightly, my teeth clenched. Nothing to see here. Certainly not a teenager feeling the after-effects of an abortion. Move along. Finally I spotted Bailey. She was rushing back to the table, her eyes alight with that mad, dangerous look she got that I knew meant trouble. Suddenly, the fact that my uterus was twisting itself into a pretzel was the least of my problems.

'Bailey, what did you do.' I left the question out of my voice.

'What's the matter with you? You look like a wounded moose.'

'Cramps. What did you do?'

Bailey's brows creased in concern. 'Are they bad? You need to go to a doctor?'

I shook my head. 'They said they would be "intense". Bailey. Tell me. What you did.'

She slapped a set of keys down on the tile tabletop with a triumphant smile. I closed my eyes. Not from the pain, which was actually lessening, but from her sheer audacity.

'No. This is not a viable solution. Put them back. We've had enough felonies for one trip.'

Bailey shook her head. 'Look closer.'

I did. And that's when I saw the 'I ♡ Veronica' key ring hanging off them. 'Are these . . .?'

She nodded, her grin growing impossibly bigger. 'Yep.'

'He's here?!' The sentence came out as more of a squeak as I scanned the room, searching for Kevin's lanky frame. But the restaurant was huge and packed with customers. I couldn't see him anywhere. Which hopefully meant he couldn't see us. 'How did you even find him?'

'He's in the back. I heard some waitresses complaining some guy had been there all day just eating chips and drinking Sprite. He'd gone to the bathroom and they were talking about giving his table away. And I just knew. So I walked over and wouldn't you know it, the dweeb had left his keys on the table.' Her grin turned maniacal. 'He was pretty much begging me to take them.'

I picked up the keys, then set them down. 'Bailey, we can't steal his van.'

'It's not stealing. We'll give it back. In Missouri.'

'Bailey, the bus is fine. We'll get back tomorrow and I'll deal with my parents.'

'His keys were on the table. This is clearly a sign from God!'

'Oh, now you're religious?'

'I'm just trying to speak your language. Come on, let's go.' But I remained in my seat.

She grabbed my hands, suddenly serious. 'Don't you see? If we take the van, we get you back in time. Your parents, your friends, none of them will find out,' she pleaded with me. 'We can still pull this off.'

She was right. Hope fluttered in my chest. A tidal wave of humiliation was cresting over me, about to come crashing down, and suddenly I had an escape. And all I had to do was 'borrow' my psychotic ex-boyfriend's car. Bailey sensed my hesitation.

'Veronica, the guy almost ruined your life. *Will* ruin it if we don't do this.'

'It might not work. He could still talk.'

'Please, you think he wants to be known as "Kevin the Condom Popper"? And even if he does talk, you're no worse off than you are now. Plus, you're forgetting one important thing.'

'What?'

'He deserves it.' I was startled by the ice-cold hatred in her voice. 'You know it. A kick in the balls and a single punch isn't nearly enough.' As she said the words, an answering anger flared in my own body. She was right. It wasn't nearly enough. Pulling away from her, I picked up the keys and dropped them into Bailey's hand.

'You're right. It's not enough. But maybe a kick in the balls, a punch *and* grand theft auto is.'

'It's a start!' Bailey crowed.

I raised my palm, stopping her. 'But we leave him some money. So he can buy a bus ticket.'

Bailey grinned. 'Done.' She clambered out of the booth and held out her hand for mine. 'Let's go commit another felony.'

We burst through the doors, leapt down the steps and ran for the parking lot. Bailey had given enough money for a bus ticket to a waitress and told her where Kevin was sitting. Then we'd run for it.

I scanned the cars, searching for Kevin's familiar van. 'There!' I pointed, spotting it in the back corner. We sprinted towards it, our bodies singing with adrenaline. A stupid smile spread across my face. It was wrong – wrong – to be having so much fun. But I was. I heard the door to the restaurant open behind us, the sound of mariachi music wafting into the night. Risking a glance over my shoulder, I saw Kevin silhouetted in the doorway.

'He found us,' I called, both panic and glee tingeing my voice.

Still several feet away from the van, Bailey unlocked the

doors with a click of the key. I heard feet pounding behind us, getting closer, breaths coming in angry grunts. Kevin was a starter on the soccer team, I remembered belatedly. He was fast.

'He's catching us!' I yelled to Bailey.

'Then run faster!' she laughed back.

Reaching the van, we threw ourselves inside, Bailey jamming the key into the ignition. The interior smelt of fast food, dirty socks and dried Slurpee. As far as I was concerned, it smelt like victory. Bailey turned the key. The van sputtered to life.

'Go go go go go go!' I yelled. She threw it into reverse. I craned my neck around just in time to see Kevin dive out of the way. 'Don't kill him!' I screeched.

'He's fine!' Bailey shouted. She threw the car into drive just as Kevin slammed himself against my window, a wad of money gripped in his fist.

'You can't do this!' he yelled through the glass.

'You can't stop us,' I screamed back, triumphant.

'Watch me!' He grabbed on to the side mirror, his feet skidding on the asphalt as Bailey drove slowly forward.

'Bailey!' I was laughing slightly hysterically. 'He's holding on to the car.'

'Not for long,' Bailey growled, and began to press on the gas. Kevin was forced to trot, then run, as Bailey angled the car out of the parking lot. I rolled down my window.

'Look at me, Kevin.' Kevin just shook his head and held on tighter to the mirror, all his mental and physical effort going into keeping up with the car. So I leant out the window a bit to make sure he could hear every word I was about to tell him. 'Face it. You owe me, big time. Like, years' worth of grovelling. But I'm feeling generous. I'll call us even after you let us borrow this van. And just to be extra super nice, when I text my friends and tell them we broke up, I'm going to say it was mutual. That we didn't want to be tied down for college, blah, blah, blah, and not something like, you're a lying, manipulative stalker whose penis smells like cheddar cheese. So you're welcome for that. Now, if you agree to my terms, I suggest you let go of the car.'

I watched the quick play of emotions over Kevin's face: anger, embarrassment, defeat, resignation. With a grunt, he let go of the mirror and stumbled to a halt. I turned to Bailey. 'Gun it.'

Bailey nodded and pressed down on the gas. The minivan leapt forward. As we turned on to the main street, I watched Kevin dwindle away to a speck in the rear-view mirror.

'Wow,' Bailey said. 'Wow wow wow wow wow wow. Remind me to never get on your bad side.'

I smiled. 'Well, we don't have time to mess around. We have nine hundred miles to drive in, like, fourteen hours.

Think we can avoid stopping at a strip club this time?'

Bailey pretended to think. 'Well . . . I suppose so. If you answer me one thing.'

'What?'

'Does Kevin's penis really smell like cheddar cheese?'

'Gross! No!' I screeched, then thought about it for a second. 'Well, maybe a little?'

'Ewwwwwwwwwwwwwwwwwwwwwwww!'

MILE 1102

'Eeeeeeeeewwwwwwwwwwwwww!'
    'Bailey! Stop!'
    'No. Can't.'

MILE 1432

'Eeeeeewwwwww – Oh, look, there's Mermaidz!'

   'Bailey, why are you switching lanes?'

   'No reason.'

   'Bailey.'

   'Just one song!'

   'Bailey, I will recite every sexual encounter I had with Kevin *in detail!*'

MILE 1433

'You know, if you really need to pull over and stretch your legs, this looks like a good place.'

'No.'

'Aw, come on. You can say hi to your friends.'

'They are not my friends. They almost killed me.'

'Moo. We miss you, Bailey. Moooooooo.'

'Stop that.'

'Moooooooooooo.'

MILE 1502

'We're filled up on gas.'

'Great. Here you go.'

'Wait. What's this?'

'A Slurpee. Half blue raspberry, half cherry, with a splash of Coke. And the latest issue of *UFO Encounters*.'

'I love you.'

MILE 1519

'OK, I texted them.'

Bailey and I hovered over the screen, our faces bathed in its blue glow, and waited for a response. The message read, **Kevin and I broke up.** We'd pulled over to the side of the road. The occasional lorry lumbered past, but other than that it was quiet.

'They're not answering,' Bailey said.

'Give them a minute.'

My phone exploded with a thousand pings, nearly vibrating out of my hand as the screen flashed with text after text.

Emily: WHAT????

Jocelyn: This is a joke, right?

Kaylee: Not funny Ronnie.

Emily: Seriously what's going on?

Jocelyn: Do you need us to call you?

Kaylee: I still don't believe you

Emily: What happened?

My fingers hovered over the keyboard. I looked at Bailey. 'It feels weird lying.'

Bailey snatched the phone from my hand. 'Nuh-uh. Nope. I appreciate the sentiment, but now's not the best time to break out the New and Improved Veronica. Not when we're about to pull the whole thing off.' Bailey was right. I'd come so far. What was the point of ruining it now? Bailey was thumbing something into the phone. She showed me the screen.

'We had a fight about college. He was upset I was going so far away,' I read.

'It's true,' Bailey pointed out.

'Just leaving out a few details,' I said.

Bailey nodded. 'You're right.' She typed something else and showed me the screen.

'His dick smells like cheddar cheese,' I read. 'Bailey!'

'You said you wanted to be truthful!'

'Take it out.'

'It's a salient detail!'

'Bailey . . .'

Bailey huffed, disappointed. 'Fine.' She handed the phone to me. I read the message once more and pressed send. There was barely a delay before the texts poured in again.

Jocelyn: But he's known ur going to Brown forever

Kaylee: Why not wait till the end of summer?

Emily: I get it. Why let things drag on when it's going to end anyway?

Kaylee: I guess. But . . . his arms. They're just . . .

Jocelyn: She'll survive. There are probably guys with way better arms at Brown.

Kaylee: If he's free, do you mind if I take him for a spin this summer?

Emily: KAYLEE! Lock those hormones down and show a bit of sensitivity.

Jocelyn: Yeah. She needs to mourn. Ask her Monday. jk. 😊

Emily: 😂

My phone continued to vibrate with a string of texts. Clearly I wasn't needed for a discussion of my break-up. I let it drop to my lap.

'Looks like they're taking it pretty well,' Bailey said.

'Yeah,' I said, a little deflated. Their reaction was what I should have expected. Jokes, but no real concern. Though that was as much my fault as theirs. Being Perfect Veronica meant never needing any help.

'At least they're not suspicious.'

I snorted. 'Why would they be? This is exactly the sort of thing I would do.' My phone had stopped vibrating. I checked it. At the end of a long list of texts detailing Kevin's charms and their plans for finding me a hot lifeguard this summer, there was a half-hearted offer of leaving the lake house early and picking me up. I quickly told them no. I turned to Bailey. 'Let's get going.'

'Hold on. Let me borrow your phone.'

'No. I already told you. No cheddar cheese jokes.'

'It's not always about you, Veronica. Jeez. I just have to make a call.' Bailey huffed. I handed it to her, slightly confused. She dialled a number and waited. Finally . . .

'Hey, Mom,' she said. There was a burst of sharp, angry words on the other end. Bailey winced. 'Yeah. I'm sorry I yelled at you before you left for your shift.' She waited as her mom continued ranting for a moment before interrupting. 'Um, you should know, I went to see Dad.' There was a beat of silence. 'Yeah. In Albuquerque.' Bailey held the phone away from her ear as another torrent of angry words followed. 'Chill, OK! It was a waste of time anyway. I'm almost home. I'll explain then. Yes! I'm with a friend! Yes! I do actually have friends! Yes, of course I brought the Taser! God, Mom! Anyway, I just wanted to let you know . . . I'm OK.' She listened to her mom continue to harangue her, a small smile on her face. 'Yeah. You're right. We're better off without him. Love you too.'

She was about to hang up, then stopped. 'Wait? What? Trav's car?' Bailey looked at me. I looked back, panicked. We mouthed *shit* at the same time. Bailey turned back to her phone and played innocent. 'Wow. Weird. No, it was there when I left, but you know, now that I think about it, the keys were in it.' A few words from her mom and Bailey crumbled. 'Fine! I stole it! But then some other guys stole it, and then they wrecked it, and it's somewhere in Oklahoma, OK?'

I goggled at her. Bailey saw my reaction and quickly added, 'Also my friend had nothing to do with it!' There was a long beat of silence as Bailey listened to her mom. 'Right? Totally! Dipshit shouldn't have cheated on you. You ever think about playing for my team?' Bailey laughed along with her mom. 'Right. See you soon!'

She clicked off her phone. 'At least I have one good parent.'

'I . . . You . . . Your mom . . .' I stopped, trying to gather my thoughts. 'I could never be that honest with my parents.'

'Yeah, well, she doesn't know everything.' Bailey threw the car in gear and pulled back on to the highway. 'She doesn't know about the weed in my Hello Kitty dolls, or that I try to catfish all her boyfriends to see if they're paedos – only one so far – or the time I French-kissed my cousin Cooper—'

'You kissed a boy?'

'Yes, whatever, I'm not through. She doesn't know about the time I stopped up the toilet flushing my

SpongeBob figurine – he wanted to go back to the pineapple under the sea – or the time I fed my hamster – named Snickers – Snickers for a month. He died. Or the time . . .'

MILE 1869

The featureless landscape rolled past my window, endless and dark. I could see a vague hint of my reflection in the glass. I didn't look happy, but I didn't look terrified any more either. I looked at peace. It could have been because of the second industrial-strength ibuprofen I'd swallowed ten miles ago, but I didn't think so. When I returned to school on Monday, everything would be different, true. There would be whispers and stares, but they would be the kind I could handle. Honesty was important, but not having anyone know what I went through was going to be so much easier. I could concentrate on my finals. Enjoy graduation. Not disappoint my parents.

As each yard of asphalt disappeared under our tyres, I felt better and better. A Veronica who broke up with her boyfriend over college was the Veronica I was supposed to be. Not New Mexico Veronica. Not Abortion Veronica.

And now every mile closer to home made me feel more at ease. Exhaustion disappeared under a wave of relief. And I owed it all to Bailey. I turned to her and smiled.

Bailey took a final swig of an energy drink and chucked it into the back of the van. 'What?'

'You.'

Bailey belched. I rolled my eyes, then snuck another look at her. She was glassy-eyed and her hair was sticking up in every direction. She'd had a handful of hours of sleep.

'Sorry we didn't make it to Roswell.' It came out softer than I intended, heavy with all the other apologies I owed her.

Bailey shrugged. 'It's OK. Don't know whether you caught on, but I kinda went on this road trip in order to see my dad.'

I snorted. 'You don't say!'

Bailey smiled at my faked surprise. 'I know. Total shocker.'

I stared out the window again. The desert had been replaced by empty rolling plains, which had now given way to lush, tree-covered hills. Above us, the stars shone brilliantly, dancing in an infinite sky. The only sign of humanity was the occasional billboard that flashed past, promising food, relaxation or God. One caught my eye.

'Pull off here.'

Bailey looked at me, surprised. 'Wait. Seriously?'

I grinned. 'Seriously.'

MILE 1870

We stood in front of the chain-link fence next to the sign announcing, 'Closed at Dusk'. Beyond, the oversized elephant and cow loomed majestically in their sea of grass. The only sounds were the screech of night insects and the occasional distant hum of a car whizzing down the highway. And my heart thudding with anticipation.

I gripped the cold metal with both hands and started to climb, the fence rattling softly. 'You coming?' I asked over my shoulder.

Bailey stayed on the dirt. 'What about the dogs?' she asked coyly.

I grinned. 'We'll be ninjas.'

A moment later we were over the fence. With a quiet whoop of delight, Bailey ran for the elephant. She launched herself at the trunk and started hoisting herself up. I craned my neck, back, back, back, to study the cow. How was I going to climb that? It didn't matter. Because I was going to.

With abandon, I flung my arms around Bessie's knee, wrapped my thighs around her leg, and heaved myself upwards. I slid a bit, but gripped tighter and pulled again. I inched up. Another heave, another inch. My shoulders burnt. My thighs quivered. But I kept going.

And I made it. Mainly because halfway up I realized there were metal rungs clearly meant for climbing the thing.

I stood on the back of the third-largest cow in the state, the world spread out below me, my hair ruffled by the damp night breeze, my face bathed in starlight. I turned to look at Bailey. Six feet away on the back of a pink elephant that stood twelve feet off the ground, she twirled, chin tipped towards the heavens.

'Best vacation ever!'

Sensing my gaze on her, Bailey stopped spinning. Her eyes caught mine. With a grin, she extended her arms.

I did the same.

We stood on our statues, arms like wings, bridging the gap between us. Our fingertips couldn't quite touch, but it was close enough. I could still feel her.

Later, we lay on the backs of our respective beasts, arms cushioning our heads. The stars were splashed across the sky, white and endless. Without any town nearby to drown out their light, they looked close enough to touch, the whole universe spread above us, ready for us to dive in. 'I know it's not Roswell,' I continued, 'but—'

'Shhhhh.'

We lay like that, silent and still, the ground far below.

Finally, Bailey turned to me, her face lit by the stars. 'You did it. You're going to get back without anyone knowing.'

'I know.' I waited for the rush of giddiness, but this time it didn't come. Instead I just felt a hollow sort of ache. 'I can't really believe it. It seems crazy that in a couple hours we're going to pull up to my house and this will have never happened.'

Bailey continued to examine the stars, raising an arm to trace a constellation. 'Look, there's Gemini.'

'I mean, I guess Kevin could tell.'

Bailey snorted. 'He won't. He's a coward.'

She was right. Kevin might threaten, but he'd never really say anything. He had almost as much to lose as I did. My secret was safe. I could feel it.

'Bailey—'

'You know, since everything's going back to normal, I want you to know I don't expect to, like, hang out, or anything. You don't need to high-five me in the halls or whatever.'

It was a punch to the stomach. All the air rushed from my lungs. 'Oh, come on, I'm not going to ignore you,'

I stuttered.

Bailey turned away from the stars to face me. 'So me and the girls are all gonna eat lunch together? Talk about how we all got As on our physics final?'

'Well, actually, I haven't studied all weekend, so I probably won't get an . . .' I trailed off. She held my gaze, waiting. She was right. When I'd been imagining my newly recaptured life, why hadn't I been imagining Bailey? Or if I had been, why was she just there, somewhere on the edges, hazy? Why hadn't I imagined walking down the halls together? Eating lunch?

I sat up, crossing my arms, hunching against the cold night air and Bailey's excellent point. 'Yeah. I don't know. Why not?' But Bailey continued, sure and implacable. 'And you don't think suddenly being besties with me might look a little weird? Raise a few questions?'

'We could say we, I don't know, reconnected or –'

'You're the valedictorian –'

'– possible valedictorian –'

'And I bark at people.'

For a moment I hated her. Hated her for what she was giving me. Because she knew how badly I wanted my life back – the shiny happy life that she had no place in. And I knew what it would cost her. And she was going to do it anyway. For me.

'But . . .' The feeble protest was all I could muster.

Bailey sat up and looked at me. 'I'm not going to be mad if you don't say hi.' She said it simply. Truthfully.

I nodded once. 'OK.'

She nodded back. 'OK.'

I looked down, at my shoes, at the ground, anywhere but at her. 'But . . . we're still friends?' I asked, the words tumbling out before I could stop them. After everything she'd done, was going to do, I didn't deserve to ask. My cheeks flamed. 'Sorry, I – If you don't, it's—'

Bailey huffed. 'Of course we're still friends. We're always going to be friends, dummy.'

I smiled.

Suddenly, Bailey jerked forward, pointing a finger to the sky. 'Wait. What's that?'

I followed her finger to the section of the sky she was indicating. 'Bailey . . .' My voice quivered from the shock. 'Bailey, that's a—'

Bailey started shaking her head. 'No. No, it's not.'

'It is! It is!' I insisted.

'No. No way. Not possible.'

In the distance, moving through the stars, was a glowing, twinkling . . . something. Too oddly shaped to be an airplane or a helicopter, it moved slowly across the sky, trailing a soft greenish light behind it. For a moment it hovered above us, then seemed to rotate once, twice, and winked out of existence.

I turned to look at Bailey. Her eyes were still glued to the spot in the sky where the . . . whatever it was . . . had disappeared, her mouth open in a silent O of wonder.

'Wow.'

'Yeah,' I agreed.

She turned to me and grinned. 'Maybe it was taking Kevin back to his home planet.'

We both burst into giggles, laughing so hard we almost tipped off our animals. 'Come on. Let's go home.'

MILE 2012

I woke to the sensation of drool running down my chin. Squinting into the bright sunlight, I attempted to regain my bearings. Sometime in the early morning, after our last stop – gas for the minivan, some extra ibuprofen washed down with Slurpee for me, and energy drinks for Bailey – I must have fallen asleep, rocked to unconsciousness by the white noise of the engine and the gentle motion of the road. But now the van was pulled to the kerb, the engine off. The houses lining the street were achingly familiar. I was home.

'Hey, sunshine. I let you sleep for a bit. Didn't want you to get home too early.' She waved a magazine at me. 'Did you know Kevin has, like, fifty old dog-eared copies of *Men's Journal* in the back seat? He's really into supplements.' Bailey's voice rasped with exhaustion. She had circles under her eyes and was covered in Pringle crumbs.

'We made it.' It was all I could think to say. I tried to

smile but felt tears spring to my eyes instead.

'Yeah. We did.' Bailey's smirk faltered. She sniffed and scratched the back of her neck. She didn't look at me. Suddenly it was uncomfortable. Should I just get out now? Say goodbye and walk into my house? Should we hug? 'Thanks' didn't even begin to cover it. And once I climbed out of this van, it was over. I didn't want it to be over.

'Uh, your house is around the corner,' Bailey said abruptly. 'I didn't want your parents—'

'To see the van. Thanks. Good idea.'

'Yeah. Be a shame to mess it up now.' Another silence. Bailey picked at a Pringle crumb on her leg.

'We're probably going to sleep for a month, right?' I cringed. I sounded so insipid. So flippant.

Bailey waved an empty can at me. 'Nah, I got like twelve empties of these in the back. I'm so wired I think I can feel my arm hair growing.' We both laughed at her lame joke. It sounded forced. 'Oh, hey,' she said, 'I picked up this while you were asleep. I got us each one.' She shoved a rectangular piece of paper at me.

It was a postcard – the giant pink elephant and black-and-white cow standing nobly in a field of waving grass. 'Greetings from Missouri,' I read.

'Yeah. I know. Feels a little flat. They could've thrown a pun in there.'

'Greetings from Moo-souri,' I offered.

'Keep on Trunk-in,' Bailey added, with a laugh that died off quickly.

I shoved the postcard in my backpack, blinking rapidly. 'Thanks. It's pretty much the perfect way to remember . . .' I stopped myself before I said *us*. It seemed too final. 'To remember the weekend,' I finished.

'Yeah. Cool. Whatever,' she replied, suddenly interested in digging the remnants of smashed Sour Patch Kids off the ignition.

'So, I guess I'll just go, then.'

'Yeah. OK.'

'OK.'

So I went. I grabbed my backpack. Climbed out of the van. Closed the door. The slam reverberated through my body. It sounded like . . . punctuation. Should I just walk away now? My feet didn't move. Maybe Bailey would drive away first. Then I could go. But Bailey just sat in the van, her hand on the key in the ignition. She didn't turn it. I waited for Bailey to leave. She didn't.

It had to end. I couldn't stand there for ever. It wouldn't change anything. I turned around and began to walk down the sidewalk. I listened for Bailey to start the van. She didn't. I reached the corner – my street. I kept walking. I didn't turn around. I rounded the corner, still waiting to hear the start of the engine.

I heard birds. And someone's TV.

I kept walking. I could see my house now. It looked no different than it had two days ago – the same faded play equipment in the yard, the patchy dry grass, the American flag. I'd walk through that door and this would be over.

But it was over already. Bailey wasn't going to come flying around the corner, open the door and yell at me to climb in. We weren't going to drive off into the sunset on another madcap adventure. That would ruin everything. I didn't want to ruin everything. I didn't. It was time for me to go inside, say hi to my parents and start living the life I'd driven two thousand miles to keep.

I opened the gate.

I walked up the front steps.

I did not listen for the sound of a van tearing down the street.

Because it wasn't coming.

Because it was over.

I opened the door and stepped inside.

My mom was making her special spaghetti sauce. The one she simmered all day. I could smell the garlic and oregano as soon as I walked through the door. It was my favourite. I closed the door behind me.

'Ronnie? Is that you?'

'Yeah. I'm back.' I tried to sound casual, a little tired. Normal. I totally failed. There was no way she wouldn't hear the lie in my voice. Just from those three syllables she'd know I was hiding something. She was a mom, after all. They do that sort of thing.

'Go unpack. And that doesn't mean dumping all your clothes on to the floor and leaving them for me to put away. I want the dirty clothes in the laundry, all your toiletries back in the bathroom and anything clean back in your dresser. Got that?'

'Uh, yeah. Got it.' I ran up the stairs to my room, grateful but confused.

'Ronnie!'

Oh no. 'Yeah?'

'Take a shower. You girls always come back smelling like a lake bed.'

In the bathroom, I stepped out of my Slurpee-stained clothes and kicked them into a pile on the floor. Next, I peeled off the giant mesh underwear and supersized maxi pad they'd given me at the clinic. I wadded them up and began to wrap them in layer after layer of toilet paper. I'd have to bury them deep in the trash can.

There was a knock at the door and it began to open. The bundle bobbled in my hands, brushing the tips of my fingers. For a moment, it floated in mid-air. Then my hands clenched around it and I whipped it behind my back.

'What?' I asked, my voice steady.

'Give me your clothes,' my mom said. 'I want to wash them separately.' Keeping my hand hidden, I passed her the clothes through the crack in the door. She wrinkled her nose at the stench. 'Ugh. What do you girls do up there?' she said as she walked away.

Once she was gone, I shoved the maxi pad deep under the layers of trash, then added more toilet paper to the top, not satisfied until it was completely covered.

Ten minutes later, I was still in the shower, the water pounding down on me. I'd used half a bottle of shower gel trying to clean the accumulation of the weekend from my skin. I'd washed and conditioned my hair twice. I was raw and pink and new. I smelt like cucumbers and melon. It was a familiar scent and I breathed it in with the steam.

Towelling off, I slid into crisp, clean clothes that felt stiff against my skin and smelt of laundry detergent. My favourite T-shirt and shorts. They felt like a costume. I did my hair, blowing it dry until it hung in shining waves around my face. I added a few gentle curls with my straightener. Next came my make-up. I added slightly more than normal, lining my eyes and filling in my brows. Then a pink blush on my cheeks, a cherry lip stain. I stared at myself in the mirror.

I looked exactly the same.

Veronica Clarke. Straight-A student. Likely valedictorian.

I didn't recognize myself.

I hid in my room, unpacking, organizing what was left of my notes, but eventually there was nothing more to do. My parents were waiting. I had to go downstairs.

My dad was sitting in the kitchen in his usual chair, sipping a beer as he waited for my mom to put dinner on the table.

'Ronnie! All ready to ace those exams?'

'Yep.' I nodded. My tongue felt too thick to say more. I sat down across from him. I'd prepared all sorts of amusing anecdotes: an unexpected fall in the lake, too much candy, a rundown of all the movies we watched. I waited.

'Good,' he grunted, and picked up the true crime novel he was reading. 'We're proud of you, honey.'

And that was it. Dinner was no different from any other dinner we'd had. My brother went over every play he'd made in baseball that weekend. My mother shovelled more food on to our plates. My dad made noises at appropriate times to make it seem like he was participating in the conversation. They didn't even bother to ask any more about my weekend. They weren't interested. I was a known quantity. The good daughter. The hard worker. I should have been grateful. I was angry. They didn't see me. If they did, they would have known something had happened. Instead they only saw the pieces I was made of. A question already answered.

'Kevin and I broke up!' I blurted as my mom was

standing to clear the dishes. The lines on her face instantly rearranged themselves into something proclaiming 'sympathy' and 'concern'.

'Oh, honey. I'm sorry. Are you OK?'

'Yeah. Fine.' I shrugged, instantly regretting telling them anything.

''Bout time,' my dad sniffed.

'Dave!' my mom chided.

'What? I never liked the guy.' He looked back towards the refrigerator. 'Any ice cream for dessert tonight?'

'Dave, our daughter just broke up with her boyfriend of three years; can you show a little sympathy?'

My dad sighed. 'Fine.' He turned to me. 'I'm sorry you broke up with the boy you were obviously too good for. I'm sure you'll find another one who's also not good enough for you once you get to college.'

I wasn't stupid. 'Not good enough' only counted if I wasn't pregnant. If I had been, Kevin would have immediately been husband material. After all, no one liked Pete and he was still part of the family.

'That is not what I meant,' my mom hissed. She turned to me. 'What happened?' my mom asked, still using her soft 'I care about your problems' voice.

He poked holes in the condoms we were using. I got pregnant and I got an abortion. Could I say it? Suddenly I wanted to. How would they fit that piece into their picture of me? Or would it shatter it entirely? All I had to do was say the words. I opened my mouth.

'Nothing. We just couldn't agree about college. We're still gonna be friends,' I mumbled.

'Well, I'm sorry. Let me know if you need to talk,' my mom said, her mind obviously already on the dirty dishes in the sink and the reality TV dancing show she was going to watch later.

My dad grunted and wandered off to the living room. My brother disappeared upstairs to play video games. My mom scrubbed the plates. And I sat at the table alone.

I felt guilty. Why? I didn't understand where the feeling was coming from. It wasn't because I'd lied to my parents. I could tell that much. I was familiar with that guilt. It was a tiny sting, nothing more. No, the guilt was for some other reason that I couldn't name. I pushed the feeling aside, concentrating instead on feeling elated. They hadn't had the slightest suspicion that anything was different. It couldn't have gone better. Everything was perfect. This was exactly what I'd wanted.

The guilty sensation returned. The weight of it pressed me into my chair.

'Ronnie?' my mom asked.

'Yeah?'

'If you're just going to sit there, I could use some help with the dishes.' I mumbled something about needing to study more and hurried to my room.

I lay on my bed imagining the water stain on my ceiling was the Milky Way and feeling the weight of the guilt press me into the mattress.

'Hey! There's the single lady!' Emily rushed over to me, trailed by Kaylee and Jocelyn. I shoved my tattered textbooks into my locker and slammed it shut. I hadn't slept for more than a few minutes at a time last night, too worried about what I'd face today. Hiding what had happened from my parents was one thing; they saw what they expected to see. And now, after a fitful night's rest, I was grateful for that. But my friends knew me. It would be far more difficult to keep the secret from them.

'Hey.' The girls surrounded me and I was engulfed in a cacophony of concern.

'Oh my God. You poor thing! We need more detail! Those texts were not enough.' 'Did Kevin cry?' 'Did you cry?' 'Was there break-up sex?' 'What are you going to do now?'

'Uh . . . finish high school, I guess.'

The girls looked at me blankly.

'But . . . everybody knows that you broke up,' Kaylee said. 'It's, like, the talk of the school.'

It was my turn to look blank. 'What are they saying?' I kept my voice carefully neutral.

'Just what you told us. Being at separate colleges was going to be a problem so you broke up now rather than let it drag out all summer. And I heard Kevin was late today. And he looked really sad.' Probably more like really tired, I thought. But at least he seemed to be keeping up his end of the story. I wondered if Bailey had managed to return his van.

'*Everyone* is talking about it,' Jocelyn repeated, in case I hadn't appreciated it the first time. I shrugged.

'OK. Well, thanks for letting me know. Shouldn't we get to homeroom?' The girls looked disappointed and confused. Suddenly the problem was obvious. I wasn't acting like myself. Breaking up with my boyfriend would have been huge – devastating – to me last week. I could see the beginnings of suspicion swirling in Emily's eyes. There was a reason she was only half a grade point behind me in the rankings. I quickly faked a trembly smile. 'Sorry, guys. I'm just kinda out of it. It's just been a lot to process, you know? I need my girls.'

The performance earnt me a round of 'awwwws' and hugs. I walked to homeroom surrounded by love and support, my friends loyally by my side. I forced myself not to turn around when, from the corner of my eye, I thought I saw a flash of teal hair.

They announced the graduation honours after the principal's morning address. I got valedictorian. I waited to feel something as I accepted my classmates' high fives and congratulations. The only thing I managed was grim satisfaction.

I saw Kevin for the first time on the way out of calculus. He was standing with a group of guys from the soccer team, high-fiving and laughing. Seeing him there, I remembered how much I'd loved his popularity. His status. The attention he brought me. And that someone who had all that seemed to need me so, so much. I'd thought that was love. I knew now it wasn't. He gave me a quick jerk of his head and mumbled, 'Congratulations.' I managed to say thanks. Apparently this interaction was enough to fuel gossip for the next two periods, at least according to Kaylee.

By AP Physics, I needed a break. I sat in a bathroom stall, staring at the tiles on the floor, figuring out exactly how many minutes I had left until the day was over. It wasn't fair. I'd made it. I'd got away with everything. I was back to being plain old Veronica Clarke. Good student, reasonably popular, now even freakin' valedictorian. So why did every congratulations on my achievement or sympathetic smile over my break-up make me want to scream? Why did I still feel guilty? It was then that I noticed the graffiti on the bathroom wall. I was sitting in the same stall. That stall. The one that started it all.

The door to the bathroom opened. I sat up, listening,

my heart suddenly thudding in my chest. The familiar *clomp clomp* of boots sounded on the linoleum.

Bailey.

I burst from the stall, the door swinging wildly, banging into the wall. The girl at the sink jumped.

Not Bailey.

Just some girl I vaguely recognized from art class. I barely heard her cheery 'Congratulations!' as I ran from the bathroom.

Lunchtime. I made my way through the throng of students, looking for the girls at our usual table. I prepared myself for thirty minutes of sympathy and pointless worrying about finals. Of course we weren't going to fail. Why had I ever worried that we would? It suddenly seemed absurd, all the energy we wasted over it. Even if we did the unthinkable and got a B or even – the horror – a B minus, we'd pass our classes, our colleges would accept us and life would continue. But I'd have to keep talking about it and worrying over it endlessly, because that's what Veronica Clarke did.

Skirting around a few freshmen who eyed me with something akin to awe, I spotted my friends perched at our table. Talking to . . . Kevin. My best friends of four years. Emily's hand was placed delicately on his arm and she was looking up at him with a mixture of sympathy and invitation.

I must have made a noise because they all turned at the same time. Emily flushed and jerked her hand away. Kaylee looked guilty and Jocelyn was attempting to stifle a nervous laugh.

'Ronnie,' Emily stuttered, 'it's not what you think!'

'He was just so upset,' Jocelyn said.

'He wanted to know how you were doing,' Kaylee added.

'I just needed some ketchup,' muttered Kevin.

They watched me, waiting for my explosion. An explosion that was never going to come. Because it was all so small. And trivial. And whatever. And were they really expecting me to fly into a rage because one of them was flirting with my ex-boyfriend? A boyfriend whom they'd all been jokingly lusting over the whole time we were dating? Probably. Because if Veronica Clarke were faced with the betrayal of her best friends, she would confront them. She'd be hurt. There would be tears. Long, heartfelt conversations. Eventual forgiveness.

Clearly I wasn't Veronica Clarke.

Maybe I never was.

The guilt I'd been feeling suddenly lifted.

I looked past my trio of ex-best friends and ex-boyfriend to a forgotten corner of the cafeteria. I could just make out a lumpy form sprawled on a table, a shock of teal-and-black hair sticking up every which way. I smiled.

Taking my tray, I edged my way around the foursome, feeling their eyes follow me as I went. I could sense the moment they relaxed, thinking I'd opted for an injured but dignified retreat. I stopped, enjoying the sensation of their panic flaring up again. Turning, I stepped towards them. Kevin – who obviously knew me better than the girls did – took this as a sign to bolt. Without so much as a goodbye to Emily, he hurried from the cafeteria. She stared after him, trying to hide her hurt. I waited for her to turn her attention back to me.

I wanted to laugh. I'd worked so hard to save a girl who no longer existed. Been so afraid to lose something I didn't really want. I didn't know who I was yet, but it didn't matter. The cafeteria practically sparkled in my new-found clarity, every detail sharp and true. Colours were more vivid. The sounds of lunch – cheap cutlery hitting plates, students' laughter and yelling – rang bright and clear. And I knew the words I'd been so terrified to hear said aloud would be easy now. I looked my friends in the eye. My stomach didn't flutter. My heart didn't pound. My hands were steady. I spoke.

'Look, I don't care what you do with Kevin.' Emily opened her mouth to protest, but I held up my hand. She quieted. 'Seriously. I don't care. We broke up. It's over. But you should know, he poked holes in our condoms to get me pregnant so I wouldn't go away to college. I spent the last three days driving to Albuquerque with Bailey Butler to get an abortion because that's the closest place to get that done around here. So public service announcement: if you're gonna let him stick it in you, I'd recommend birth control.'

Their stunned reaction was immensely, pettily satisfying. I turned on my heel and walked off, not bothering to look back as they started whispering among themselves. I made my way to the back corner, to the table I'd been drawn to as soon as I entered the cafeteria.

Bailey was asleep. Beside her, an empty energy drink lay on its side, a few sticky drops pooling on the table. She snored softly, her cheek pressed flat against the cool, smooth surface of the lunch table. The draught from the air-conditioning duct blew her hair gently, making it flutter like it had on the road. Still in motion. Still free.

My friend.

When she woke up, I'd be there. She'd make a snarky joke. She'd roll her eyes. But she wouldn't be able to stop smiling. And neither would I.

Putting my tray down, I sat next to her. I laid my head on my arms and closed my eyes.

My hair blew gently in the breeze.

ACKNOWLEDGEMENTS

When you tell people you're going to write a funny book about abortion, most of the time what you get is a blank stare and a few cautious steps backwards, so it's really important that we thank everyone who not only didn't do that, but instead cheered us on.

Brianne Johnson, our wonderful agent, thank you for being the first to think a comedic abortion friendship story with lots of cursing was not only worthy of becoming a book, but was an important story to tell. Alyson Day, our editor, thank you for your guidance, knowledge and support. You kept our girls on track and made them shine. The team at HarperCollins: Erin Fitzsimmons, Alexandra Rakaczki, Jessica White, Manny Blasco, Megan Ilnitzki, Jacquelynn Burke, Ebony LaDelle and everyone else, thank you for lending your talent, effort and time. Laura Breiling, thank you for your gorgeous and irreverent cover illustration for the US edition. Ava Mortier, thank you for your valuable input. To the rest of our team at Writers House, Cecilia de la Campa and Alessandra Birch, thank you for making Veronica and Bailey's road trip not just an American one, but a global one. To Alexandra Levick, thanks for all your hard work and for being our Twitter buddy. And to NARAL Pro-Choice America and Planned Parenthood for doing the actual hard work of fighting for the rights of women to have control over their bodies.

And now, because there are two of us, some personal thank yous.

Jenni: Warren, thank you so much for your inflated opinion of my writing skills and for being a husband and partner who happily took over kid duties so I could go back to work. I love you and I couldn't have done this without you. To my friends, you were my inspiration. Whether we met in high school, our kids' pre-school, or any time in between, thank you for being there. And finally to my mom, who when I was sixteen, sat in our church parking lot after mass and explained that the priest was wrong — parental consent and notification laws for abortion are, in fact, dangerous. Because, while she hoped I'd feel safe talking to my parents, not every child was privileged enough to be in the same position. (Dad, I love you, too.)

Ted: It's quite possible I've been writing all these years just in the hope that I could finally say this to my amazing wife: all of your suffering was worth it. The innumerable pretentious, ill-fated, half-baked stories you've had to read over the years was for this. I couldn't have done it without you, your brutal criticism, or your boundless love. Also, watching you give birth to our two amazing children made it very clear that no one should be forced to have a baby.

I want to acknowledge my incredible parents. My mom

was a reading teacher who couldn't get her kid to read. Yet, she sowed the seeds of writing even when it looked like I wasn't listening. And let's not forget my dad's 'self-proclaimed' benign neglect. It gave me the space to find out who I was (just as he'd always planned).

The encouragement from my friends Aaron, James, Tristan, Teresa and my sister-cousin, Kerrie, kept me deluded enough to persevere. And much thanks to Chris Mills for being the first one to believe my writing could be worth actual money.

Finally, a great big thank you goes to Loyola Marymount University, without which I would never have had the chance to meet Jenni, who I'm now going to acknowledge in the same 'Acknowledgments' that she is also writing. And since I'm writing this 'Acknowledgments' after she's finished hers, she can't go back now and acknowledge me. So I win.

But, also . . .

She's freakin' amazing. If you ever stumble upon someone who has the same sense of humour as you but with a stronger work ethic, better fashion sense, and is a way better writer, trick them into writing a book with you. I did, and look at me!

Jenni: Dammit, Ted, always showing me up. Thank you too, even though most of that is bullshit, except for the part about better fashion sense.

Finally, an apology from both of us to the patrons of Panera Bread. We are sorry for making so many foetus jokes while you were eating your salads.

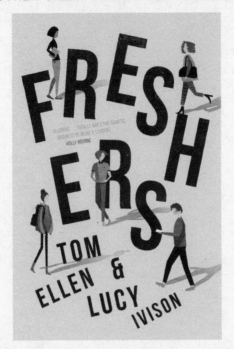

FRESHERS by Tom Ellen & Lucy Ivison

Phoebe has been waiting all summer for uni to start and her life to finally begin. And knowing Luke Taylor is going to be there too makes the whole thing even more exciting . . .

But Luke's relationship is secretly falling apart and campus life isn't proving to be the escape he thought it would be.

When the two collide in the madness of Freshers' Week, everything changes – and they both get sucked into each other's worlds in the most messy, intense and hilarious ways imaginable . . .

'Hilarious, heartfelt and honest – FRESHERS makes the university experience universal.'
NON PRATT

Paperback, ISBN 978-1-910655-88-7, £7.99 • ebook, ISBN 978-1-911 077-45-9, £7.99

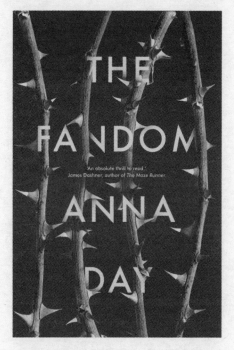

THE FANDOM by Anna Day

Violet loves *The Gallows Dance* – like every fan, she dreams of being a part of her favourite story.

But the dream becomes a nightmare at Comic-Con, when Violet and her friends are catapulted into the *Gallows Dance* for real. Trapped in a violent, dangerous dystopia, Violet and her friends throw the original plot off course by accidentally killing its hero, Rose.

There's only one way to survive in this world of thorns: Violet must fill Rose's shoes, put the plot back on track, and get out fast.

> 'Compulsive, intricate and genre-busting:
> I am most definitely a fan.'
> KIRAN MILLWOOD HARGRAVE

Paperback, ISBN 978-1-910655-67-2, £7.99 • ebook, ISBN 978-1-911077-43-5, £7.99

PRETTY BAD THINGS by C. J. Skuse

I know what you're thinking. Tearaway teens. Yadda yadda. Maybe you're right. But we're all out of choices.

Last time we made headlines, Beau and I were six-year-old 'wonder twins'. Little kids found alive in woods after three days missing, looking for our dad.

We've just hit sixteen and life's not so wonderful. In fact, it sucks out loud. Still no Dad. Still lost. Still looking.

But now we've got a clue to where Dad could be. Everything's changed. It's a long shot but we've nothing to lose. In the words of Homer Simpson, seize the donut.

'It's so good, I'd even recommend it
to people I don't like.'
KEVIN BROOKS

Paperback, ISBN 978-1-906427-25-2, £6.99 • ebook, ISBN 978-1-909489-22-6, £6.99